TAKE ME FOR *granted*

K.A. LINDE

Cover Designer: Najla Qamber Designs

Editor and Interior Designer: Jovana Shirley,
Unforeseen Editing, www.unforeseenediting.com

Visit my website at http://www.kalinde.com

ISBN-13: 978-0996053013

Contents

I didn't remember the number of women I'd fucked.

Yeah, that might sound cocky or maybe a bit disgusting even, but I'd never given two fucks. I wasn't about to start now.

Whoever was lying beside me needed to get the fuck out before I could remember her name.

Did I remember her name?

Lany.

Lacy.

Lucy?

No.

Fuck.

I didn't give a shit. She just needed to leave, so I could get back to sleep.

"Babe," I grumbled, nudging the chick in the ribs. "Darlin'."

"Mmm," she groaned. "I love when you call me darlin'."

I'd already known she liked it. She had lost her clothes quickly enough to the sound of it last night. Now, I was pretty sure I'd never say it again if it meant that she would get out quicker.

"Time to go home."

The girl turned on her side and tucked the comforter under her arms, covering her tits. *Well, there went her best quality.* She gave me a come-and-get-me look and pouted her lips as if that would change my mind. *Not likely.*

"Oh, come on, Grant," she whispered throatily.

Her hand slid down my chest and then farther south. *Yeah, not happening.* I wasn't interested in another mediocre performance on her part. *Maybe a blow job. Then again, probably not.* She stroked my cock, and I was reconsidering that blow job. She had to be better at sucking dick then fucking. It was some unwritten rule. Either they sucked, or they fucked.

"No, honey. It's time for you to go home." I rolled onto my back and reached for the joint and a lighter on my nightstand.

"That's not what you were saying last night."

I flicked the Zippo to life and took a drag on the joint. "That's what I'm saying now. You knew how this was going to go when you came back with me. So, save me the headache and just leave."

"Baby…" she whined.

She tried to shimmy closer to me, but I pushed her away.

Man, her voice grates on my nerves. "This was fun. Nothing more."

"Can't we have fun again?"

"No. I'd rather have fun with someone else," I told her point-blank, taking another drag.

Her jaw dropped, and she hopped out of bed. "Whore," she snapped. She snatched up her clothes and then stormed toward the door.

I waited until it slammed shut behind her before blowing out the smoke.

It wasn't the first time I'd heard that. I preferred the term *manwhore.* I'd earned that title, and I was fucking proud of it.

"It's just not working."

Four words—and I was completely detached from every single one of them.

It hadn't been working between Benjamin and me for a while. It wasn't just because I wasn't willing to lose my virginity to him. Though, I was sure that had factored into his decision. I just didn't like him more than my perfect 4.0 GPA, and that was a low blow to his ego. I guessed the fact that I wouldn't lose my virginity to him was a blow to his ego, too. *Oh well…*

"Aribel, it's not you. It's me."

Uh-huh.

"I don't want to hurt you."

Too late.

Sort of.

Did I finish that chemistry assignment?

I couldn't remember. I was pretty sure I'd gotten through the last two problems. They'd been the most difficult. Maybe if he hurried this up, I could double-check them.

"I hope we can still be friends," Benjamin continued.

"That's okay," I said, my voice indifferent. My hands were hanging at my side. "I mean, we weren't really friends before, and we don't have any classes together. Actually, we have very little in common."

"Aribel, this is what I'm talking about. You always just spit out the first thing on your mind."

I was already bored with the situation. I reached up and started fiddling with the top button of my peach cardigan. His eyes flicked to the movement, and his face hardened further.

Oh well.

The day a guy held my interest longer than my chem lab, I'd probably marry him and have the requisite two-and-a-half children, like my parents.

"I just feel like sometimes…I don't know. Sometimes, I feel kind of like you just don't care. You get so wrapped up in everything else that—"

"What?" I asked, trying and failing to keep from snapping at him.

"I'm just saying that maybe you should stop and smell the roses."

"I don't like roses." I crinkled my nose.

Benjamin blew out his breath heavily. "Just forget it."

"Okay."

When Benjamin left, I walked over to my desk and rechecked the chemistry assignment on my MacBook. *Finished. That's a relief.* Now, I wouldn't have to worry about that.

It was early September, and I was in my sophomore year at Princeton. I was taking my first upper-level class in the chemistry department. I wouldn't want to fall behind—not that it was likely. But with the homework off my mind, I could reflect on what had occurred.

Benjamin had dumped me. I wasn't sad exactly, not really. I was more disappointed. He was exactly the kind of guy I was supposed to be with—bright, a junior at Princeton, parents still happily married and part of the high society in Boston my parents frequented. He was driven, motivated, and ambitious…like me. I just didn't know why it hadn't worked, why it never worked.

Walking out of my bedroom, I turned toward the kitchen to make myself a pot of tea. Some honey lemon chai would make this all a little better.

"Hey, Aribel. I just saw Benjamin leave," one of my roommates, Shelby, said with a smile. She was standing by the open refrigerator across the room. Her shoulder-length brown hair was up in a ponytail, and wearing Nike running shorts and an oversize T-shirt, she looked like she had just come from class. "You still making him wait?"

"I guess he'll have to wait a lifetime," I responded dryly.

"You should just give it up. It's really not a big deal. Cheyenne is going to make fun of you for the rest of your life."

"I don't care what Cheyenne thinks," I said stubbornly.

Cheyenne might be one of my closest friends, but the girl was a real nuisance when it came to my love life.

"So, for real, why not Benjamin? Doesn't he fit the list of things you want in a guy?" Shelby leaned her hip against the refrigerator and waited for my reply.

I looked up into her dark brown eyes. "I don't have a list."

Shelby snorted. "Well, if you had a list, wouldn't he fit?"

I shrugged noncommittally. "Sure."

"Oh my goodness, she agrees with me without arguing. The world has ended as we know it."

"You're hilarious, Shelby. You should be a stand-up comedian," I said, crossing my arms over my chest.

"You haven't answered my question. Sidestepping won't work on me. Why not Benjamin?"

"Because he broke up with me."

"What?" Shelby all but shrieked. "When? Just now?"

"Yes."

"Oh God, I'm sorry. I was a jerk, and Benjamin just broke up with you." Shelby rushed forward and enveloped me in a hug.

She was taller than me by a few inches, and her stooping over me made me feel even more uncomfortable than I already was.

Sympathy—my favorite.

I stood there awkwardly as my roommate tried to console me for something I wasn't even sad about. Yeah, I was disappointed that it hadn't worked out, but it wasn't like I was a blubbering mess. Shelby needed to pull herself together.

"I'm fine, Shelby." I patted her back.

"You're not *fine,* Aribel. You always act like you're fine, but you're clearly not. Who is fine after her boyfriend breaks up with her? No one."

"Really. It's okay." *Please drop it.*

"No. You know what? I'm going to call Cheyenne and Gabi. You're coming with us tonight to the ContraBand show at The League, and we're going to find you a rebound."

I fiercely shook my head from side to side. I didn't need a rebound. More importantly, I wasn't interested in rebounding off of someone I hadn't cared that much about. "No way, Shelby. I am not going to a dumb bar to see a dumb band. That is not my thing."

"That's exactly why you should go. And ContraBand isn't a dumb band," she scolded. "Even if you don't like the music, you will appreciate their talent."

"All I know is that you guys drool all over them," I said.

"That's because the whole band is smoking hot."

I rolled my eyes. That was just what I wanted to do—spend my precious sleeping hours at a party with some crappy college band. "Count me out."

Shelby narrowed her eyes at me and gave me a look that said, *Just try to argue with me.*

I'd seen that look before. It was never followed by something I would be happy about.

3 GRANT

We hopped off the small stage at a local Princeton bar, The Ivy League.

"That was a fucking good set!" Vin yelled. He flexed his bulging biceps and set his black guitar down on a stand.

"You're telling me," Miller cried, high-fiving him. The bassist was the brains of the operation. He was tall, clean-cut, and put together with short brown hair and a quiet confidence.

McAvoy flipped his drumstick in his hand and nodded. His shaggy blond hair fell into his eyes, and he swished it to the side. His green eyes were perpetually bloodshot from smoking too much weed. He was tall and lanky with an I-could-not-care-less attitude, but he always managed to mellow us out. "Killer. I need a beer."

"Me, too," I said, nodding at my bandmates and sticking a pick into the front pocket of my jeans.

"Beer first and then bitches," Vin said. He clapped me on the back and made his way toward the stage door that exited to the bar.

As soon as the door opened, the screaming began. I smiled and ran a hand back through my dark brown hair. After the music, this was the best part. I lived and breathed the music, but damn, the chicks I would get from doing what I loved didn't hurt a damn thing.

I followed the rest of the guys out the door, and I was immediately surrounded by a crowd of girls. I had my pick of the litter at this party. I liked when my biggest decision of the night was blonde or brunette. The Princeton crowd was one of the best. As smart as the chicks were, they would all act dumb and turn to putty in my hands.

Even though none of us had actually gone to Princeton, I considered the League our home base. Miller had hooked us up with a semiregular deal. Now that we all lived in the area, we would play shows every other week or so. We'd moved here from the Point Pleasant area after graduation and stayed. I wasn't even from Jersey, like the other guys. My parents had relocated from Knoxville when I was ten. That was before shit had hit the fan.

A beer was passed to me almost instantly, and as I took a swig, I slung my arm around the closest girl to me. "What's your name, darlin'?"

"Kimberly," she peeped. Her tits bounced in her top as she pressed herself against me.

My mind wandered, and I started thinking about how fast I could get her out of that top and get those tits in my hands. She looked to be a handful, but I wouldn't mind a little bit more to motorboat tonight. *Maybe one of her friends.* I scanned the other girls around her. I wasn't that picky as long as they were hot.

"Well, Kimberly, do you know that girl right there?" I asked, pointing to a girl with a nicer rack.

"My friend, Kristin?"

"Kristin, darlin', come on over here." I crooked my finger at her.

Her eyes widened, and she jogged over. It was a beautiful sight.

"Oh my God, you're Grant McDermott," Kristin groaned. Her hands went to her chest as she bent her knees and stared up at me with big brown eyes.

"That I am." I finished off my beer, and another appeared in my hand.

A second later, Miller and McAvoy showed up with a girl carrying a tray full of shots. After tossing back a couple, I decided to cut the small talk and get down to business. Neither girl protested.

Big Tits had her tongue down my throat before I'd even wrangled her and her friend into a corner. I knew the place wasn't crowded enough to push the other chick to her knees, but the alcohol was kicking in, and I was contemplating it. It wouldn't be the first time I got a blow job in the League. As if she'd read my mind, the chick started working on my belt buckle, and I just fisted her hair as a thank you. At least I knew how the night was going to go. *One who sucks and one who fucks. Perfection.*

"Bro!" Vin called.

I broke away from Big Tits long enough to send Vin a fuck-off look as he jogged up to where I was standing. "Kind of busy right now."

Vin scoffed at me. "You can do better."

The girls gasped. I took another look at them and wondered why they were acting all offended. Vin was probably right. I *could* do better, but I'd been heading toward something pretty nice.

Oh well. Later perhaps. I nodded my head at Vin. "Truth."

"Pig," Kimberly grumbled, standing swiftly. She grabbed Kristin's hand, flipped me off, and dragged her away.

I bet they'd still fuck me if I asked.

"Sorry to cockblock, but I totally just drugged some chick," Vin said, smiling like a total dope while crossing his arms over his chest.

"You just did what?" I furrowed my brow. "What the fuck did you do that for?"

"So, look, I know this chick Cheyenne. She follows us around when we tour, and she brought her fucking hot roommates with her tonight. I picked one out, but she turned me down flat."

My eyebrows shot up. I loved pussy as much as the next guy, but even I could admit that Vin was a good-looking guy. He had the Italian guido look going for him—tan skin, shaved head, and built like a tank.

"You finally meet a chick who says no, and your response is to slip something into her drink? What the fuck is wrong with you? You don't drug girls to get them to have sex with you. You move on to the next one. Seriously, Vin, you're the fucking scum of the earth."

"Yeah, bro. Are you just figuring this shit out?"

Vin cracked up, laughing at himself, and all I could do was shake my head at my bandmate's insanity.

"You're a fucking imbecile, Vin."

He shrugged like he didn't fucking care, but this was low, even for him. Although he couldn't get *any* girl he wanted like I could, it just seemed unnecessary. Not to mention, adding date rape to his record sounded pretty shitty.

"Just take a look at this chick though, man."

"All right, show me which piece of ass turned down my man."

Vin pointed out a small blonde chick standing against a column surrounded by a few other girls, nursing a pint of beer. She looked completely out of place but coherent. I watched as she buttoned and unbuttoned the top of her cardigan. She didn't seem to be showing any side effects I would assume she'd have if Vin had really drugged her. Actually, she just appeared really uptight and vigilant. She looked like a cork, and I wanted to be the corkscrew—uncap that pressure and help her explode.

"No wonder she turned you down. The girl has a boyfriend," I told him automatically.

"She could be a closet nymph, and I bring out her inner sex kitten," Vin said, raising an eyebrow.

"No way. Boyfriend. I'll find out how serious it is." I winked at Vin and then started walking over toward the girl.

"Bro!"

I turned back around with my signature smirk already fastened into place. I was ready to go in for the kill.

"You actually going to give her to me, man?" Vin asked, concerned.

"Sure. After I'm done with her."

I heard Vin cussing me out, but I tuned him out as I was striding toward the blonde. Vin wouldn't mind sloppy seconds. Plus, no one kept me interested very long anyway.

"Grant McDermott is walking over here," Cheyenne whispered. "Grant McDermott is walking over *here*!" She grabbed Shelby's arm and started bouncing up and down. Her curly red hair flounced all around her. She was tall, confident, and outgoing with a killer body to boot.

Gabi paced a little. Her blonde pixie cut was as unruly as ever. She was generally quiet and had a bit of an up-in-the-clouds personality, but I still loved her. "Oh my God, he's so gorgeous."

"I just can't believe it." Shelby swished her brown hair over her shoulder. "He looks even better up close."

"Do I have to be the one to ask?" I messed with the button on my cardigan. "Who is Grant McDermott?"

All three girls turned and stared at me at once. *Yeah, I guess I'm that person.*

"What planet do you live on?" Cheyenne asked. "I mean, I know Benjamin just broke up with you, but I can't believe it addled your brain *that* much."

"Aw, that's cute, Cheyenne. You think *my* brain is addled." I let my dark blue eyes grow wide as I tried to play the innocent act through my sarcasm.

"Don't even start with me," Cheyenne snapped.

"All right. It doesn't matter," Shelby said, jumping between Cheyenne and me.

"Didn't you watch the show, Aribel?" Gabi asked.

"Um...kind of?"

Okay...I hadn't really been paying attention. I'd had no interest in attending the concert in the first place, so I'd been going over the calculus lecture from yesterday in my head while I sipped on my beer. This just wasn't me. I preferred quiet places, like libraries, classrooms, and the privacy of my own room. Plus, the beer was disgusting. I'd just been staring at my new pint since that creepy guy had put something in it after I refused to suck his dick—his choice of words, not mine.

"Grant McDermott is the lead singer of ContraBand," Cheyenne filled me in with an eye roll. "He's practically the whole reason we show up. I can just see his fingers playing across that guitar and imagine what they would do to my body."

I held up my hand. "TMI, Cheyenne."

"And he's walking over here," Gabi whispered, unnecessarily pointing him out.

I took a good, long look at Grant McDermott. He swaggered more than walked over to us with his dark-wash jeans hanging low, hugging him perfectly. Tattoos peeked out of his charcoal gray T-shirt, and dog tags hung loose from his neck. He was muscular but lean. His hair was long in the front, but it was shaved short on the sides, and looked purposely messy. His smirk was cocky and his eyes inviting.

His entire appeal from the clothes to his demeanor was contrived. Looking at my friends obsessing over him, I was pretty sure they were too far lost in a Grant McDermott haze to see through the playboy attitude.

Grant walked right through a crowd of women clamoring for his attention and straight toward me. I just stared at him with furrowed brows. He smirked when he saw that he'd caught my attention. I almost looked away, but his attention only infuriated me. I tilted my chin up and held my ground. *What the hell did* he *want?*

"Hey, Grant," Shelby said when he finally stopped in front of us.

He nodded in Shelby's direction, but his eyes were fixed on me. "What's your name, darlin'?"

I couldn't help it. I laughed. "Darlin'? Really?"

He took a swig from his pint, unaffected by my laugh. "I still didn't get your name, babe."

"Grant, this is my friend Aribel," Cheyenne said. "I'm Cheyenne, and this is Shelby and Gabi. Did Vin tell you that I know him?"

Grant outright ignored my friends and continued to talk to me as if there hadn't been an interruption. "So, Aribel, you don't like darlin'?"

"I might like it if you happened to be from a fifties Western movie," I said.

Grant cracked a smile. "Not a Western, darlin'. Try Southern gentleman. Rhett Butler."

"Are you going to try to peddle *Gone with the Wind* to me?"

Shelby bumped me. "Um…Aribel, now might be the time to *not*."

I ignored her. "No, really," I said, "have you ever read anything longer than a *Penthouse* magazine?"

Shelby smacked herself on the forehead and turned away.

"There are articles in *Penthouse*?" Grant asked.

I snorted and turned away. I had standards, and if he thought that calling me darlin' and talking about Rhett Butler would make me fall all over myself to be another one of his groupies, he was sadly mistaken. I started walking back to the bar. I needed to get rid of this drink and then get out of here. I was over this scene and wanted to get back to my life.

"Hey, where are you going?" Grant asked.

He tailed me as I walked to the bar.

I groaned. "Why are you following me?"

"Mouthy little thing, aren't you?"

"Okay," I said, stopping and shaking my head. "Let's get this straight. I am not your darlin' or babe or little thing. My name is Aribel, and usually when a girl walks away from you, you should get the hint and leave her alone."

"I'm not good with hints."

Grant's smirk turned into a full-blown smile. The arrogance was still there, but what was underneath made me pause. The smile was genuine, not contrived like his smirk. I'd actually amused him, and he'd reacted in a way that showed me that few people did. His eyes lightened, and the gold ring around his pupil was more prominent. There was an openness, a vulnerability, in his expression as he dropped some of the playboy look that I was sure he didn't actually want people to see. It kind of took my breath away.

He took the few steps to clear the distance between us, and I retreated, my back pressing into the bar. I placed my beer down and tried to avert my gaze from his face, but it was a struggle with him staring at me so intently.

"So, how about you ditch the hints and just admit that you're interested in me?" Grant asked matter-of-factly.

I opened my mouth to slap a retort back into his face, but for once in my existence, I had no idea how to respond. Most people weren't as blunt as I was, and no one came up to bat when I was on the defensive. He was using my own techniques against me, and I was finding it hard to look away from those big brown eyes ringed with gold. I felt like he'd blown my carefully constructed world into tiny pieces.

"Aw, come on, princess. Words failing you?" He dragged his hand gently down my jawline.

I brought two fingers up to his hand and forcefully brushed it aside. "I'm not a princess. My name is Aribel. We've covered this. Keep up."

He leaned forward, and I watched as he put his beer down to the right of my glass. His face was only inches from mine, and I could practically taste the alcohol on his breath. I should have been disgusted, but it kind of smelled good on him.

I had no idea who the person was thinking these traitorous thoughts. I was not attracted to someone like *Grant McDermott.*

"All right, Aribel it is." He drawled my name across his tongue, like he was experimenting with the taste of it.

"Are you always this forward with someone you just met?"

"Only women."

"How flattering," I muttered sarcastically.

"Isn't it? I could have picked any girl in the room, but I'm talking to you."

Grant had said that as if I was supposed to appreciate the fact that he had just openly admitted that he was willing to sleep with any of these other girls, but lucky me, I was the winner for the night.

Um…no, thank you.

"Wow. I get the princess reference now. I feel like a fucking Disney princess who Gaston chose instead of whoring himself out to the rest of the town," I said, crossing my arms.

There was that goddamn smile again. He needed to cut that out.

"Belle wasn't a princess," Grant corrected me.

"Another thing we have in common."

"I'm going to kiss you now."

His hands tangled loosely in my blonde hair before I could even get a response out.

His lips were soft and tender, but they had a certain authority to them that I had never experienced. It was like being led through a waltz. We were both dancing, but he had absolute control of the situation. I found myself wanting to kiss him back.

No, I am *kissing him back.*

And just as I felt my entire body practically quiver with desire, he slowly released me, his lips lingering oh-so invitingly in front of me.

As soon as I opened my dark blue eyes again, my body straightened, and I snapped out of my trance. *Oh, he's good. He's really, really good.* But if he was going to be a total douche bag and then think he could kiss his way out of anything, he had another thing coming.

"So, are we getting out of here then?" Grant asked.

"Yeah," I said, plastering on a fake smile. I reached for the drinks on the bar and handed him the beer that had been spiked earlier. "Finish our drinks, and then we'll head out?" I even giggled for added effect.

I raised my glass to cheers, and then I started chugging.

When I woke up, my head felt like it had been split open. *What the fuck had I drunk last night?* I couldn't even fucking remember, and I always did. I might not have a knack for names or faces, but alcohol and I were old friends. I must have gone way over my personal limit.

Then, I something came back to me—a flash of blonde hair…a pair of dark blue eyes…a giggle.

I reached over to check out who was in bed next to me. I didn't think I'd taken someone home, but if all I could remember when waking up was a chick, it was a pretty safe bet that she was in my bed.

The girl rolled over and smiled at me, and I had absolutely no recollection of who she was.

Brown hair, brown eyes. No, this couldn't be the same person. Then, who is the girl from last night? I'd kissed her. I'd tasted her. She'd been mine for the taking. And if I remembered her so vividly, then why the fuck hadn't I fucked her last night?

I swung my legs over the bed and stood. I was going to fucking find out.

"Hey, where are you going?" the chick asked. "Aren't you interested in round three?"

Round three? Shit, had I fucked that girl twice?

"Not interested. Find your own way out," I said, throwing on a pair of jeans and a sweatshirt.

"Grant! We had such a great time last night."

"I don't even remember fucking you." My dog tags swung around my neck as I surged out of my room.

I probably shouldn't have left a crazy bitch unattended in my bedroom, but the only things of value I had in there were my half ounce of weed and a 9mm.

I barreled down the stairs and banged on Vin's door until he answered. Sweat pooled on his brow. He must have already started his morning workout.

"What the fuck, bro?"

"What the fuck happened last night?"

Vin scratched his head and looked at me like I was out of my mind. "We played a show at the League. What do you mean, what happened?"

"I know that, dipshit. I remember the show, but then everything else is fuzzy. I have some chick in my bed, but all I remember is another girl."

"Whoa! Is my main man, G-man, G-money, G-dog, the one and only man in this house who cares to hit the G-spot, *pining* over a girl?"

"I don't even know who the fuck the girl is, Vin. You can't pine after someone you don't know. I just want to know what the hell happened. I remember one blonde chick, but I have another dumb brunette in my bed."

Vin laughed in my face. "Blonde chick, huh? That's real specific."

"Fuck you, man. I'm going next door to see if Miller or McAvoy will be more helpful than your ass."

I slammed my palm down on the doorframe, then turned and walked toward the front door just as the chick from upstairs stopped on the landing.

"Why aren't you out of my house yet?" I demanded.

The girl glared at me. "Aren't you at least going to give me a ride back to campus?"

"Fucking walk home for all I care."

"You know, I didn't believe my friend when she said you treated girls like dirt after sleeping with them, but damn, she was right."

I shrugged, and she started to walk out.

Then, I had an idea. "Hey!"

"Yeah?" She turned and batted her eyelashes at me.

Even after I had just been a total dick to her, she was still interested. *Why would I act any other way?*

"Do you remember me talking to a blonde chick last night?"

"Oh my fucking God, Grant," she cried, throwing her hands in the air. "You are at an all-time low. If you weren't amazing in bed—"

"Yeah, but I am. So, do you remember?"

"There were a ton of blonde girls at the bar last night, and even if I cared to remember, I don't." She started typing on her phone as she stormed away.

Useless.

"Bro, you're acting crazy," Vin said. He was standing in the living room with his arms crossed over his bare chest.

"I don't remember anything but this girl."

Vin looked at me like he thought I was losing it, but he filled me in nonetheless. "We walked offstage and drank some beers. You started making out with these two chicks, but I interrupted. I spiked some girl's drink, and you were going to find out if she had a boyfriend. Since you're fucking piece of shit, you decided to snag her from me after I'd done all the dirty work. But don't worry, bro. I found another chick who did want my dick last night."

I didn't care about Vin's conquest. I just wanted to know about the girl. "So, what happened with the blonde chick?"

"I think she bailed with her friends, and then you left with that other chick."

It hit me like a two-by-four to the chest—blonde, dark blue eyes, mouthy spitfire. Aribel—that was her name. She'd been playing hard to get. I'd known off the bat that she hadn't taken a sip of Vin's drink. And she had been fucking hot under that prim-and-proper attitude. Then, after I'd kissed her, she must have given me the drink Vin had dosed.

What the fuck?

"Do you remember now?"

"Yeah." I felt like an idiot, and it was an emotion I wasn't used to. No way was I going to let Vin know that chick had gotten the better of me. I'd never fucking hear the end of it.

"Maybe try a new kind of weed or lay off the heavy liquor. You're freaking me out." Vin started walking back to his room, probably to do another hundred push-ups or something.

I couldn't get Aribel out of my mind. *Why had she given me that beer? What kind of girl would go to such extremes to get rid of me?* I wanted to find out.

"Hey, Vin. That girl you dosed—you said you knew her friend, right?"

"Her roommate Cheyenne," Vin offered. "Yeah, I know her. Why?"

"You got her number?"

Vin shrugged. "Yeah."

"I need it."

"You want to fuck her? Because I'm already moving in on that," Vin told me.

"Keep her. I want the roommate."

6 Aribel

Gabi rubbed her eyes as she walked into the kitchen. Her blonde pixie cut was slightly askew, and as always, she looked a bit like she was up in the clouds. "What are you doing up so early?" she asked softly.

"Going over my calculus assignment." I'd completed it two days ago, but I'd woken up in the middle of the night, realizing I'd done something wrong.

She nodded and then went about pouring herself some cereal before collapsing into a chair. A minute later, Cheyenne appeared with plenty of makeup and her curly red hair managed. She sank into the chair next to me and fixed me with a direct stare.

"Do you need something?" I asked, glancing up from my homework.

"Will you *please* tell me what happened last night? I *have* to know. I'm literally dying on the inside. I could hardly sleep," she said dramatically. "Imagine failing a chemistry test."

"I can't imagine that."

"Exactly. That's how terrible I feel because you're keeping this from me. I *have* to know." Her green eyes were wide as she reached out and grabbed my hands in hers. She was acting like this really *was* life or death.

I just rolled my eyes.

"Leave her alone, Cheyenne," Gabi peeped. "Her boyfriend just broke up with her, and she had to deal with whatever happened with Grant. Can't you cut her some slack?"

"But it's Grant McDermott!" Cheyenne cried.

Gabi shrugged her petite shoulders and returned her gaze to her cereal.

"So spill," Cheyenne said.

I set my pencil down on my paper with a thwack. "If you want to find out what happened, ask Grant…if he even remembers this morning."

"What does that mean?"

I cracked up laughing and then immediately covered my mouth with my hand. I shouldn't have taken so much enjoyment from watching Grant drink that beer, but I had. *Let the asshole get a dose of his own medicine for a change.*

"Oh no, I know that look," Cheyenne groaned. "What did you do?"

"Some guy slipped something in my drink last night. I saw him do it."

"What?" Cheyenne asked in shock. "You saw him? What did he look like?"

"Yeah, I did. I don't know who he was. He was beefy with a shaved head, and his shirt was too tight. I think you were talking to him at some point."

"You mean Vin? The guitar player in ContraBand?" she asked in disbelief.

"Sure."

"Bastard!"

"Anyway, Grant propositioned me, and then when I said no, he wouldn't leave me alone. So, I gave him my glass instead of his. He probably doesn't remember any of it."

Her friends' mouths dropped open. Maybe I should have felt remorse for what I'd done, but I didn't.

"You drugged Grant McDermott?" Gabi asked in a soft tone.

"I'm sorry. I didn't hear you correctly," Cheyenne said.

"Yeah. He deserved it."

"Okay, that's pretty ridiculous," Cheyenne said. "Grant propositioned you, and you said *no*?"

Oh, of course. That's why she's freaking out. Typical Cheyenne. "What did you *think* I would say, Cheyenne?"

"Still processing here. You could have lost your virginity to Grant McDermott, and you didn't? I kind of want my virginity back, so I can lose it to him."

I couldn't resist laughing at Cheyenne. I loved her to pieces, but she was totally outrageous.

"Why did you say no? I mean, we all saw you kiss him. I just figured he changed his mind after he found out how blunt you were or maybe he thought you sucked at kissing."

"Thanks for the vote of confidence, Cheyenne."

"You don't need to know why," Gabi said, smacking Cheyenne's arm.

"Yes, I do." Her phone started buzzing in her purse. She held up a finger to me and then answered it. "Hey, Vin."

That sounded like my cue to leave. I packed up the rest of my homework and started carefully placing it into my messenger bag.

"Sure, I don't mind talking to Grant at all."

I slung my bag over my shoulder to leave, and Cheyenne just shook her head. She pointed her finger at the chair.

Yeah, that *is going to keep me in the room.*

"Hey, Grant."

Cheyenne listened into the phone for a few seconds. A smile grew on her face. I could only guess the sweet nothings he was whispering into her ear.

"Oh, Aribel?" Cheyenne said into the phone.

I had only made it halfway across the room when I stopped dead in my tracks.

"Yes, she's right here."

I turned around and fiercely shook my head. "I'm not here." My hands were out in front of me, gesturing wildly, signaling for her to tell Grant that I was away or incapacitated or dead. *Anything.*

"Yeah, let me get her for you." Cheyenne stormed across the room and grabbed my wrist as I tried to retreat. "Just talk to him."

"No. I talked to him last night. I'm not doing it again."

She thrust the phone into my hand. "He's a nice guy, Aribel, and he's gorgeous, plays guitar, fucks like a god. Talk to him on the fucking phone, or we're no longer friends."

"What a threat," I said sarcastically. "Plus, nice guy? Really?"

Cheyenne fixed me with a death glare.

"*Fine*," I groaned, taking the phone. I took a breath before speaking. "Hello?"

"Hey, darlin'," Grant drawled.

I rolled my eyes and sighed. "I really thought we covered this whole darlin' thing last night. It's not going to work."

"Work on what?"

"I assume it works on the other women you attempt to seduce."

"Attempt?" he asked with a chuckle. "Baby, give me some credit."

Ugh, baby. Seriously get over yourself. "Were you calling for a reason?"

"Several."

"Care to share? I have to get to calculus, and I'd really like to get this conversation moving."

"I guess I'll start with, why you drugged me?"

Grant just laid it out there. *Who calls the girl who drugged you the night before? This isn't Cinderella. I didn't lose my glass slipper.*

"Because you deserved it," I answered.

"What did I do to deserve it?"

"Besides treating me like a whore?"

Grant laughed at my comment, but I wasn't sure why it was funny. He had treated me like a whore, which was basically the opposite of the kind of person I was.

"What are you doing tonight?"

I narrowed my eyes. I wasn't going to play this game. "Curing cancer. What about you?"

"Taking you out," he answered, not missing a beat.

"That's strange because I just said I was busy."

"Busy out with me," he said smoothly.

"I appreciate the offer, Grant, but no." I hoped that I'd sounded firm, but this guy was so persistent. *Good Lord!*

Cheyenne smacked me on the arm. I'd completely forgotten that she was standing there.

"Are you out of your mind?" she hissed.

I shrugged my shoulders and turned away. I didn't want to hear her nonsense right now. I just wanted off the phone.

"Come on, princess. What do you have to lose?" Grant asked.

"My self-respect?" I said dryly.

"From one date?"

"My answer is no. Good-bye, Grant," I said and then ended the call.

As I handed the phone back to a shell-shocked Cheyenne, it started ringing again.

"Don't answer that."

"What just happened?" she asked.

"Grant asked me out, and I told him no."

This probably killed her, but it didn't kill me. I had no interest in someone like Grant. I'd grown up in a wealthy suburb of Boston. My father was the CEO of a prominent bank in the city. My entire family were Princeton alums. That was the kind of person I was supposed to bring home to my parents—not Grant McDermott. Not even one date.

He didn't care about me or respect me. He just wanted to sleep with me.

It was Gabi's turn to look astonished. "He asked you out?"

"Grant McDermott does not ask people out!" Cheyenne cried.

"Well, he just did."

I crossed my arms and leaned back against the pillar in front of the math building, which I'd tracked down after Aribel had hung up on me. *Fuck, I'd even called her back.* I didn't know if I was more pissed or intrigued. The combination was making me crazy.

When had I ever staked out a chick's class to see her?

Never.

But I wasn't fucking leaving now. *How much longer could she possibly be?*

Just as the thought crossed my mind, a stream of people exited the building, and at the back of the group was my target. She was as hot as I remembered—short with stick-straight natural blonde hair. Her nose was buried in a book, and her lips moved as she read the words while she absentmindedly picked at the top button of her cardigan.

I took a step toward her right when some other guy walked up to her. *Who the fuck is that? Her boyfriend?* Well, that wasn't the biggest obstacle, but I thought I'd gotten that one out of the way when I'd kissed her last night.

When he spoke to Aribel, her head popped up, and she snapped her book closed. They exchanged a few tense words, and she shook her head a lot, but he kept speaking and gesturing in short, sharp motions. Her frown deepened.

All right, enough is enough.

I strolled across the small courtyard to the front doors where Aribel was standing. "This guy bothering you?" I asked.

They both turned to look at me. Aribel pursed her thin lips and hugged her textbook to her chest. The guy just looked irritated that they had been disturbed.

"What are *you* doing here?" Aribel asked.

"You know this guy?"

"Benjamin, just leave it alone."

"Yeah, Benny, leave her alone," I said with a chipper smile.

"Benny?" he retorted, clearly offended.

"Good Lord," Aribel said.

"Who is this guy, Aribel?"

I stuck my hand out to Benny. "Grant McDermott. Nice to meet you."

Benjamin stared down at my hand, but he apparently had the manners to shake my hand anyway. "Benjamin Curtis. How exactly do you know Aribel?"

"Oh, recent acquaintance." I winked at him because I couldn't resist poking at his jealousy.

"I don't have time for this. I'm going home," Aribel said.

She turned to go, but Benjamin stopped her. "Aribel, wait, I really want to talk about last night."

"And I think I'm done talking about it."

"Last night?" I asked.

She didn't seem like the type to bed-hop. She was clearly a bit uptight. I needed to shrug her out of that cardigan because there was only one thing I liked tight about my women.

"I don't want to talk about last night with *either* of you," she snapped and started storming across the courtyard I'd just crossed.

"Aribel, were you with this guy last night?" Benjamin asked, grabbing on to her wrist.

"Yes," she spat, snatching her hand back. "And why should it matter to you, Benjamin? You broke up with me. I told you I didn't want to be friends, but you did. I don't think any of my *friends* would act like a jealous ex-boyfriend if they found out I'd been with someone else last night. In fact, all of my friends are encouraging me."

I cracked up, and Aribel sent me another stern glare. Her eyes dropped to my mouth for a fraction of a second, and something in her softened.

Benjamin drew her attention again. "Fine. I thought I'd made a mistake, but if you're already hanging out with someone else, then I guess I didn't."

Her eyes turned stony dark blue, like the sky in the middle of a hurricane. She looked fucking fierce, and it was turning me on.

"I guess you didn't," she agreed.

I jogged lightly alongside her as we left Benny behind. "Ex problems?"

She held her book tighter against her chest and blatantly ignored me.

"So, after your phone died earlier today, you didn't call me back."

Aribel rolled her eyes and picked up her pace, carrying us out across an open field.

"Do you need my number for next time?"

She humphed and kept walking.

Jesus, what is with this chick? "You don't take jokes very well, do you?"

"Excuse me, but did I lose a glass slipper or something?" she asked.

"What?"

"A glass slipper. Do I look like Cinderella to you? Are you some kind of prince trying to sweep me off my feet? What is this whole charade, Grant?"

"No charade, babe. I just wanted to see you and take you out."

"Uh-huh. Where exactly are you taking me?"

I smirked at her. "Dinner." *My bed.*

"Why do I have a feeling that we're not talking about eating the same thing?"

I chuckled to myself. She had me there.

"Oh, come on. I didn't even say that." Though, if I had it my way, I'd be doing more than that tonight.

"You didn't have to," she called over her shoulder.

I caught up to her again and started walking backward in front of her. I was probably making a spectacle of myself, but I didn't really care. She didn't even seem to notice that people were staring at us.

"Look, I really do want to take you out. I'm not one to deny myself the things I want, but I *was* talking about eating food with you."

"No. And anyway, how did you know to find me? Are you stalking me or something now? Should I invest in a rape whistle?"

"No, but you can blow my whistle, baby."

"Oh, dear Lord."

She tried to push me aside to continue walking, but I circled her wrist and pulled her back toward me. Her hand landed on my chest, and she lightly tugged on the dog tags there as she tried to regain her balance.

"All joking aside, I want to go out with you. Why won't you go out with me?"

"Because I don't *want* to," she snapped defiantly, taking a step back.

"What can I do to change your mind?"

"Enroll at Princeton, get a higher IQ, stop having sex with the entire school," she ticked off on her fingers. "Oh, and be someone else—someone who cares about his future, his career, and not just some stupid band."

I leaned forward into her until our noses were almost touching. "For someone who doesn't even know me, you're incredibly judgmental."

The hiccup in her breathing was the only thing that gave away her racing heart. Her eyes were fiery as if my words only fueled her, and saying no was her challenge as much as getting her to say yes was mine.

"It's hardly judgmental when everything I said was true."

"Just give me a chance," I whispered, releasing her wrist and snaking my hand down to her waist.

She was skinny but soft everywhere I was touching her. She had smooth skin with just enough extra padding, and she wasn't too muscular. I trailed my hand down lower and knew that her hips would fill out something beautiful in the next couple years. I wanted to grip them as I slammed into her. I wanted to see her pale skin flush as I fucked her.

Fuck, I'm getting turned-on again.

Her pupils were dilated as she stepped away from my touch. Whatever had just torn through me, she was feeling it, too. If she said she wasn't, then she was a fucking liar. She wanted me, and I was going to fucking give her what she wanted.

"You have a million other girls dying to fall into your bed. Give that chance to someone else."

"I'm giving it to you."

"Then, you're only going to be disappointed, so just leave me alone."

She scurried away, and this time, I let her. I glanced around and saw just how many people had been staring at us.

"Nothing to see here people," I called out to the crowd.

Everyone's eyes shot back to whatever they had been doing before and left me to stand in the middle of the field, looking out after Aribel.

What the hell am I going to do now?

My hands were shaking as I dashed across the open quad. People were staring at me from all directions. I *hated* the spotlight. I was supposed to be invisible. I was supposed to get high marks in all my classes, graduate at the top of my class, and then start my career as a lab researcher. My parents expected me to eventually meet the right kind of guy—someone confident and ambitious, a Princeton alum preferably. These things were important to me. I couldn't forget that the next time I was trapped in Grant McDermott's heated gaze. Better yet, he just needed to leave me alone.

When I made it to the chemistry building, I plopped down into the first available seat in the lecture hall, and I placed my hands flat on the desk to keep them steady. *What is wrong with me?* I'd never acted like this before.

Cheyenne's words rang in my ears. *Grant McDermott does not ask people out.*

That had to be an exaggeration, right? Because he had just asked me out again.

"Aribel," Kristin said in welcome. With a big smile, she took the seat next to me. "I just saw you with Grant McDermott on the quad!"

"Oh," I said softly. "How do you know Grant?"

"ContraBand, duh! Like, everyone knows who Grant is. If you don't follow the band, how do *you* know Grant McDermott?" she asked, her brown eyes wide.

I debated if I should just tell her that I didn't know Grant, but she would probably want more details if I gave her that kind of answer. "My friends dragged me to the band's show last night after Benjamin broke up with me."

"Oh, I'm sorry. I was wondering what that was all about with Grant since I knew you were taken. That sucks so bad," Kristin said.

I hated sympathy, and I hated false sympathy even more. Kristin and I coincided in the same group of mutual friends, but that didn't mean she knew me well enough to be this sorry about my breakup.

"It's for the better. It's not a big deal."

"I still can't believe you were yelling like that on the quad," Kristin said.

Had we been yelling? "He was bothering me."

"He's gorgeous. He can bother me all he wants."

"I'd prefer that," I said dismissively.

"So…you have no interest in him at all?"

"Did I look like I did when I walked away?" I asked. I was getting irritated again. *Is everyone going to be in my business about this?*

"You guys looked like you were going to kiss."

"Well, we didn't."

"Okay, jeez, I was just asking," she said, pulling up her laptop.

At that moment, the professor walked up to the front of the lecture hall and clapped his hands. "All right, class, let's get started."

I tried to push aside the events that had transpired. I'd gotten rid of Grant McDermott. That was all that mattered. People would forget about our encounter on the quad. Everything would go back to normal.

I reached into my bag and pulled out my chemistry assignment. I passed it over to Kristin for the TA to collect.

"Hey, darlin'," I heard as I ducked my head under the table.

My head snapped back up and smacked into the desk. "Shit," I cried, rubbing the back of my head. I saw Grant's standing in the aisle and nearly groaned. "What are you doing here?"

Grant smiled back at me broadly with his eyes wide and innocent. I knew that he was *anything* but innocent. His eyes averted to Kristin sitting next to me. Her mouth was hanging open.

"Babe, you mind relocating? I'd like your seat," he said, laying on the Southern charm thick.

"Um…sure," Kristin said breathlessly. She picked up her laptop and started shuffling her papers together.

"Is there a problem back there?" the professor asked.

"Sir, we're just getting our seats situated, sir," Grant spoke up confidently.

"Well, get situated quickly. I have a class to teach."

"Yes, sir."

Kristin stared back at me in disbelief before scurrying to a seat across the aisle. I didn't even know what to say as Grant slid effortlessly into the vacated chair. He slunk back and tossed his arm across the back of my seat. Some of his dark hair fell forward across his forehead, and he wore his sexy smirk like a god.

"What are you doing here?" I hissed as the professor started teaching.

"You told me to enroll at Princeton. I'm not bad at chemistry, but I thought I'd sharpen up."

"Grant, seriously, this isn't a game."

"No, princess, it's not. Now, shh…you're interfering with my learning experience."

"Interfering?" I managed to gasp out.

"Shh…" he said, pressing his finger to his lips and looking at me with his peripheral vision.

I snapped my mouth shut and tried to focus on the class, but my mind wasn't in it. I was too busy trying to figure out Grant's motive. I wouldn't suddenly go on a date with him because he stalked me to my chemistry class.

Partway through the lecture, Grant's hand slid from my chair to my side and landed on my thigh. I swatted at him, and he moved his hand away, but then he replaced it a minute later.

"Ever heard of sexual harassment?" I growled at him.

"Nope."

"You should look into it," I said, pushing his hand away again.

He turned to face me again, and his gaze felt hot on my face. I tried to focus on the professor.

"Go out with me."

"No," I groaned. "Find someone else, and leave me alone."

"I don't want anyone else. I want you."

"Tough shit! You don't always get what you want."

"Fine. Just come to my show in the city this weekend."

"If I won't see you here, why would I drive to New York City to see you?" I demanded.

"Because it's the city that never sleeps, and neither will you."

"Oh my God." *Where the hell did he come up with this stuff?*

"Just go out with me. Anywhere. Dinner, the city, coffee. I'll fucking sit out on the quad with you, and we can let people stare at us again. Just give me a chance."

"Why?"

What I wanted to ask—but I was actually holding back for the first time in my life—was, *Why me?* I wasn't some slutty sexpot. Even if we went out, I wasn't going to give him what he wanted. I understood that I had said no and so that had made me appealing to him in some way, but it wasn't enough to justify all of this.

"Because I know what I want."

"You don't even know me."

"I know I want you."

"And that's enough?" I asked desperately.

"For me."

We were staring at each other so intently that I hadn't even noticed the professor had walked up the aisle to stand in front of my desk.

"Since you two seem unable to contain your conversation, perhaps you should continue it outside."

My mouth fell open. "I'm so sorry. We'll be quiet."

"Sir, it was my fault," Grant said, taking the fall.

That surprised me a bit.

"I don't care whose fault it is. I expect you to pack up your things and leave. Return when you will not disturb the class," he said before turning and walking back to the front of the room.

I grabbed my things and rushed out of the classroom in shame. I had been kicked out of class. I couldn't believe it. By the time I exited the room, I was fuming.

Grant followed behind me a minute later. "Aribel, I'm really sorry."

"You got me kicked out of class!" I yelled at him.

"I know. I'm so, so sorry. I didn't think—"

"That's right! You didn't think. You have *no* idea what this means to me or how this could affect me. All you care about is your stupid game. Newsflash, Grant—I'm not going to sleep with you!" I screamed in his face. "I've known you for less than twenty-four hours, and you're already messing up my life. So, do me a favor, and just get out of it!"

Thirteen years.

It had been thirteen years since I last pushed too hard for what I wanted...since the last time I had failed. All of that came crashing down around me as I stood there and let Aribel lay into me like I was no better than the scum on the bottom of her shoe.

In all honesty, I probably wasn't, not compared to someone like her. She seemed like a package deal—smart, really fucking smart, hot, and feisty. *Why the hell would she want to go out with a guy like me anyway?*

And that should have made me back the fuck off. It should have made me want to walk dick-first into the next easy pussy I stumbled across. But it didn't. As she rambled on about my utter douchiness, all I could think about was how I could fix this. So, I let her walk away. I was already going to be late for rehearsal, and if I were late one more time, Miller would have my ass.

Arriving just on time, I hopped out of my lifted dark blue F-150 and strolled into the garage. When I'd first bought the place, I'd renovated the garage, so we would have a place to rehearse. I'd only left enough space for my sleek red Ducati.

"Bro, where the fuck have you been all morning?" Vin asked.

"With your mother."

"Fuck off!" Vin yelled back at me.

I sauntered over to my baby and picked her up from her stand. She was a cherry red Gibson SG that I loved more than anything else on the planet. She had gotten me through the rough times, and every day that went by when I wasn't strumming her to life made me feel like I was dying.

"Seriously though, Grant," Miller started his best reprimand, "can't you ever manage to be on time? You'd think a label scout coming to our show tomorrow night would get you to be more serious about rehearsals."

"Miller, chill the fuck out. I'm serious about rehearsals."

"Then, can we fucking get started?" McAvoy leaned back against the wall, balancing precariously on two legs of his stool. He flipped a drumstick between his fingers.

"Yeah. Are we playing 'Hemorrhage'?" I asked.

McAvoy started the beat to our lead song.

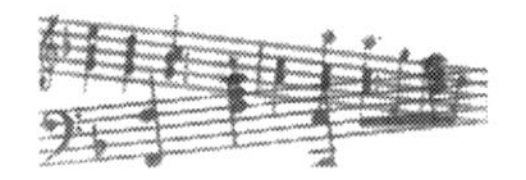

The words were spilling out of my mouth. My hands were flying across my baby as I coaxed the chords and rhythms out of her. My body was super heated from the bright lights on the stage, and sweat collected on my brow and the back of my plain black V-cut T-shirt. My dog tags hung loose around my neck, moving in time with me.

McAvoy was shirtless and fully tatted with his hair swinging as he slammed the sticks down on the drums in front of him. Miller's bass beats were thumping into my body. He looked completely unfazed in his crisp jeans and polo as the heat intensified through the set. Vin's shirt was a size too small, and somehow he was flexing as he played his shiny black guitar next to me.

We were killing it tonight. Most nights, I'd felt like we were in sync, but nothing could compare to tonight. It was a Saturday night in September, and the dive bar in New York City where Miller had gotten us a show already looked like they were breaking the fire code with how many swaying, drunken bodies were crammed into the small space.

A blonde chick was standing in the front row in the lowest cut shirt I'd ever seen. Her tits were nearly bouncing out, and I could almost see her nipples as she danced and jumped to our music. She hadn't looked away from me for one second the entire set, and I was sure we'd be fucking in the restroom before I even knew her name.

As I finished off our last song, the light panned across the room, and the crowd cheered to a deafening volume. Performing was an adrenaline rush unlike anything else. I felt perfectly in control and in my element.

"We're ContraBand. Thanks for coming out," I called out to the crowd before swinging my guitar onto my back and exiting the stage.

The venue actually had a real backstage, unlike The Ivy League, and the other bands were lounging on couches and chatting with fans. McAvoy immediately made friends with the dudes who had gone on first, and Vin was already fondling a chick near the stage door.

Miller shrugged. "Feels weird, not being bombarded."

"We would be if we took one step out that door." I pulled a joint from my pocket and lit it up. *I didn't typically smoke in public, but who the hell is watching now?*

"You going for the blonde in the front row?" Miller asked intuitively.

The guy was sharp. He always picked up on the moods of the guys, and he was able to keep us cohesive.

"We'll see."

About ten minutes later, the next band started their set, and a wave of girls ran backstage. A crowd was forming for us, and Blondie was at the lead.

"Hey, sexy," she said, walking right up to me and running her hand down my dog tags.

"Hey, darlin'."

"I *loved* your show." She stuck her chest out, and her tits pressed against me, emphasizing how much she would enjoy an aftershow.

"Thanks, babe. This your first ContraBand show?"

"Mmhmm...I sure hope it's not my last."

I smiled down at her in a way that I'd heard melted panties and nodded my head toward the back room. She arched an eyebrow and winked. All the confirmation I needed.

"You made it, Cheyenne," Vin called out next to me.

My head snapped to the side, my conversation with Blondie completely forgotten. *Cheyenne? As in, Aribel's roommate? Is she here?* She might have been pissed with me, but maybe her friends had dragged her along. It was wishful thinking maybe, but I had to know.

"Will you just give me a minute?"

She pouted with her gloss-coated full lips. For a second, I envisioned the mess that would make on my dick, and I shuddered. Blondie had a nice rack, but she needed to take that shit off.

"Come on, baby," Blondie purred.

"Just one minute." I held up a finger, pulled myself from her grasp, and walked over to where Vin was standing with a tall, curly-haired ginger.

I looked around, but I didn't see a short blonde in a cardigan. Maybe she was hidden behind the mass of people who had just come backstage. "Cheyenne," I said in greeting.

"Oh, Grant, hey," she said, smiling warily at me.

Not the reaction I was used to. I wondered if Aribel had told her what had happened or if gossip had traveled to her.

"Bro!" Vin said, trying to nudge me out.

He still didn't realize that I had no interest in the girl in front of me.

"Hey, is Aribel with you tonight?"

"Aribel? Hmm…" Cheyenne glanced back at the two girls standing behind her.

One of them, a nondescript brunette, shook her head, and her eyes bulged slightly. *All right, so they are going to play it like this.*

"She's not with us," the other girl with a blonde pixie cut said so softly.

I barely caught what she had said.

"Oh, she didn't show?" I couldn't hide my disappointment. *How the hell am I going to get to this girl?*

"We tried to get her to come, Grant," Cheyenne spoke up.

The brunette chick smacked her.

"What, Shelby? We did! Nothing wrong in telling him."

"She's not interested in him," Shelby whispered.

"She's an idiot for not being—"

"Ladies, it's fine," I said, shutting them up.

I didn't want them to keep bickering, and if they kept talking about her, it was going to bring me down from the high I was on from the show. I liked to hold on to my adrenaline rush for as long as I could.

Blondie was making her way over to me, and she had a scowl on her face that did nothing for her. After just talking about Aribel, the thought of fucking Blondie in the restroom stall didn't sound that appealing. *Who the fuck am I?*

"Guys," Miller said. He had a huge smile plastered on his face. "The scout wants to talk to us!"

"What? Really?" Vin asked.

"Scout?" Cheyenne asked curiously.

"A label scout," Vin told her. "We're gonna get fucking signed. We're gonna be fucking famous!"

"Vin, keep it down," Miller said, punching him on the arm.

"Sorry, girls," Vin said. He leaned forward and planted a bold kiss on Cheyenne's lips. "Next time you see me, I'll have graduated to rock god."

Cheyenne laughed and shook her head. *Yeah, she wants him.*

I nodded at the girls and didn't even glance at Blondie before turning and following my brothers to where we would meet with the label scout. Anticipation buzzed through every inch of my body, and by the time we made it to a private back room, I was practically bouncing from the shot of adrenaline. This was my future right here, my boys' future. Our moment for fame was dangling before us on a string, and all we had to do was walk into this room and take it.

"Welcome, gentlemen," a guy in a black suit said.

With greasy short hair, a fake smile, and beady, observant eyes, he looked exactly how I'd pictured label scouts.

"Please, sit. You want beers or water or something?"

We all shook our heads.

McAvoy was last into the room. He shut the door and took a seat.

"Great. We're all here. I'm Frank Boseley with BankHead Records. I'm glad that I was able to come out and hear you guys live. Look, I'll just cut to the chase. I'm not sure you're exactly what our label is looking for right now."

My stomach plummeted. *Shit!* The boys deflated around me. I knew that this was just the first of many rejections we would likely see in this industry, but we had *killed* it tonight. *If a label didn't want us off of that performance, when would they want us?*

"Thanks for inviting me out. I wish you luck in your future."

Miller, always the best of us, walked up and shook Frank's hand. Miller handled the business side of the band, so he'd had the most contact with Frank. It must have hit him the hardest even though it was clear we all felt like someone had punched us in the gut.

"Thank you for the opportunity," Miller said and then he turned back to us. "Come on, guys."

I stood in dismay and started to leave with my friends. I couldn't believe what had just gone down. My high was diminishing quickly, and I was going to need a drink and at least a blow job to get over this.

"Grant," Frank called, stopping me in my tracks. "My man, do you mind staying after for a minute?"

What the fuck did he want? Miller, McAvoy, and Vin looked like they wanted to know the same damn thing. I was too curious not to stay though even if the man gave me the creeps.

"Yeah, sure. What's up?"

"Just close that door for a minute."

I nodded at the guys reassuringly before shutting the door. "What's up?"

Frank crossed his arms over his chest and smiled. "I know I said that the label isn't interested in ContraBand, Grant, but that's only partially true."

"What do you mean?" I asked, confused.

"They're not interested in ContraBand. They're interested in you."

Oh. Motherfucker thought I was a sellout?

"The reason I'm here today is because of you. We're looking for a front man. Solo acts are selling right now, Grant, and I'm offering you the opportunity of a lifetime to sign with BankHead Records."

"What about the other guys?"

"Fuck the other guys. You don't need them. You carry that band. You're the *it* factor, and you're the person fans come to watch. The screaming crowd was for you, my man. People were cramming into this bar for you. You're filling a dive bar, and we'll fill arenas together."

I laughed and scratched the back of my head. *Arenas. Shit.*

"So, what do you say, Grant? You with us?"

"What do I say?" I said. I looked straight into that fucker's beady eyes and told him exactly what I thought, "No. I'm going to have to say no."

"No?" he asked in shock. "You have no idea what you're missing out on."

"You're a fucking piece of shit if you think I'll ditch my brothers for you. I'm not a sellout. I'm not a fucking dick you can jack off with the delusional promise of sold-out arenas. If I'm fucking selling out arenas, then it's happening with my boys behind me. Without them, this business isn't worth the headache of dealing with pieces of shit like yourself."

I stormed out of that room like someone had lit a fire under my ass. I pushed past the guys and ignored their questions. They could see the murderous look on my face, but I didn't have it in me to tell them the audacity that prick had.

Blondie was waiting for me as well, but I wasn't in the mood for that bullshit tonight. I'd barely been in the mood for it before Frank Boseley had fucked up my entire night.

Now, I was only in the mood for one thing.

"Where do you live?" I asked Cheyenne as soon as I reached her.

I was *not* sulking just because my roommates had all gone to the ContraBand show in the city and left me behind. I hadn't wanted to go, and I certainly hadn't wanted to see Grant McDermott.

But I couldn't concentrate on my homework, and for the first time in forever, I felt a bit silly for doing homework on a Saturday night. My shoulders ached from hunching over my desk all day. I rolled them back a few times and closed my book. I might as well try to get some sleep.

As I was about to change into something more comfortable, a knock on the door stopped me short. *Who the hell is at my door?* I hoped it wasn't my drug dealer neighbors. The last time they had stopped by, they had asked if they could stash their weed in our house until the cops passed through, and then they'd had the nerve to be angry when I'd refused.

I looked through the peephole in my door to see who it was, and my eyes widened in shock. Grant McDermott was standing on my front porch. I flattened myself against the door and took a few heaving breaths. I didn't care that I had been thinking about him all night—or all day, for that matter. I couldn't answer the door.

"Aribel!" Grant called, banging on the door again. "I know you're in there. Cheyenne said you would be home."

Cheyenne! That traitor!

"Aribel! Are you there?"

I sighed heavily. *Well, what should I do now?* He looked like he might stand out there all night. Not that it would really bother me, but I did want to get some sleep tonight. Just as he started attacking my door again, I pulled it open with a scowl.

I smoothed my blonde hair back and then tried to stop fidgeting. "What do you want, Grant?"

"Can I come in?"

"To my house?" I asked incredulously.

"Where the fuck else would I *come*, babe?" He arched an eyebrow, and the first hint of a smirk crossed his face.

Is everything sexual with him?

Yes.

"No, you can't come in. Aren't you supposed to be in New York?"

"You're not in New York," he said plainly.

"How observant. Didn't you have a show?"

I was stalling, and he could tell. He took a step toward me. I stood my ground, which took real effort because of his nearness.

"I finished my show," he growled. "Now, can I come in?"

Jesus, what is up with him? He seemed even more…primal than normal.

"I already told you no."

"I drove all the way from the city to see you. Doesn't that count for something?"

"Not sure what you want it to count for. I thought I made myself perfectly clear after you got me kicked out of my class yesterday."

"So, you won't let me in then?" He hovered mere inches away from me.

"I'm not sure how many more times I have to tell you that you can't come inside," I said irritably.

A smile crossed his face, the same one that had done me in the last time we'd been together. I could feel the tension crackling between us, like a struck match or a zap of static.

"Fine," he said.

Then, he grabbed me around the waist, yanked me outside, and dropped his mouth down onto mine hungrily. I lost myself in his lips. His hands ducked under my sweater, and his fingers dug into my soft flesh beneath. And without even realizing it, I was grasping his T-shirt for dear life and feeling the cold metal of his dog tags in my hands.

Holy shit! I'd never been kissed like this before. My whole body was on fire, and his lips were just fueling the flame. Burning desire snaked through me, starting in my fingertips, scorching through my chest, and settling in my core.

Grant walked me backward into my apartment and slammed the door shut. My back hit the wall, but our lips never broke apart. His hands ventured up my shirt, and I stopped breathing as he trailed his fingers lightly along my ribs. He skimmed the underside of my breast, and a groan escaped my lips. I squirmed against him, wanting what he was offering and silently freaking the fuck out.

"Grant," I groaned.

His mouth left mine, and he started kissing down my neck. My chest rose and fell heavily.

"Yeah, darlin'?"

"Darlin'?" I repeated mockingly.

He pulled back and stared down into my eyes. "Princess, Aribel, Ari, whatever you want me to call you."

Bending slightly, he seized the backs of my thighs and hoisted them around his waist. I gasped out and instinctively wrapped my arms around his neck.

"What are you doing?" I cried in shock.

He started walking toward the living room without answering me.

"Grant, put me down!"

Once we were standing over the couch, he lowered me onto it and covered my body with his.

Oh my God, he is rock solid. I could feel every inch of him as he lay there on top of me. He wasn't overly built, but he was all lean muscle, and the way his body was moving against mine was making me forget sense.

His lips found mine again, and then I felt his erection slide up against the thin material of my yoga pants. My mind immediately started firing on all cylinders again, and I knew *exactly* what he'd wanted when he laid me down on the couch.

"Grant, stop!" I said, pushing at his chest.

Holy shit! How had I let myself get this carried away? I never got carried away. His kisses had done things to me that I didn't understand. I'd completely lost myself…and I'd liked it. But as much as I'd liked it, I couldn't let it continue.

My breathing was ragged as I tried to get myself under control. His body still covered mine, and I was sure he knew exactly what he had done to me.

He groaned and pulled back to stare at me with his pleading brown eyes. His body was still aligned with mine, and when I shifted, he gripped my hip tighter in his hand.

"Oh, come on. You want me."

I shook my head and swallowed. I didn't want *this* even if I had gotten lost in his lips.

"You seriously want me to stop after you kissed me like that?"

At least I knew it had affected him, too. Actually, as I shifted out from under him to sit up, that became *very* clear. "I didn't kiss you like anything."

"Bullshit!"

"Well, are you happy? You got what you wanted."

"I got a tenth of what I wanted, princess."

"A tenth is all you're going to get. Now, you should probably go," I told him.

"Go?" His eyebrows shot up. "You're kicking me out after I just got permission to enter?"

"I didn't *give* you permission."

His hand ran down my jawline. "How many other people do you kiss like that when they ask to come inside?"

I swatted his hand away. "What are you really doing here, Grant? Besides the other nine-tenths that you want."

"I thought you would be at the show."

"I bet plenty of other girls were at the show, offering a lot more, that you didn't have to drive home to see."

"Would you prefer I was with them?" he asked.

He was waiting for me to contradict him, but that smile on his face held my tongue.

"You answer my questions with questions a lot."

Grant shrugged and glanced away. "Do you really want to know? I haven't even told the guys yet."

I hadn't expected him to actually answer when I asked him the question, but he wasn't advancing on me at this point, so that was a positive.

I might as well keep him talking. "Sure."

"We had a scout for a label come to the show tonight."

"That's good, right?" I asked uncertainly.

He didn't look like it had been a good thing.

He scoffed. "It should have been. Fucking prick."

I fiddled with my fingernails and tucked my legs up underneath me. "Did the scout not like your band?"

"He liked *me*," he said plainly.

He was fuming and trying desperately not to show it. I wondered how often he talked to people about the shit in his life because he seemed incredibly uncomfortable with it. I couldn't blame him though. It wasn't like I was particularly forthright about my own life.

"I'm not following."

He jumped out of his seat and stomped angrily across the room. He pushed the sleeves of his shirt up, and the muscles in his arms bulged. I noticed a tattoo peeking out of his shirt on his bicep, but I couldn't really see what it was.

"They wanted me but not the band. They offered to sign me if I left ContraBand."

It sounded like a pretty shitty deal if he was that invested in the band, but maybe he just wanted to be famous. Looking at his scowling face, I couldn't see that being the case.

"I'm guessing you didn't do it?"

"Do I look like a fucking sellout to you?"

I glared at him. "Don't yell at me! I was just asking. You're the one telling me about your shitty night. I don't have to listen!"

"Fine. I didn't mean to blow up. I'm just…I'm not a fucking sellout."

"I never said you were. I just thought you might want this as a career, and someone offered it to you, so it makes sense that you might have taken it. I guess I was wrong." I crossed my arms and gritted my teeth.

I had asked him one simple question, and he didn't have to be such an ass about it.

"As long as I have my guitar, I'm fucking solid." He mirrored me and crossed his arms. "The band isn't just a band. Those guys are my brothers. It would be like getting rid of family, and I'm not fucking doing that."

That was probably the nicest thing I'd ever heard come out of Grant's mouth, and we'd managed to have a semblance of a conversation without him making some dick sexual reference.

"Then, it sounds like you made the right choice. Why are you so pissed off about it?"

He shrugged and turned.

I stared at his profile. His jaw was strong and defined with stubble growing in. His lips were full, and his nose was angular. I could make out his high cheekbones and the intensity of his gaze.

"Grant?" I prompted.

"I don't know how to explain it."

"Are you just going to stand there all night and try to figure it out?"

"I'd rather get back to my nine-tenths, princess," he said, walking back over to me and sitting down.

I stood hastily. "I don't think so, Prince Charming."

Grant laughed at the nickname and leaned back casually on the couch. "Charming, huh?"

"Or maybe you're actually a frog."

"Does that mean I get to kiss you again?"

"I don't think so."

"You know, I think what irritates me is that I can't release my frustration. Are you sure you can't help with that?"

I rolled my eyes. *Nice try.* "Not a chance. You should probably go actually, so I can go to sleep."

"Want some company?" He stood and his fingertips circled my waist, drawing me toward him.

How did he do that so easily?

"Um…no company."

Seeing that I wasn't going to change my mind, he grumbled something under his breath. "All right."

He trudged across the room, and I followed him.

He reached for the door. "So, Ari, can I see you again?"

I smiled despite myself. He'd used my name. Even if it was a shortened version of it, it was *my* name. *Improvement.*

"Do I have much of a choice?" I asked, knowing that it wasn't likely.

"No, not really."

"Relentless, aren't you?"

"Yes," he said, slipping my hand into his and pulling me into him.

I didn't even fight him this time.

My arm wound around his neck as he dipped his head and placed a kiss firmly on my lips. It wasn't the fiery passion and deliriousness of the last one, but this one was a promise. He was telling me that I would be seeing more of him whether I wanted to or not, and my answering kiss betrayed the fact that I wanted to.

It was official. Aribel fucked me up. The asshole at the record label be damned, Ari was the one driving me mad. I'd kissed a lot of girls, and not a single one of them had I thought about longer than a fleeting moment. I'd say I didn't fuck girls twice, but I couldn't remember them long enough to know if that were true.

So, why had I driven all the way from the city to see Aribel without the promise of some ass? In fact, I'd been certain she would turn me down. But something about her had made me want to try for it anyway. Maybe it had been the way she put up a fight, her reactions to me kissing and touching her, or her fucking bullshit banter.

And who is the pussy that had taken over my body when I opened up and told her about the band? Any other girl, I would have just fucked until I forgot about it, but no, not Ari. She wouldn't let me forget about it. She wouldn't even let me keep kissing her.

I'd thought that maybe since I told someone about what had happened with the label, it would be easier to tell my boys about what had gone down when I stayed behind. But it wasn't.

I walked into the garage for our regularly scheduled band rehearsal the next afternoon, and all the guys were sitting around on couches, not touching their instruments. *Yeah, I'd seen this coming.*

"Rehearsal is canceled. We're going to get beers," McAvoy told me with a nod.

"All right," I said. "Want me to drive?"

Miller shrugged as he walked past me and out of the garage. *So, he's pissed. Well, aren't we all?* Last night hadn't gone down how any of us anticipated.

"That means, yes, dick," Vin said, punching me on the arm, as he followed Miller out.

"Are they going to hate on me all night?" I asked McAvoy.

"It'll blow over, dude," McAvoy said, holding a joint between his fingers. "Want some before we go?"

He handed off the joint to me, and I took it graciously. *I fucking need this.* After taking a few long drags, I passed it back to McAvoy, and we walked out to my truck.

I headed to a hole-in-the-wall Mexican restaurant that we frequented in town and pulled my truck into the run-down parking lot. They had good food and cheap beer, which was all that mattered. We took our normal seats in the back of the restaurant and ordered a few pitchers.

"So, what happened last night?" Miller asked, getting straight to the point.

"Yeah, you ran out of the fucking place like some motherfucker was chasing you with a gun," Vin said.

I shrugged. "The label offered me a solo gig."

The guys nodded like they had been expecting that. They still looked pissed, and I couldn't blame them.

"I told him to fuck off and that I couldn't be in this business without my bros."

"I told you," Vin said, smacking Miller upside the head.

"We all thought that, Vin," McAvoy said. "It was just a shitty night for everyone, and then you just disappeared."

"Yeah. Where did you go?" Miller asked.

"You know he went to get himself some ass," Vin piped up.

"Of course I did." I didn't want my boys to think I was losing my game.

"No one knows Grant here like I do," Vin said. "Man needed some pussy. Nothing wrong with that."

Miller and McAvoy shook their heads at Vin just as the pitchers arrived.

"Anyway," Miller said, already shrugging off the weight of my disappearance, "what do you guys want to do from here? We don't have a show for another two weeks. I haven't heard from another label. I was thinking we could take a breather. Just take some time off and regroup. In your case, Grant, fuck yourself out of disappointment."

Sounded about par for the course.

Aribel's dark blue eyes flashed before my eyes, and a small smile snuck onto my face. She was the only thing I wanted to be fucking over the next week. A streak of blonde hair, her groans as I'd touched her tits, her lips making my whole body hard as a rock crossed my mind. I shook my head and tried to get her out of my thoughts. *What the fuck is wrong with me?*

"I want to fuck myself out of disappointment," Vin said, "with that fucking ginger, Cheyenne. I'm ready to find out if the carpet matches the drapes."

"So, how long are we talking?" I asked, ignoring Vin's vulgar comment.

"A week?" Miller offered.

A week sounded good. I needed to stop obsessing about Aribel, so maybe the next time I saw her, I wouldn't try to attack her.

"Cool. I think I'm going to call Sydney then and go visit her," I said.

Vin whistled. "Bring her back with you. I've never seen a nicer ass. You know exactly what I'm talking about."

I slammed him back into the booth and cut off his windpipe. "Pipe the fuck down, and remember who you're talking about."

Vin glared and pushed me off of him. "All right, bro! Fuck off! I'll stick with my redhead."

"Yeah, you fucking will."

I'd made out with Grant McDermott in my own house—willingly. *Who the hell am I?*

Aribel Madison Graham did *not* get caught up in guys, let alone in a guy like Grant McDermott.

And now, I'm referring to myself in the third person. I was seriously going off the deep end. I was way too smart for all of this.

The girls had stayed in town with Cheyenne's family and didn't get back until late Sunday night, when I had already been in bed. I'd made sure I was up and out of the house the next morning before anyone could talk to me. I'd known that Cheyenne had spoken to Grant about coming here, and I wasn't looking forward to her harassing me about what had happened.

When I couldn't avoid my roommates any longer, I finally returned home. Prepared for the worst, I tried to act like nothing was different, but Cheyenne had decided to stake out the apartment. I passed by her on my way to my bedroom, and she jumped over the couch to block my path.

"Where have you been all day?"

"At school," I responded, trying to walk around her.

"Not with Grant?"

"Grant who?"

"Don't play coy with me! I need details! Grant asked me for our address, so he could come see you Saturday night. What happened?"

"You gave some random guy the address to our apartment?" I shook my head, just thinking of the absurdity of it all. "What if he came here to kill me?"

"So, he was here?" she squeaked.

Gabi and Shelby sheepishly walked out of their rooms. Shelby waved at me and bit her bottom lip as if it would keep her from demanding details just like Cheyenne. Gabi looked as far off in her own world as ever.

"Yes. He was here. He came, he saw, he conquered. Can we move on now?"

I tried to walk around her again, but she grabbed my arms and started jumping up and down.

"Conquered? As in, you had sex last night?" Cheyenne asked.

"Do you know me at all?" I asked, flabbergasted.

"Oh my God, don't spare us the details!"

I stared at them in disbelief. They actually thought I'd gone through with it. *How could they think that I would give it up that easily?* It wasn't like I was forty and had never had sex. I was only nineteen years old. *What's the big deal?* I hadn't been interested in any guy enough to give myself up, and since it hadn't happened yet, I just wasn't willing to let it all go so freely. I wanted there to be a reason to do it. I wanted to *want* to do it. And all I'd ever felt was nervous, disgusted, and to be totally honest, scared.

But I wasn't about to tell them that. It was easier to deflect the conversation.

"Did *you* hook up with that guy you were talking about?" I asked instead of answering Cheyenne's question.

"No, but that's not the point. Grant McDermott was in our house. He came here to see *you*!"

Shelby stepped forward. She tossed her brown hair over her shoulder and piped up, "You know Cheyenne is never going to let you do your homework until you tell her what happened."

And neither is she obviously.

Fair point. Nice move, Shelby.

"Grant came over and knocked on the door until I answered. We kissed, we talked some, and then I made him leave." I left out the part about the record label and the second kiss. I wasn't sure if I was supposed to talk about the former, and I kind of wanted to keep the latter to myself.

They all looked stunned. *What did I say?*

"He just left?" Gabi whispered.

"Well, he asked to see me again, but yeah, he just left."

"Okay, you're like a Grant McDermott virgin, so let me fill you in," Cheyenne said.

I scrunched my eyebrows together. "Aren't all of you Grant virgins?"

"We follow him around to his shows. We know him and how he operates," Shelby explained.

"How he operates?" I asked. I thought I knew where this was going, and it wasn't going to be pretty.

"Grant can have whoever he wants. Yeah, he plays guitar and sings, but there's more than that. He has a presence onstage, and if you had paid attention the night we went, you'd understand."

"Okay," I drawled the word out.

"But he doesn't date, Aribel," Gabi said.

"Right!" Cheyenne cried. "He doesn't date. He doesn't just kiss a girl and leave unless he's not interested, and he must be interested because he never leaves a show empty-handed."

"Are you supposed to be endearing him to me? That sounds disgusting."

"Okay, maybe a little, but he drove over an hour to see you. After just a kiss, he asked to see you again and then left. Grant McDermott is not acting like himself with you, Aribel."

"So?"

"So, are you going to see him again?" Shelby asked earnestly.

"Everyone in New Jersey might die if Grant starts dating," Gabi murmured to herself.

"Look, I'm not dating Grant. If anything, you have all convinced me that I shouldn't see him anymore."

"But you want to," Cheyenne said with a wink.

Maybe I did.

It was the strangest feeling in the world, but I kind of *did* want to see Grant again. He hadn't been so bad once he actually stopped and talked to me about something other than getting in my pants. *And that last kiss.*

I shivered slightly at the thought of it. Kisses like that made me lose touch with reality, and I knew that if I saw Grant again…I wasn't going to stop him from kissing me.

13 GRANT

Luckily, no one had questioned my motives for driving back to Jersey to get ass when plenty of women who'd been more than willing were at the venue. I'd never been happier for my manwhore title than at that moment.

But the only way that I could escape a repeat appearance at her place had been to get the fuck out of Jersey, so I'd packed my shit and gotten the hell out of there. On the ten-hour drive to Knoxville to visit Sydney, I'd done nothing but convince myself that I'd been an idiot for storming into Ari's house after the show.

A week away had been exactly what I needed. I'd needed to forget Ari and blow off some steam after the disappointment from the label. Then, when I'd come back, I'd fallen seamlessly into the daily band rehearsals and the routine we'd perfected since we formed the band. I had been glad to be back, and it had seemed the guys were too.

Miller had written a new song during the break, and we had been messing around with it all week. He'd wanted to open with it, but I'd thought it would do better as a closer.

Since we were playing at The Ivy League, and the regulars loved our normal opener, "Hemorrhage," everyone agreed to add the new song to the end. After we put together the set list and ran through the entire show a few times, we packed up the van to head out to the show.

After the show, I'd have to decide what to do about Ari. I'd thought that getting away and sinking myself into my music would make me forget her, but she was still on my mind two weeks later. I'd wanted to go see her since I got back, but I hadn't let myself. I hadn't cared that she thought I was stalking her, but I didn't want her to think that I was more attached than I was. No matter how much I'd thought about her since I walked out of her place.

On Saturday night, I slung my guitar over my shoulder and walked into The Ivy League. The bar already had a bunch of girls crowding the counter, and when I walked inside, a few pointed in my direction and giggled. I shot them a smile, and that only made them giggle more.

By the time we were finished setting up, the bar was full of students crawling into the League after classes had ended. I usually saw a number of the same faces over and over again at our shows. I hated to admit that I missed the larger crowds from the city. Nothing would compare to the energy from our home show, but I loved when I could look out across the room and not be able to calculate how many people were in attendance.

The guys got into position just as the lights dimmed. I walked onto the stage last, and applause hit me from all sides.

I smiled confidently, owning the stage, and then stepped up to the mic. "What's up, Leaguers? I'm Grant McDermott, and we're ContraBand." I waited until the screams died down before speaking again. "It's fucking good to be here again. For the first-timers in the audience, my virgins, here's a taste of what I'm going to be giving you all night." I winked for added effect. "This is 'Hemorrhage.'"

McAvoy started up the backbeats, and then Miller, Vin, and I came in after an eight count. We'd played this song so many times that I could perform it in my sleep, but I tried to give it the same feel every time. The crowd bobbed along with beat, and I could hear girls singing along with me.

Just as I started on the second chorus, I saw her. The lyrics stuck in my throat, and I faltered through the line before recovering. Miller looked at me like I'd grown horns, but I just kept singing into the microphone as if nothing had happened. My eyes darted back to her, and she smiled at me.

Shit! Aribel.

What is she doing here? I'd thought that I would have to go to her if I ever wanted to see her again. Now, her hot little body was at my show and only ten feet in front of me. I was done for.

We ended "Hemorrhage" and moved into the next song easily. Her friends pushed her forward through the crowd until she was only a couple of rows away from me. And she wasn't in a cardigan. She wasn't even in a sweater. In fact, she was in some tight black dress, showing off her figure in ways that had my mind thinking about anything but the lyrics to this song.

I wasn't sure my eyes left her for the next couple of songs. And as embarrassed as she clearly was by the attention and her friends whispering in her ear, she held her head high and watched the entire set. She wasn't like the groupies in the first row—grinding their bodies to the music, singing along to every song, and reaching out for me—but she seemed to be enjoying herself.

"We have a special treat for you tonight," I called into the microphone. "We're playing a never-before-released track just for you. We're calling this one 'Letting You.'"

The only thing I could think about as I moved on to our last song was how fast I was going to get her backstage when I was finished.

Okay, I'd underestimated how good he is. Why didn't I pay attention the last time I was at the ContraBand show? His voice was smooth and sexy, captivating the audience with the clever lyrics and easy rhythms.

Grant moved across the stage—guitar forgotten, microphone in hand—as he belted out the bridge of the song. His stage presence was the male equivalent to a Siren entrancing and capturing its victim. He owned the stage, the music, the lyrics, the people, the lights, and the sounds. The whole fucking room belonged to him, which inevitably meant that I belonged to him.

His eyes swept the crowd, making every single person around him feel like he was singing the song specifically for to that person, but then his eyes would return to me—intense, enthralling, and alluring.

I could feel people looking at me, assessing me, wondering what was holding Grant's attention. I'd thought that I would make some kind of splash by showing up tonight, but more like a ripple and less like a tidal wave.

It had been two weeks since Grant had basically broken into my apartment and kissed me. I'd kind of been expecting him to continue stalking my existence until I was sick of him, but just when he had made me promise to see him again, he'd disappeared. And, well, I wanted to know why he'd disappeared. It was more morbid curiosity about why the man who had taken my life by storm had cleared out just as quickly. *Why would he push so hard and then fall off the face of the planet?*

His silence intrigued me, and I wasn't easily intrigued.

Cursing myself for wanting to figure him out, I'd told my friends that I was going to the ContraBand show with them. Shelby had looked stunned, Gabi had worn a knowing smile on her lips, and Cheyenne had jumped up and down while insisting on dressing me. That was how I'd ended up in a fit black dress and heels when I preferred cardigans and ballet flats.

Grant finished out the lyrics to the last song, which had to be my favorite. "That's our show. Thanks for coming out to see us. We're ContraBand. See you in a few weeks."

The crowd cheered, and I joined in with the applause. My eyes were still trained on Grant, and after he put his guitar back on its stand, he found me again in the crowd. He crooked his finger at me, and my cheeks heated. Cheyenne nudged me forward through the dispersing group of people to the side of the stage.

"Hey," I managed to get out over the noise in the room.

"Come here you," Grant said, holding out his hand.

I wavered for a second before the girls made up my mind for me and pushed me forward. I walked straight up the stairs to Grant.

He smirked. "Hey, Princess."

Oh, those goddamn nicknames! At least it isn't darlin'!

"I didn't wear my glass slippers tonight."

"Then, I guess that means you won't be leaving me at midnight either," he said, taking my hand and walking me toward the stage exit.

I glanced over my shoulder for a brief moment and saw my friends freaking out along with a whole lot of other girls glaring at me. I raised my head and attempted to look like I belonged exactly where I was going. It was what I'd been raised to do. Though, my parents had probably instilled it in me for when I would meet politicians and CEOs, not for when I was walking backstage at The Ivy League.

The backstage area actually wasn't much of a backstage. It was more like a long hallway with a restroom, a closet, and two exits. The other guys in the band were standing in the hallway. I only recognized Vin because he had tried to drug me, and he was now interested in Cheyenne.

"Picking early, Grant?" Vin asked, eyeing me up and down.

Oh, dear Lord, did he actually think I was a groupie? I opened my mouth to make sure he knew that I wasn't, but Grant was already pulling me down the hallway.

"Something like that," he said over his shoulder.

"Are you going to let them think that we're coming back here for a reason?" I hissed as we walked away.

"That's exactly what I'm going to let them think." He wrenched me through the closest door.

The room was bigger than it looked from the outside. It looked more like an employee break room.

"I'm not some groupie," she said, trying for a playful attitude. I fluttered my eyelashes at him, placed my hand on his chest, and mockingly leaned into him as if I were. "Oh, baby, take me now," I purred.

Grant reached for me, and I slithered out of his grasp. I twirled slowly in a circle, knowing his eyes were on me, and then I beckoned him forward. When I backed away and tried to sidestep him again, I almost got past him, but he was too fast, and I was in heels. He pinned me back against the table, and I was lost in his dark brown eyes.

"If you keep teasing me like that, I'll make you one," he growled.

I laughed softly, trying to slow my thudding heart, as he nipped at my ear.

"I was just joking." I pushed him off me and straightened out my dress.

"Darlin', joking about sex with me when you're not offering it up might not be in your best interest."

He had a playful glint in his eye, but I knew he was serious.

"So, you came to my show."

"Well, you stopped stalking me, so I thought I'd give it a go."

He raised his eyebrows. "Oh, yeah? How's that working out for you?"

"I think it's working out better for me than it did for you."

"I like that." He dropped his hands to my waist and ran his hands down my sides and before landing on my hips. "I've been thinking about you."

I took a step forward, startled by his honesty. "You've been thinking about me?"

"Mmhmm…about this."

His lips touched mine, and just like last time, I felt myself giving in to him. I thought I'd imagined how intoxicating his kisses were, but my memory hadn't done this justice. The only thing I could focus on was the electricity between us. Heat pooled in my stomach and radiated from my center.

Grant moved me to the couch to sit next to him. He dragged my bottom lip between his teeth and then captured me in another searing kiss. My breathing was ragged. My arm was around his neck, the other grasping his side. My leg was nestled against his, and as he drew me closer, it slipped over his knee. His hand dropped down on my bare leg. I didn't even have a mind to move him. His kisses were keeping me completely occupied.

He positioned me to straddle him. My dress rode up dangerously high, and I squirmed, wondering if I was letting this go too far. But he kept his lips on mine, and that energy was burning its way through me.

Both his hands were on my legs now, and I could feel his calloused fingertips trailing up my thigh. They were featherlight touches at first, making my whole body hum, as he traveled higher and higher. His hand slipped under my short dress, and I let out a soft gasp against his mouth. He grinned at my response as he slowly traced the line of my underwear. My body quivered at the touch, and I seriously contemplated letting him do whatever he wanted with me. *How did he get me this flustered?*

He distracted me with his mouth, but this time, he pressed his luck, tugging lightly at my underwear. His finger slid under the material, and he swiped it down my core. That brought me back to my senses. I jumped out of his lap faster than I'd thought I could move in these heels and yanked my dress back down.

Jesus, I was about to become a groupie if I couldn't get a hold of myself. Gripping the table, I took a few deep breaths. I didn't care if he saw how worked up he'd gotten me. I just had to stop.

Grant casually leaned back, looking completely unperturbed that I'd run away. Well, aside from the large bulge in his jeans.

I averted my gaze quickly. "I should probably get back to my friends."

He stood and moved so that he was in front of me again. He tucked a loose strand of blonde hair behind my ear and planted another kiss on my lips. "Are you sure?" he asked, his hands finding the hem of my dress again.

"Sure, um…yes," I said.

"Your body disagrees."

He started to slide my dress back up over my hips, but I stilled his hands.

"My friends," I said more confidently.

He sighed. I guessed he was realizing he wasn't going to get anywhere else with me right now.

He checked his watch. "Ten minutes."

"What?"

"Nothing. Don't worry about it."

I didn't wait to figure it out as I walked toward the door.

"Hey, Ari," he said, catching up to me.

"Yeah?"

His hand reached out for mine, and he threaded our fingers together. My heart skipped a beat, but I tried not to get caught up in him.

"I'm really glad you showed up."

A smile broke out on my face. "Me, too," I admitted shyly.

He gave me that heart-wrenching smile that had started it all. "And I'm going to see you again?"

His brown eyes stared deep into mine, and I couldn't think of a reason to deny him, so I just nodded. His broadening smile was worth it.

We walked back down the darkened hallway and out the door to the bar. The band was standing with a cluster of girls, my friends among them. The guys looked at us with various forms of surprise.

"You done already, bro?" Vin asked with a cackle. "Quickest quickie ever."

As the other guys cracked up, I glared at Vin.

"Seriously?" I asked in frustration.

I was ready to contradict them when Grant bent down and whispered in my ear, "Ignore them."

"Ignore them?" I hissed. "Are you kidding me right now? They think we just had sex, and you're just going to—"

"They wouldn't believe me even if I told them that we hadn't," he told me plainly.

"Oh, how your reputation precedes you."

"You and I both know what happened. Why does it matter what anyone else thinks?"

"Because I have a reputation, too, and I don't want you to make me look like one of your sluts."

Grant laughed at my comment, but I didn't think it was very funny.

"Sorry, babe, but it's a hazard of being around me."

I opened my mouth to say something smart back, but he wasn't finished.

"And you've already promised to see me again. I'm not letting you back out now."

"You're going to make me regret this, aren't you?"

He winked at me. "Not a chance."

Two guys I didn't recognize walked up to us. "Grant," one of the guys said, "Hurst said tonight was the biggest crowd we've had."

"Epic," Grant said.

I glanced between them and wondered why I was left standing here awkwardly. So, I thrust out my hand and introduced myself. "Hi, I'm Aribel."

Both guys looked at me in surprise and then back at Grant.

After a second, one of them took my hand slowly, like he had never been introduced to anyone before. "Miller."

"Nice to meet you."

He quirked a smile at me. "You, too. This is McAvoy."

McAvoy's eyes were bloodshot, and he looked really out of it, but he still managed to nod at me.

"Hi," I peeped. "Who is Hurst?"

Both guys' eyes bugged, and they turned to Grant. *What the hell is wrong with them?*

"He owns the bar," Grant informed me without glancing at his friends.

"Oh, well, that's great for you guys, right?"

"It is," Miller said. "Bigger the shows, the better the business is for him."

"Bro!" Vin called, barging in between them.

I was thrown back into Grant and grunted as I slipped on my high heel. He put his arm around me to help me regain my balance.

"Bro, where is Sydney? I thought she was going to come to the show."

I raised my eyes to Grant, who still had his arm around me. *Who is Sydney?*

"She couldn't make it," Grant said.

"Dude, you spend all week with her and can't even bring her back to share with me?" Vin asked.

He was clearly cracking himself up, but Grant looked like he was about to pummel him.

I moved away and crossed my arms. *So, that is why he had been gone.* He had been away, visiting someone else. If I had to wager from Vin's comments, she was probably someone who was a lot easier than I was.

"What the fuck have I told you about talking about her like that?" Grant growled.

"I'm an ass man. You can't fault me."

"Um…who is Sydney?" I managed to get out.

Grant took his eyes off Vin for a second to look at me, and his anger dissipated. "Oh, no. She's not…" he said, fumbling for the right words.

"She's not what?" I asked. *Why am I getting defensive?* It wasn't like we were dating.

"Ari, Sydney is my cousin."

"Oh."

Well…shit. I really am an idiot. I had gotten worked up, thinking he had hooked up with some girl all week when he just went to visit his cousin. I wasn't sure why I had even been getting worked up over him. It wasn't like we were together or anything—or that I was even interested in that. He'd intrigued me, that was all. *God, maybe I* am *judgmental.*

"I, um…okay," I said. My face heated, and I turned to walk back to my friends. *I should probably get back to my quiet, invisible life. Calculus is way easier than this.*

"Ari," Grant said, following me into the crowd. "Aribel, will you stop?"

"What, Grant?"

His eyes were fixed on me, but all I could see was everyone else staring at us. It was like the quad all over again, except all of our friends were here this time.

"I'm starting to think you're going to back out of our arrangement."

"What arrangement is that?"

"You said you'd see me again. I want some collateral on that," he said, stepping closer to me.

I just narrowed my blue eyes. "What kind of collateral?"

"I was thinking your phone number."

The people around us had gradually grown silent. Everyone was giving me the same expression that Miller and McAvoy had given Grant when I introduced myself. *Maybe Grant actually didn't go on dates with* anyone…

"You want my phone number?" I whispered now that the room had quieted.

"Then, I can make sure I can find you." He was so close to me now that his lips were nearly grazing mine.

"Just kiss her already!" Vin called out.

Grant smirked, and my heart stopped. His hand found the back of my head, and then we were kissing. Full-on making out in front of all these people, and I didn't even care. I just wanted to let this desire course through my body and live in the moment. Live the moment that I'd never allowed myself before.

Two days later, Vin and I were playing Madden on my Xbox.

"You going to call that chick?" McAvoy asked, plopping down on the couch in the middle of my living room next to Miller.

"Of course he isn't going to," Vin said. He was bobbing and weaving with his players as he spoke.

"I don't know, man," I said.

My player sacked Vin's quarterback in the last play of the game. I'd won again. Vin flipped me off.

"What do you mean, you don't know?" Vin asked. "She's just some chick that you had a quickie with in the back room of the League."

"She looked like a little bit more than a quickie," Miller observed.

"Bro, Grant doesn't do more than that."

"Vin, you blind?" McAvoy asked. "He pulled her onstage, and she introduced herself. How many groupies you know that do that?"

"There was that one girl," Vin said dismissively.

"Who?" Miller probed.

"Fuck, if Grant doesn't remember their names, why would I?"

"Guys, chill," I said, relaxing back into the recliner. "It's no big deal."

"Is that code for the three-day rule?" McAvoy asked.

I shook my head. "What the fuck is the three-day rule?"

I needed to get out of this real quick. These fuckers knew me too well not to realize that I was in over my head about Ari. I had a fucking reputation to uphold.

"When you get a chick's phone number, you wait three days to call her. Just long enough to make her think you're not interested, but not long enough to actually look disinterested," Miller filled in. "It's more of a guideline."

"Anyone actually follow that standard?" I asked.

"Looks like you are," McAvoy teased me.

I set the controller on the coffee table, stood, and stretched out. Now would be as good a time as any to make up some shit, so they'd leave me alone. "Nah, I've got plans tonight with a hot Puerto Rican chick. I'm going to be getting laid while you assholes sit around and play video games."

"See?" Vin said. "My man, Grant, isn't some pussy worried about when to call some bitch. He tapped that last night. Wham-bam-thank-you-ma'am."

A muscle twitched in my jaw, and for a second, I thought I might throw Vin through the window. *Who the fuck does he think he's talking about?* Aribel wasn't some slut who fucked every dude in her path. If I hadn't done more than kiss her yet, then I was sure she wasn't letting just anyone dip into the honey pot.

"Vin," Miller said in the voice he would use when Vin wasn't paying attention during rehearsal.

I relaxed my jaw, but it was too late. Miller had seen what I was thinking as clearly as if I had laid it out in front of him. The motherfucker knew me too well.

"What?" Vin asked, oblivious.

I walked through the living room and grabbed my brown leather jacket. I didn't know where the hell I was heading to now that I'd committed myself to going out, but it would be better than sitting around and getting shit about Ari.

I uncovered my motorcycle in the garage and steered it across town. Soon, I was out on the interstate—hitting eighty, a hundred, a hundred and twenty in the blink of an eye. My pulse rose with the speed of the bike between my legs, and a sense of control settled over me. This was what

I'd needed—speed, adrenaline, power—to make me forget everything I was constantly running from.

My cherry red baby, the booze, the girls—they were all the things I'd gotten used to needing in my life. But Ari was different. She was the new distraction to my uninterrupted self-torture. And I didn't know what the fuck I was doing. I had *no* control with her, yet I didn't feel the pain when I was around her.

Everything else did nothing but dull the ache. Ari might have started as a conquest, but I'd never met anyone else like her. Girls would put up with my shit, but she would push my buttons as much as I'd push hers. She'd give shit back to me tenfold and glare at me with those hurricane dark blue eyes, like she was going to chew me up and spit me right back out.

And she was so innocent. She hardly let me touch her, and fuck, did I want to touch her. I had a reputation to protect, yet I'd gone and made a fucking idiot of myself by asking for her phone number in front of everyone. Now, Miller and McAvoy were catching on, and I didn't want to deal with any of it.

But I'd still call her.

I knew I would. Like an addict, I'd take the morphine hit to forget the pain—even if it was temporary. I had always needed more and more of everything else in my life to stall the pain of what one argument, one kiss from her completely eradicated.

I kicked up the speed on the bike, trying to drown out her face and everything else that originated from being interested in someone like Aribel.

The rain came as unexpectedly as Aribel had into my life—a dribble and then a downpour.

I cursed under my breath, but it was soon lost to the wind howling in my helmet. I checked the next sign and groaned. I was over an hour away from home. I pulled off on the next exit ramp and cut my bike back toward

Princeton. I hoped I could outrun the worst of the oncoming storm.

I felt the shift in the weather just as I was making it onto my street. The wind picked up, the rain came down in sheets at an angle, and lightning ripped out of the sky from every direction. I'd never been happier to park my bike in the garage. It had been a cold, miserable hour, and I just wanted a steaming hot shower and to jack off in peace.

I pulled my phone out of my jacket pocket and took the stairs two at a time. I stalled on the landing when I saw that I had two missed calls from Aribel. *Fuck!* I couldn't believe she'd called me while I'd been out riding around in this shit. Actually, I couldn't believe she had called me at all.

When I dialed her number, she answered on the first ring. "Oh my God, you called me back," she said in that bitingly sarcastic tone she used all the time.

"Hey, darlin'. You miss me?"

She snorted, and it made me smile.

"Grant, I'm stranded."

"What?" I asked. "Where are you? What happened? Are you okay?"

I probably sounded a bit frantic, but I'd only just met her. I didn't want anything to happen to her.

"Yes, I'm fine. My car broke down right off campus, and my roommates are in the middle of a movie. I-I don't know what's wrong with my car. Do you think you could, um…maybe come help me?"

I stared down at my drenched clothing and shrugged. I was already soaked through. It wouldn't hurt me any to go check on her.

Who the hell am I kidding? I wanted to see her, and I'd drive through this madness to do it.

"Sure. Where are you?"

Aribel gave me the nearest intersection, and I was happy to hear that she was only a couple of miles from my place. As soon as I hung up, I was out the door and in my truck, but the storm had managed to get even worse since I'd been inside. With the wipers on high and my brights lighting my way, I could still only see a few feet in front of me.

A three-minute drive took me nearly fifteen minutes, but then I saw a black BMW sitting on the side of the road with its flashers on. "Fuck. She drives a Beamer?"

I parked behind her, shaking off the questions of why someone would give a college student a BMW, and then I dashed out of my truck. When I reached the driver's side, I tapped on the glass. I saw her jump in the front seat, and then she smiled when she recognized me. *That smile is going to be the death of me.*

I opened the umbrella I'd brought with me as Aribel rolled down the window. "Take the umbrella and go get in my truck."

"What about my car?" she asked like there was a better plan.

"Pop the hood. I'll take a look, but you won't see a tow truck tonight. Not in this mess."

She sighed and then nodded. She didn't even argue with me. *Miracle of all miracles.*

After she exited, she slid the keys in my hand, took the umbrella, and then made a dash for my truck. It only took me a couple of seconds to realize she had a busted radiator. She'd have to leave it until the morning. When I finally made it back to my truck, I didn't think there was an inch of me that wasn't sopping wet.

"Thanks," she said softly once I was settled in the seat.

"No problem," I said. "I mean, I thought I might have gotten lucky, and you wanted a jump."

I winked at her, and she just rolled her eyes.

"Seriously, everything is sexual with you."

"I just saved your hot ass. I think you can handle a joke."

She sighed and then seemed to agree. "All right. Could you tell what was wrong?"

"Cracked radiator."

"Great," she groaned.

"Yeah, but it won't be too bad. I have a friend I could hook you up with. He does great work for cheap."

"My parents will probably want me to take it to the dealer."

"Ah." I didn't know what else to say, so I shifted into reverse and backed away from her car. I made a U-turn in the middle of the street and started back the way I had come.

"Wait, my house is that way." She pointed behind her.

"I know, Princess. It would take an hour to get to your house in this. It takes fifteen to get to my place, so that's where we're going."

"Um…I don't think so."

"Look, if we're driving the hour to your place, then I'm staying there because I'm not driving the hour back."

Aribel opened her mouth as if she as going to contradict me, but then she didn't. I glanced in her direction twice, waiting for her to say something, to tell me that I'd fucking drive her to her house and back because she said so, but still nothing came out.

"My parents are going to be so angry," she whispered.

"Why? It's not your fault."

She shrugged her little shoulders and stared determinedly out the window. "I don't know."

"Seems like a silly thing to get angry about."

"Well, you don't know my parents. What would your parents say?"

"Nothing," I said, tensing at the question.

"Really? You're so lucky." She sank back into the seat and crossed her arms.

She looked really young. I'd never given a thought to her age until that moment.

"How old are you, Princess?"

"Nineteen," she said without skipping a beat.

Shit! Really young. I mean, I'd fucked girls her age and younger, *but shit!* Ari wasn't just some fuck. She seemed so mature. I definitely would have guessed a solid twenty-one at least. Maybe that was just what I'd been hoping for.

"How old are you?"

"Twenty-three."

Her eyes widened. "Oh."

"What?"

"You're my brother's age. He'd kill me right now if he knew what I was doing."

"What exactly are you doing? Getting a ride home from a guy who just helped you out of a tough position. Yeah, what an asshole!"

"That's not what I meant," she said, trying to backtrack. "He's just…protective."

"Doesn't want his little sister to turn out like the girls he's fucking?"

"Aaron is *not* like that!"

I cracked up laughing because there was nothing else to do in the situation. I was certain her brother was exactly like that.

"It's not funny."

Aribel smacked me on the arm, but I caught her hand before she could yank it back.

"If you're going to be such a jerk, I'll reconsider making you drive across town to take me home."

I turned onto my street just as she said it. After stopping in front of my house, I unbuckled her seat belt and pulled her across the cab to me. "Ari, at this point, you'd have to walk home. You're not fucking leaving."

Her eyes found mine, and I saw the anger leaving her body as she stared at me. She still looked a bit like she wanted to slap me around, but I was good with that as long as I could get her inside.

After a minute, she conceded. "You're right. I'm not."

Well, damn. This was going way better than I'd thought it would. She had fought me tooth and nail for every second of her time up until this point. *When did we turn a corner?*

I kissed her softly on the lips. I didn't want to get too into it before we went inside, but fuck, when she responded to my touch, I had to fight myself not to lay her out in the cab of my truck.

She pulled back first, and her cheeks heated when I looked down at her.

God, I want to fuck her.

"Let's go," I said, nodding toward the house before I actually acted on that.

We jogged through the rain until we were inside. I gestured for her to take the stairs, which she did without a single snide remark.

"I like your house," she said.

"Thanks."

My eyes were fixed on her body in the light from my bedroom. She was wet, and her clothes were clinging to her in the most tempting way. All I could think about was what it would feel like to peel them off of her, to get my hands on her soft skin again. I felt my body stiffen at the prospect. "I need a shower…if you're interested."

She shook her head. "I'm sure you can have enough fun all on your own."

"But you're already wet, babe." I couldn't hold back my smirk.

She snorted and crossed her arms over her chest. "Is *everything* sexual with you?"

"Not everything," I told her. "But you are torturing me with your body right now."

I watched as she shifted uncomfortably from my compliment. She wouldn't even meet my eyes. For someone who looked like *that*, I would have thought that she could take compliments better.

"No, I'm not going to shower with you, but some dry clothes would be appreciated, so I can stop torturing you," she responded softly.

"Who said I wanted you to stop torturing me?"

She leveled me with an eat-shit-and-die look, and I just laughed.

"All right, all right."

I found her some clothes before reluctantly retreating to the bathroom. It took a solid ten minutes for the cold to leach out of my skin and another ten until I felt human again. I hated making Aribel wait that long, but I had spent the better part of the last two hours in the rain. I deserved a twenty-minute shower.

Grabbing a white towel off the rack, I wrapped it around my waist and then confidently strode out into my bedroom. *This is going to be fun.* I was naked from the waist up, and I knew what my body looked like. Even though I wasn't a gym rat like Vin, I spent time to keep myself in shape. I had defined muscles in my arms and chest, not to mention a six-pack and that V that made sane women crazy.

Aribel's eyes bulged when she saw me. She hadn't expected me to walk out like this, and it was clear as her eyes raked my body. They flickered from my abs to the tattoo on my shoulder and stretching across my collarbone. *Who would guess Princess Cardigan would be interested in my tattoos?* Apparently realizing that she had been gawking, she hastily looked away like she wasn't supposed to see it.

"Um…sorry," she whispered.

I wasn't sorry though. I'd wanted her to see.

All I saw was that she was sitting around in my clothes—*my* T-shirt and sweats. She looked fucking amazing in them. I liked her wet clothes, but something about seeing her in mine turned me on. I'd never let a girl wear my clothes before.

"I'll just...yeah," she said, swiveling in place to completely face away from me.

I dropped my towel to the ground, and I watched her fidget. *Yep, completely nude here, honey. Just turn around.* But she didn't. I found a pair of boxers and some basketball shorts, but I didn't bother with a shirt. She had been interested in my body, and I wasn't going to give her an out when her eyes had widened like that.

After I changed, I wrapped my arms around her from behind, and she jumped at the unexpected touch. I dropped my lips down onto her neck and tasted her soft skin. She tilted her head slightly, and I took that as an okay to continue. My hands slid up under the T-shirt I'd let her borrow, and I pulled her hips back against mine.

Then, she groaned.

Fuck. Fuck. Fuck. Aribel was here—in my room, in my clothes. Her skin was still wet from the rain, and her body was lush and ripe for the picking.

I thought my brain shut down at this point, and all I could do was feel the woman in my arms. This, right here, was what I'd wanted.

"Ari," I whispered against her skin.

She moaned an incoherent response.

"Bed." My voice was strained from holding back.

All I wanted was to fuck her until she couldn't walk the next morning. She was driving me batshit crazy, and I was starting to believe that she had no fucking clue what she was doing to me.

"Grant, no."

She tried to pull away from me, but I still had her hips in my hands. I yanked her back against me hard, and she squeaked.

I turned her around to face me and repeated myself, "Bed."

For a split second, I thought she was going to turn me down. Then, I saw her eyes soften, and she swallowed.

"I, um..." She bit her lip and stared up at me under thick black lashes.

Fuck me.

"Get in my fucking bed, woman."

"Don't order me around."

I smacked her ass with a flat open palm, and she yelped, her eyes widening in surprise.

"What the hell?"

"Get in the bed."

Just as I reached for her, ready to make her listen, she scrambled under the covers. *Perfect.* I slid into place next to her, and I could feel her tension from a mile off.

I ran my hand slowly down her side. She tried to remain perfectly still, even as I coaxed shivers out of her. I trailed across her flat stomach to her hip bone, and I adjusted her so that she was on her side, facing me.

"Grant," she murmured, her eyes wide.

She was fighting with herself, and it looked like I was winning. I tangled our legs together and dropped my mouth onto hers. It was like turning the key in the ignition. Suddenly, I couldn't get enough of her. I couldn't stop touching her. I just wanted her. I wanted to feel my dick slide into her. I wanted to see her face when she hit climax.

I started tugging the sweats over her hips, and then I grabbed her ass in my hands. *Good God.* I was an ass man, and she had a great fucking ass. Yanking her hard against me, I knew she could feel what she was doing to me. I groaned into her mouth as her hands slid across my bare chest. Her touches were featherlight at first, like she was just testing the water. I pressed my body against her, craving her touch.

Her hands were trembling, even as they moved across my abs. I tried to slide the sweats farther down her legs, but she wasn't having any of it, and I gave up. They were far enough. I could reach everything I wanted. I slipped my hand in between us and then into her underwear. Her body was on fire, and even better, when I slid my finger across her, it came back really fucking wet. My cock twitched just at the thought of plunging into that.

She squirmed against me, but I couldn't tell if she wanted me to stop or keep going. It seemed like she wanted more to me. I gently swiped at her again, probing, until I heard her faint gasp. *Fucking fuck, that's hot.*

"Ari," I groaned, "you're so fucking wet for me."

She ducked her head into my shoulder, seemingly embarrassed, but she didn't stop me. I rolled her over onto her back and yanked the pants down to her ankles. I needed this. *Fuck, I need this.*

My hand reached for her underwear, but she put her hand out. "Grant…I can't. Oh my God, I can't do this." She frantically pulled up the sweats I'd lent her.

"Ari…" I begged.

I adjusted my erection right before her eyes, and she tried not to notice.

"I'm not going to have sex with you."

I wanted to show her exactly how wrong she was about that.

But the pleading look in her eyes, rather than the aloofness she would normally send my way, fucking broke me down. I'd give her whatever she wanted even if she wasn't giving me everything I wanted.

I sank down onto the bed next to her, and I tried to get my head on straight. She'd turned me down. I wasn't sure that had ever happened…yet I still wanted her here. I still wanted her in my bed.

"You know what?"

"What?" she breathed.

"I want you, Ari."

"I gathered that."

"Yeah, I want to have sex with you. What guy wouldn't? I mean, I want you here, like this. I want you to stay the night. I want you to just be here…with me."

She didn't know how much those words really meant. I'd never fucking wanted that in my entire life.

"Then, I want you to let me take you out to dinner. I'll pick you up, I'll take you out, we'll walk through the park, and I'll even get you home before midnight, so your coach doesn't turn into a pumpkin."

She giggled, actually fucking giggled, and I knew I had her.

"What do you say?"

She licked her lips as if she were considering. "All right, Grant. I'll go on a date with you."

We kissed until I thought I might combust from the energy coursing between us. How she held such composure was beyond me, but I wanted to respect her. I *did* respect her. It was the strangest thing that had ever happened to me.

Soon, Aribel nuzzled her head into my shoulder, her breathing slowed, and then she was fast asleep. I wrapped my other arm around her and held her tight.

I'd never had a girl spend the night just to sleep.

After I'd fallen asleep in Grant's arms, the rest of the world kept spinning at its normal speed, but my life felt like it was moving in fast forward. I'd been shocked at how far I let things go with him, but it had also seemed so easy to just let it happen. I had thought I was going to give myself up. I had never felt like that before in my life. When I was with Grant, I felt safe and secure. Although not completely comfortable in my skin, I was definitely more so with him than I'd ever felt before. And as much as my defenses were normally up, I could feel him crumbling them with ease.

I was glad that Cheyenne had planned to visit her parents in the city for the weekend, so she wasn't there to see me getting ready for my date on Friday afternoon. I chose a dark blue dress and paired it with my jean jacket and ballet flats. I'd even curled my hair and let it hang loose past my shoulders.

When Grant knocked on my door, I was surprised to find him out of his normal T-shirt and into a polo and dark-wash jeans. He'd cleaned up, too—freshly shaven, his hair styled, his tattoos hidden. My heart skipped a beat.

"Hey," he said, pulling me against him. "I've been thinking about you all week."

I started to chastise myself for getting giddy because he'd been thinking about me, but then I just let myself feel what was working its way through me. When we weren't at each other's throats, I kind of liked being around Grant.

We walked out to his truck, and I hopped up into the passenger seat.

"Hope you don't mind a little drive," he said.

"Where are we going?"

He smiled at me. "Down the shore."

It was an hour before we arrived at a small pizza place. It didn't look like much with a small sign that read *Duffie's* overhead, but the parking lot was jam-packed. I was a little worried about finding a table, but Grant didn't seem to have any anxiety.

We hopped out of the truck and Grant came around to my side. When he saw the concern on my face, he just laughed and took my hand. "Come on, Princess. It's the best pizza I've ever had. You do like pizza, right?"

Uncertainty crossed his face for a moment, but then it disappeared as soon as I nodded.

We walked into the building together, and a hostess greeted us. Every single table in the place was filled. Waiters were carrying trays of drinks and pizza and joking around with customers. The restaurant had an energy about it that made me relax. I hadn't known what to expect with Grant, but I was kind of glad he hadn't taken me anywhere fancy. That was what I typically went for, but that didn't seem like Grant to me.

"Great. Thanks," Grant said to the hostess.

"This way," she said.

We followed her through the crowd, out a set of double doors, and onto a balcony overlooking the ocean. Exactly one table was unoccupied, and it had to be the best seat in the place. *How are we so lucky?*

I sat across from Grant and waited for the hostess to leave before speaking. "This is…really nice. How did you find this place?"

"I used to come here a lot when I was younger."

"Oh, really? Are you from the area?" I asked, leaning forward. For the first time, I realized that I knew next to nothing about the man in front of me.

"Moved here from Knoxville when I was ten, and I've been here ever since." He looked a little sheepish before admitting, "This was actually my first job. I worked here through most of high school."

I'd never pictured him working, which was out of the ballpark of normalcy for me. *What do you do?*—that had been the only question that really mattered in my parents' circle of friends.

"I bet you brought all the girls here," I said lightly. *Yes, bringing up other girls is smart on the first date.*

"Uh…no, not really."

"No?"

"I didn't have to take girls out. I guess this would be the first time."

I gaped at him.

"So, how am I doing?" Grant asked, spreading his arms wide.

The first time? Like, his first date ever?

No. No way. That can't be right.

Surely, someone like Grant had had tons of girls flocking for his attention in high school. He'd had to date someone…sometime.

Right?

The longer I stared at him with that smirk on his face, the more I saw the layer underneath. He was…nervous. Grant McDermott was nervous to be on a date with me.

"You're doing great," I reassured him. I couldn't believe it, but so far, this was better than the dates I'd gone on with guys from Princeton.

"Grant!" an older man said as he walked up to our table. "So good to see you home again and with such a beautiful date."

"It's good to be back, Randy. This is my friend Aribel."

"It is a true pleasure, Aribel." The man took my hand in his, large and strong from use. He had kind eyes and a welcoming smile.

"Randy's the owner," Grant filled in for me.

"Oh, well, I love your restaurant."

"Bah! You haven't even tasted the food!" He glanced at Grant and laughed. "I like her."

Grant seemed completely comfortable when his eyes shifted from Randy's back to mine. "I like her, too."

My cheeks heated, and I looked away from him. I couldn't figure out how Grant made my stomach flip the way it did. I'd always been so logical, practical…and he threw those qualities out the window with only a smile.

"We'll have the special and some water. Unless you want something else?" he asked me hesitantly.

"That sounds fine."

Randy picked up the unopened menus from the table. "Don't be a stranger, Grant," he said before leaving.

"You've been incredibly accommodating tonight," Grant said. "I keep waiting for a snarky comment."

I shrugged. "Well, you haven't made any asshole sexual comments yet."

"I could if you like."

"Oh, yes, my dream in life is to be sexually objectified every chance I get."

He cracked a smile. "There she is."

"Does it ever get tiring?"

"What?" he asked, leaning in closer to me.

"The sexual objectification, the constant stream of girls. Don't you ever just want more?"

"Babe, I'm usually getting more."

"Ugh! Not what I meant," I said, turning my face out to the ocean. "You've never been on a date before. From everything I've heard about you…you sleep with women and then never talk to them again." I could feel the heat of his gaze on my face, and I forced myself to look at him. "Haven't you ever thought there was more to a relationship than that?"

Grant stiffened at my question. There I had gone again. I couldn't keep my mouth shut. I couldn't keep myself from asking exactly what was on my mind. I was messing this thing up, whatever it was with Grant, before our first date had even come to a conclusion.

"To be perfectly honest, Ari, until you, I'd never given two shits about anyone that wasn't family."

17 GRANT

Ari and I left Duffie's after we finished dinner, and she started walking back toward my truck. I hadn't driven all the way down the shore just to get pizza. We were on my first date, so I was going to go all out.

I grabbed her hand and looped it with mine. "This way," I said, taking a side entrance to the boardwalk.

Her dark blue eyes were wide and alert as she took in the scene before her. The sun was low on the horizon and reflecting against the water for miles.

"You ever been down the shore before?"

"Yes. My roommates took me last summer. Shelby and Gabi are from Atlantic City, so they showed us around—um…me and Cheyenne, that is."

"Where are you from?"

"Boston."

"Never been there."

"Oh, you'd love it. My dad is a CEO at a bank downtown, so I—"

I straightened visibly at that word. *CEO. Fuck me. Who the fuck am I to take out a girl whose father runs an entire bank?*

"What?" she asked, noticing my discomfort.

"Nothing," I covered quickly.

She knew I was lying.

"Well, you'd love Boston," she finally said.

Silence lingered between us. I felt something crawl into my chest and spread out, like it was trying to fester through my whole body. I didn't know what the fuck was wrong with me. I liked this girl. *That has to be it.* I was completely out of my element. I'd fucked spoiled princesses whose parents had too much money. I hadn't discriminated against who landed in my bed. But this…this felt fucking different.

"You have something on your mind," she whispered finally.

"Yeah." I drew her into me and kissed her hard on the mouth. Maybe I could drown out my own thoughts.

Her arms wrapped around my neck, and she wound her fingers through my hair. She shivered in my arms, and I wasn't sure if it was from our kiss or the crisp air as winter rolled in on the boardwalk, but I just kissed her harder, more desperately. I didn't care who her father was or how much money they had or how much better than me she probably was. She was kissing me back. Whether I deserved it or not, Ari wanted this, too.

As always, Ari pulled away first. Her dark blue eyes met mine, and she giggled against my lips. Since I'd known her, she had always worn such a stern expression with a particularly prominent scowl, so her giggle made me smile.

"Something funny, Princess?" I asked, pulling back to look at her.

She shook her head. "No. I'm just surprised I'm having a good time with you."

"Ouch," I said, bringing a hand to my wounded heart.

"Oh, no…I didn't mean it…" She trailed off and bit her lip. "Sorry. I have a problem with spewing the first thing that comes to mind."

"It's not a problem," I told her quickly.

Actually, I liked it. She knew I was an asshole, and she had still gone on a date with me. I hadn't given her any other option, but still…

"Well, I'm not one to sugarcoat," Ari said.

"Me either. That's why when I told you that I wanted you in my bed, I meant it."

"Oh, I know you meant that." Her cheeks turned a soft shade of pink. "But what I didn't know was if all of this was just an excuse to get me there."

Huh. As much as I wanted to fuck this girl, that hadn't been in my game plan, not the way that she was thinking at least.

"And?" I finally asked. "What do you think?"

She took a few steps away from me and leaned her elbows against the railing of the boardwalk, facing out to the ocean. My body responded to the beautiful sight of her body pressed into the wooden railing and her tight little ass sticking out. She glanced over her shoulder and saw me checking her out.

"Well?" I prompted when she said nothing.

"I think you want me there, but you like me *here*, too."

Well, if that isn't the damn truth.

I closed the distance between us and turned her to face me. My hands slid down the sides of her dress as I whispered in her ear, "I want you any way I can have you."

She cleared her throat as I felt her body reacting to my nearness.

"I'll be sure to remember that."

Her words sounded like a promise, and I wondered what I'd gotten myself into.

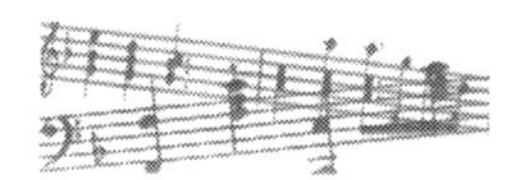

When we arrived at Ari's house right before midnight, I walked with her up to her door, all the while restraining myself from pouncing on her. Physical restraint had never been my strong suit.

Images of Ari—her lips on mine as I'd pushed her through her open doorway, her body wet from the rain, her nestled against my chest, her laughing on the boardwalk—all hit me with a fresh wave of desire. I wanted to be near her, with her, in her—and I wanted it fucking bad.

When we reached her door, I kissed her pleadingly. *Please let me stay. Please let me show you everything I can do to your body. Please let me give you what we both want right now.*

I wasn't going to walk away without trying.

She whispered something so softly that I hadn't even heard it in the breeze.

"What?" I asked.

Ari turned her head away from me, a red blush touching her cheeks and the tips of her ears. "Nothing. Sorry. Stupid of me."

I took her chin in my hand and forced her to face me again. "What did you say, Ari?" My pulse was keeping time in my ears.

Her blush just deepened. "You don't have to if you don't want to."

"If I don't want to what?"

"Come inside…" she said quietly.

I couldn't keep the smile from my face. *Fuck yes, I want to come inside.* That wasn't the only place I wanted to be coming in right now.

Aribel fumbled with the key before opening the door and leading us into her place. I'd been inside before, but it was a different experience to actually be welcomed. She shrugged out of her jacket and tossed it across the back of the couch. She teetered from one foot to the other, not making eye contact with me from across the room.

"Which room is yours, Princess?"

Her eyes widened, but she didn't answer. I could see what was written on her face—*I'm not going to have sex with you.*

"I know," I told her.

She startled as if I'd read her mind. "Grant…"

"Which one?"

She nodded her head behind her. When she didn't move, I walked across the room and guided her back toward it. I could take control. That was fine with me.

Once we were in her room, my lips found hers, and my mind went on autopilot. I needed her. I needed this.

I pushed her back until her legs met the large bed in the center of the room. It was one of those fancy-ass beds that was too high to sit on comfortably. A million useless throw pillows lay on top, and I reached out and wiped them all from their neat arrangement. Then, I grabbed her by the backs of her legs and set her down effortlessly. Her blue dress bunched around her upper thighs, and I hardened at the sight. My hands slid up under the material, and she shivered against my touch.

"Grant," she whispered.

I thought she'd meant it as a hesitation, but it had come out as a moan.

"St-stop."

"Ari, please." My voice was hoarse. I wanted something, anything at this point.

"I'm not going to—"

"I know. I know." I held back my irritation. "I'm just going to make you feel good."

"Grant," she said with a definite warning in her voice.

Well, I'll just have to fucking show her then.

I dropped to my knees in front of her and saw her eyes widen as her grip tightened on the bedspread. *Good.*

My hands pressed gently against her knees, spreading her legs farther apart. She squirmed uncomfortably, but I just ignored her. She'd be squirming for other reasons in a minute. I ran my fingertips ever so lightly from her knee to the sensitive skin hidden beneath her dress. She gasped at my touch. That did the trick. My lips followed. Each inch that I kissed brought a new wave of trembles from her body. The anticipation of what I was going to do was getting her riled up, and fuck was it turning me on, too.

When I reached her dress, I glanced up to get an okay to continue, but her eyes were firmly closed. The look on her face was doing anything but discouraging me. I flipped up her dress and kissed my way down the soft lace of her pale blue underwear. She quivered beneath my touch, and it took considerable effort to slow my racing heart and focus on the matter at hand.

I eased her back on the bed, so she was lying flat. Her eyes flew open, and she stared at me with a mix of desire and terror.

"Trust me," I told her.

She swallowed and nodded.

I pulled her underwear slowly down her legs. All I wanted to do was rip them off of her as fast as I could and bury my dick inside her, but I went slow. I wanted her to be comfortable.

Who the fuck knows if she is going to let me be this close to her again after tonight? She might come to her senses and realize that I was no prince in disguise; I was just a frog waiting for a kiss from a princess.

With the barrier between us removed, I started at her knee and worked my way back up. She was practically panting by the time my mouth found her lips for the first time. I ran my tongue down the length of her and then swirled experimentally around her clit, savoring every sound of pleasure escaping her. And I wasn't going to stop there. My tongue flicked against her until she could barely keep her hips still. I worked her into a total frenzy before finally inserting one finger into her and then another. Her body spasmed around my fingers as I worked them in and out of her.

Oh fuck. Her body was so responsive to my touch. I just wanted to feel everything that was going through her. I wanted to sink my dick into her wet pussy and ride out that wave with her, but I'd let her have hers. My own breathing was turning ragged as I brought her closer and closer to the brink.

I felt her body seize all at once around my fingers. She stiffened slightly. Her hands dug into the bedspread. When her orgasm faded out, she relaxed. No big fanfare. *Typical Aribel.*

"Why…why did you stop?" she asked breathily after a moment.

"Because I wanted to watch you come."

She blushed. "Um…I didn't."

I leveled her with a you're-kidding-me kind of look. "Um…yes, you did."

"I think I'd know."

"I'd think so, too. Want me to show you again? Because that was a fucking hot sight if I've ever seen one."

What the hell is she talking about? My dick was throbbing so hard in my pants from her orgasm, and she hadn't even known that she had one. *Am I missing something?*

She sat up and self-consciously covered herself. "Um…no."

"Hey," I said, taking her face in my hands, "it's a compliment. I'd do it all over again to watch you one more time."

She furiously blushed again. I took her hand in mine and placed it on the front of my pants. She jerked back really quick, but I grabbed it and laid it on my dick again.

"See what you do to me."

"Grant," she said softly, removing her hand again, "I don't…I've never felt like this. I'm not this…"

She splayed her hands out before her, but I wasn't sure what she'd meant. All I heard was that she'd never felt like this. *About a guy? The orgasm?*

I decided to push my luck. Pretty standard for me. I started climbing on top of the bed, and she scrambled backward. My hands latched on to her waist, and I laid her out flat beneath me.

"You know," I said into her ear, "I've never felt like this either."

I started grinding my hips against her, and she whimpered. Her hands gripped my forearms, neither pushing me away nor pulling me closer. I wanted nothing more than to loose my dick from my pants, slide it against the wetness I'd created between her legs, and ride her as hard as she'd let me. My body was literally aching to be inside her. I was sure she could feel my need as it put pressure between her thighs.

Aribel groaned and pulled me down until my lips met hers. I indulged her as I slid my hand down her bare thigh. I reached underneath her to grab her ass, and she jumped slightly. My cock twitched as she thrust upward against me.

"Please," I groaned. "Please, Ari."

She shook her head, but her eyes were filled with the same desire consuming my body. I wanted so desperately to ignore her. I wanted to take what was lying beneath me, take what was mine.

Aribel Graham is mine.

Ever since Grant had left my apartment without a word three days ago, I'd been sleeping like shit. I knew that I shouldn't agonize over what had possibly gone wrong, but I couldn't figure out what had happened. The only thing that stuck out was the fact that I hadn't slept with him. *That must be it.* He must have thought that after just one date, I'd give it up, and when I hadn't, he'd moved on. I couldn't think of another explanation.

And I was amazed, quite shocked actually, that I was physically and emotionally beating myself up about it. For a minute, I'd wanted to rush over to his house and offer myself. The logical side of my brain told me that wouldn't keep him around any more than me denying him had, but it was difficult to keep myself in check.

Deep down I'd known it was happening. When I had agreed to go on a date with Grant—maybe even before then when I had called him to help with my car—I'd known that I was falling for him. But I'd thought that one date would prove that he was everything I'd thought he was—an arrogant, conceited, manipulative, asshole, playboy rocker who cared for nothing but which bed he was landing in. While that image hadn't wavered because he was absolutely every one of those things, I'd managed to find that there was *more* to Grant McDermott…and that had been my downfall.

I'd really thought we had some kind of moment, a connection even, but it all came back to sex. *How could I ever think I would hold someone like Grant McDermott's interest? What did I have to offer that he couldn't easily get somewhere else?* Just thinking about it was irritating me all over again.

And look, I hadn't even been paying attention to my chemistry professor, so I had missed the entire slide with the homework assignment on it.

I caught up to Kristin as she exited the classroom. "Hey!"

Kristin stopped and waited for me. "What's up?"

"I forgot to write down the homework assignment. Do you think I could get it from you?"

"You? What?"

Yeah. Great. Just point out the fact that I'm not myself. "So, do you think I could see it?" I asked.

"Um…sure, hold on."

She pulled out her paper, and I started scribbling down the pages and pages of work I needed to read and all the problems I had to finish before lab on Thursday.

"So, not to be nosy or anything, but after Grant got your number last weekend, did he, like, actually call you?" Kristin asked.

Ugh! Grant.

She must have seen my grimace because she quickly said, "Never mind. He was probably just trying to get some ass, like always. You shouldn't feel bad that he didn't call you."

Breathe in, breathe out, Aribel. Think before you speak for once in your life. "Don't feel bad for me. Grant McDermott is as likely to get some ass from me as I am of getting a B on the next test."

"Wait, you mean he didn't have sex with you at the League?"

"Who told you we did?" I asked carefully.

"Everyone. I mean, everyone was talking about it. Something about a quickie in the back room."

I saw red. I didn't even know what to think or do about the situation, but it felt like in one easy swoop Grant McDermott had ruined my carefully constructed reputation.

"I didn't have sex with Grant. You can tell that to everyone else who asks you, too."

Kristin looked at me skeptically. "But you were backstage with him, right?"

"Just because I was backstage doesn't mean I had sex with him!" I snapped.

A few people glanced our way, and I reminded myself to breathe. I scrawled the last few notes into my notebook and then passed hers back. "We didn't have sex."

"Okay…you didn't have sex."

I ground my teeth together at the disbelieving inflection in her voice. I didn't even know what else to say, so I just turned around and walked away. I hadn't bothered thanking her for her notes.

I snatched my phone and dialed Grant's number. I couldn't believe that I was giving in and calling that bastard again.

He picked up on the third ring. "Hey, Princess."

Cocky, conceited, arrogant prick. I wanted to wipe the smirk right off his face. I wanted to forget ever going on a date with him or kissing him or letting him do *more.* I wanted to forget the last three days of exhaustion, wondering why he had snuck out of my house and why he hadn't called me back. I'd never had those thoughts before, and I just wanted him out of my life, so this could all stop.

"You told everyone that we slept together?" I asked, nearly hysterical.

"What?" I heard the genuine confusion in his voice.

"You told everyone we slept together!" I repeated. "Congratulations! You have single-handedly ruined my entire reputation. Now, everyone thinks I'm some dumb groupie slut. I can't believe I trusted you. I can't believe that I was foolish enough to go out with you. Why didn't I see this coming? I must be so naïve. You couldn't get any from me, so you just *told* everyone that you did."

"I would *never* do that."

"Then, why is everyone saying that, Grant? Hmm? Do you think I'm stupid? I told you I didn't want to play this game."

"Ari, would you slow down for one second? I never told anyone that we had sex. Who did you hear that from?"

"My friend Kristin told me that everyone was talking about it."

"Well, they're probably just assuming that it happened since you came backstage with me. I didn't tell anyone that. I haven't even told anyone I've been seeing you."

I didn't know why that bugged me just as much. "I'm so glad that not only does everyone think we slept together, but I'm *also* your dirty little secret. Fantastic." I reached my car and wrenched the door open.

"Ari, you need to fucking chill the fuck out right now. I'm trying to tell you what's going on, so shut your smart mouth for one goddamn second and actually listen to me."

Oh, he did not just go there. "Don't talk to me like I'm an idiot."

"No one in the whole fucking world could think you're an idiot, Ari. Just calm the fuck down," he growled. "You know what? Fuck it. Let's just meet up. I'm tired of you yelling at me through the phone."

"Fine. I'll just yell at you in person."

"I like my women vocal," he said with a chuckle. "Your place or mine, sweetheart?"

"Ugh! You're so exasperating! Just forget it."

"Princess, you should learn to take a joke. Just be at The Coffee Bean in fifteen."

19 GRANT

I dropped into a booth in the back of The Coffee Bean and tossed my helmet into the seat next to me to wait out Aribel.

Fuck. It was the one word that kept replaying through my mind. I wasn't sure how I could fucking make any of this worse.

I'd stayed the night at her place, but I hadn't slept a wink. I'd been too lost in my own train of thought, too horny to let myself relax around her. Then, I'd lost my nerve. *I'd fucking lost my nerve.* I couldn't believe it.

I'd been lying there obsessing about the fact that I liked this chick enough to give her what she wasn't giving me—leaving myself with a painful throbbing erection, dying to at least jack off—and I'd actually stayed the night. Then, I'd freaked the fuck out and bolted.

I couldn't like her this much. I couldn't fucking be in her house, lying against her soft body while holding her tight, and not want to fuck her. But I fucking respected the woman enough not to push any more than I had, and I'd been pushy as hell.

Then like a pussy, I hadn't called her after I disappeared. I'd wanted to get laid so bad, but every time I'd closed my eyes, all I would see was her face as she climaxed. I'd never jacked off so much in my life.

How hard could it be to forget someone? Clearly, it wasn't easy enough because as soon as I'd seen her number on my phone, I'd answered. I couldn't stay away from her. I'd been stupid for trying, and I was going to convince her that she couldn't stay away from me either.

The door rattled on its hinges as Ari yanked it open, and I got my first glimpse of her. A thundercloud might as well have been hovering over her head. Her eyes found me across the room. Her smile was replaced with that scowl, telling me she was going to lay into me as soon as she sat down.

This is going to be fun.

"So, I'm here," she grumbled, taking a seat. "Are you going to explain to me why you told everyone that we slept together?"

"I didn't tell anyone that," I said.

Actually, I'd purposely avoided saying anything at all about Ari. The guys had just inferred that from previous behavior.

"Then, there's no reason for me to stay here."

She started to get up, and I grabbed her wrist.

"Sit your ass back down."

She wrenched her arm away from me. "Why should I bother?"

"Look, I didn't say that I slept with you! But I have slept with chicks in the back room of The League before. We were back there for ten minutes. Vin thought that was what we were doing, and I even told you that they wouldn't believe me if I'd said we weren't fooling around."

"Fooling around does not necessarily mean sex!"

"For me, it does," I told her frankly.

She glared at me.

"What? Do you want me to tell everyone that I didn't sleep with you? Do you want me to fuck with my reputation?"

"No. By all means, I never want to see you again either," she spat. I honestly couldn't tell if she was being sarcastic or not.

"Fine. Don't fucking move."

I stood from my seat, already feeling like an idiot, but it was clear that Aribel had made me an idiot. "Excuse me," I called out to the busy coffee shop sitting just off-campus.

"Grant, what are you doing?" Aribel hissed.

Gradually, the coffee shop quieted, and eyes moved over to me. I thought I recognized some of the faces. From the flicker of recognition throughout the crowd, I was sure people recognized me.

"Sorry to take up your time, but I'm Grant McDermott."

Someone whistled, and then I heard a catcall from the other direction. At least I had their attention.

"I just wanted to make a quick announcement. This is my friend Aribel."

She blushed bright crimson as I addressed her.

"I wanted everyone to know that I haven't slept with her, that's all. Feel free to tell your friends."

I sat down and was about to open my mouth to ask her if that had proved my point, but she had already grabbed her bag and was rushing to get out of the building.

"Fuck," I grumbled. I tucked my helmet under my arm and darted out after her. "Ari!"

"Leave me alone, Grant!"

"Come on. Where are you going?"

"Just leave me alone!" she called back over her shoulder.

I jogged to catch up with her. There was no way I was letting her get away like this. "Ari, hold up."

She whirled around when I reached her. "You totally humiliated me in there! All you think about is yourself. Did you even think before telling a bunch of strangers that you didn't sleep with me?"

"I was just trying to prove that I like you, Ari. You make it so fucking impossible."

"You *like* me?" she gasped out. "That's how you want to show it?"

"I'm not a fucking flowers-and-chocolates kind of guy. If you haven't noticed, I've never done this before!"

"That's not an excuse! I've never been with an asshole rocker who thinks he's God's gift to women, but you don't see me humiliating you in public! Or better yet, sneaking out of your house and then not speaking to you for three days!" she threw back in my face.

"Well, I'm sorry, but the biggest cocktease on the planet fucked with my head, and it took me—"

"Cocktease?" she roared. "I am not a—"

"Would you shut up for one minute?" I yelled right back. "Fuck! Just let me talk, woman."

She crossed her arms over her chest and huffed.

"I was going to say, it took me three fucking days to get my head back on straight, and I realized that I can't escape you."

"Escape me? What do you mean?"

"I've never dated. I've just never cared. Never, babe," I said, running a hand back through my hair. "But I fucking care about you."

DATE TWO

Grant and I spent the next afternoon at the movies. I was prepared for one show before going home.

I was still pretty pissed about everything that had happened. Yes, he cared about me. Yes, he liked me. Yes, he had done all these things with me that he had never done with anyone else before. But still, the way he'd responded to it all made me want to throat-punch him.

The asshole had weaseled his way back in. I could no longer deny that I liked Grant. The three days without him had proven that, and once the anger from him humiliating me had fizzled out, I'd still wanted to see him.

Somehow, he'd managed to pick the movie I wanted to see. He'd said it was what he wanted and that he had been dying to see it since it came out last weekend. I hadn't even told him that I liked comedies.

Grant slipped his hand into mine as we exited the theater, and he pulled me back toward him.

"What?" I asked.

"Shh," he said with a mischievous smile.

I narrowed my eyes but held my tongue. He walked us down the hallway we had just come through. *Are we taking a back exit to the parking lot?*

When the hallway was empty, he opened up another door and gestured for me to walk inside.

My eyebrows rose. "Grant, what are we doing?"

"Just go inside."

He smacked my ass, and I glared at him.

"Come on, Princess, play along."

I didn't say anything. I just walked inside.

Grant walked all the way to the back row of the empty theater, and we took seats just as whatever movie we had just stumbled into started playing.

His arm came down across my shoulders, and he nuzzled my neck. "I think we should have come to this showing first," he murmured.

"Why is that?"

I should have been freaking out that we had walked into a movie without paying, but whatever he was doing to my neck was distracting.

"I was having trouble keeping my hands to myself in that crowded theater."

"You always have trouble keeping your hands to yourself."

"You like it."

I didn't reply. His hand ran down my side, and then he pulled me into his lap.

We made out through the next two movies.

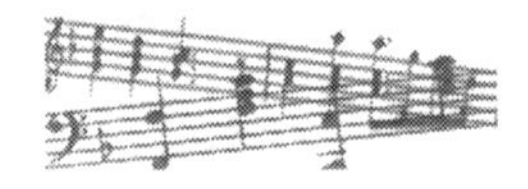

DATE FIVE

Two weeks later, Grant told me to bring a bathing suit and nothing else. It was October in Jersey. *Is he out of his mind? Where the hell are we supposed to go swimming when it was forty degrees outside at night?*

Grant parked his truck outside of a hotel. *Well, there's my answer.* His friend worked at the place and had slipped him a key card to the indoor pool. After dark, Grant and I snuck inside. Actually, it was more like Grant dragged me inside. *First, the movies, and now, breaking into a hotel swimming pool?*

"We're not *breaking in*," Grant tried to reassure me. "I have a key."

"That you basically stole from an employee."

"Darlin', if we get caught, I'll let them haul me off to jail. Just don't hurt my truck, all right?"

I rolled my eyes and slipped out of my clothes. I self-consciously covered my stomach as I stood before Grant in my blue-and-white striped bikini. He'd seen me in less, but I couldn't help it. His eyes roamed my body, and I quickly skipped into the heated pool.

What he couldn't see before, he had his hands all over as soon as he'd gotten into the pool. "Have you ever broken into a pool before?"

"You just said we didn't break in!"

His eyes shined with amusement.

"Gah! No."

"Ever done anything illegal?"

"I've drank alcohol before," I answered lamely.

"Drugs?"

I shook my head.

"Stolen anything?"

"Nope."

"Do you at least speed in your car?"

I smiled up at him.

"Damn, you're picture-perfect, Princess."

"I once slapped a guy across the face for grabbing my butt at a bar," I offered with a shrug.

He responded by grabbing my ass. *Typical.*

He held my slick body against his, and all I saw were the deep chocolate orbs and flecks of gold catching the moonlight through the windows. He seemed more contemplative than usual. Normally, he just wanted to attack me.

"What do you like to do when you're not studying?"

"I'm always studying."

"You're not right now. Are you saying you like to do me when you're not studying?" He winked.

"Wouldn't you already know if that were the case?" I shot back.

"Indulge me, Ari."

His lips grazed mine tenderly, and for the hundredth time since we'd decided to give this a shot, I thought that I was definitely going to let him do whatever he wanted.

"Horseback riding," I finally answered, coming to my senses. "I did it as a kid, and I almost always go when I'm at home."

"I could see you on a horse."

I wasn't sure if that was a good thing, but I kept going with his game. "I like to bake cupcakes."

"Coincidence—I like to eat cupcakes. German chocolate."

I giggled and shook my head. "I used to play piano, but my hands are too small."

He grabbed my hands and brought them up to his eye level, inspecting them thoroughly. His lips touched every inch of skin from my pruney fingertips to the small scar near my thumb where a dog had bitten me in high school and on to the other one.

"Your hands are perfect."

DATE SEVEN

My last class was canceled on Tuesday afternoon, which gave me free time to plan out my date. We'd been doing whatever Grant wanted for over two weeks, and I thought it was about time to plan something myself.

Cheyenne eyed me suspiciously from behind the kitchen counter while I was baking cupcakes. After Grant's outburst in The Coffee Bean, we'd thought it best to keep everything on the down low. I wouldn't lie to my roommates about what was going on, but I wasn't exactly being forthright with information, not that that was new.

"What are you doing?" Cheyenne asked.

"Making cupcakes."

"For whom?"

I shot her a look.

"Grant?" she offered.

I just shrugged. *What did she want me to say? Yes, I'm dating Grant. No, it isn't a big deal.*

"Are you guys, like…together now?"

"Something like that."

Cheyenne bit her lip and jumped from foot to foot. "How was the sex?"

"Can we not?" I asked, turning my back to her.

"Give a girl a break! I've been dying to have sex with him since the first time I laid eyes on him. I've heard he's amazing."

Heat pooled in my chest, and I ground my teeth together. I didn't want to think about Cheyenne having sex with Grant or the innumerable other women who already had.

"We haven't had sex, Cheyenne," I responded irritably.

"I mean, if you just don't want to provide details, that's fine," she said in a tone that made it seem far from fine.

I whipped around with the whisk in my hand, dripping chocolate batter onto the floor. "I'm not providing details because we haven't had sex! So, just drop the subject, all right?"

"Sorry," she whispered. "Touchy. I just didn't think Grant…did that."

"He doesn't."

Suffice it to say, that wasn't the way I'd wanted to start my first planned date night with Grant. Now, I was all grouchy when baking usually calmed me down, and all I could think about was sex.

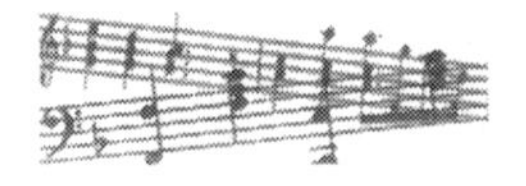

I showed up at Grant's place right after band rehearsal let out. When Vin saw me waiting outside, he snickered and punched Grant. Miller and McAvoy pulled Vin behind them, completely ignoring whatever vile comments were likely coming out of his mouth.

"Hey, babe," Grant said as he walked up to me. "What's that?" The other guys stood around apparently wondering the same thing.

"I, uh…" I began. I hadn't expected an audience. "I brought you something."

"The only thing girl's ever bring Grant is pussy," Vin said under his breath.

McAvoy smacked him across the back of the head. I just rolled my eyes and ignored him.

Grant took the box from my hands. His smile grew tenfold when he opened it up. "Cupcakes."

"German chocolate. Your favorite."

I knew I was blushing hard, but the look on his face was worth it.

"I don't think you can fuck cupcakes," Vin said loud enough for me to hear that time.

"Then, I guess you don't want one," I snapped right back.

"Wait…" Vin said, trying to correct himself to get a cupcake.

All three guys busted out laughing in unison.

Vin glared at them. "Shut the fuck up, assholes!"

"You walked right into that," Miller said.

"Who said I was going to share anyway?" Grant asked.

He slid the box under one arm and his other around me. My world spun. He was talking about more than just the cupcakes.

Grant devoured four cupcakes before we even made it to the concert I was taking him to. It wasn't even a far drive. I didn't think he'd said anything the whole trip besides mostly moans and groans about how good they were. I guessed the key to a man's heart really was through his stomach.

When I pulled up to the concert venue, Grant's eyes narrowed. "You're taking me to a show?"

I giggled. *Oh my God, Grant McDermott makes me giggle.* "I thought you would want to see what music I like."

He hopped out of the car eagerly, and before I could walk two feet, he covered my mouth with his. His hands were on either side of my face while my fingers played with the dog tags that were perpetually around his neck. He broke away first, which was unusual. His eyes searched my face, and then he kissed the tip of my nose.

"What was that for?" I asked a little breathlessly.

"Music speaks to my soul."

"So do cupcakes apparently."

He smirked. "I can see how you have an unfair advantage at this date thing. You're way better at it than me."

I laughed and shook my head. "No way."

"You have more practice." He leaned in really close to me. "I can't wait to show you the things I have more practice with."

The concert couldn't have gone on for a second longer with the heat building between us all evening.

Once we were back at his place, we couldn't get out of my car and up the stairs fast enough. I'd never felt this blind lust before. It was both terrifying and exciting. I couldn't decide which feeling was more overpowering. I tried to tell myself to stop overanalyzing every emotion hitting my body and just enjoy *being*.

Grant had the door to his bedroom closed and me laid out on his bed in a split second. My jeans hit the floor, and my underwear followed. He wasn't wasting any time. My body shook beneath him. I knew that we'd done this before, but my mind kept skipping several steps ahead. *Was I ready for that?*

When he started kissing down my stomach, my brain shut off. His breath landed hot on my opening, and he started licking and sucking me in ways that had me writhing beneath him. *Damn, he's good at that.*

His fingers slid inside me, and I squeezed my eyes tighter until the pressure lessened. Then, he was moving in and out of me, and my breathing became labored. Everything felt like it was vibrating, like I was unraveling from the inside out, and I didn't even know what to focus on.

"Ari," Grant murmured, glancing up at me, "you're close."

I grappled with the sheets and tried to hold off the intensity building inside me.

Holy fuck!

"Just let go, babe."

Let go of what?

Oh my God. His mouth. His fingers. Him.

My body pulsed as I felt something rush through me all at once. My back arched slightly, and I just let go.

"Fuck, that's sexy," Grant groaned.

I gingerly peeled my eyes open and saw he was staring at me. I knew I should reciprocate. I wasn't sure I could hold off on him having sex with me if I didn't. I felt incredible, and really he deserved to as well.

"Grant…" I whispered.

"Ari, I know. You're not going to have sex with me." He chuckled humorlessly, standing up.

I sat up, reached out, and touched his jeans hesitantly. "I thought, um…that is, if you want…maybe we could try something else."

Grant's eyes lit up like a Christmas tree. "What do you have in mind?"

I turned crimson from head to toe. My hand slid up his leg, and over his dick. He looked at me like I'd just offered him the world. *Maybe I had?*

"Yes, whatever you want, yes."

I laughed lightly. He was so eager, and I was so hesitant. *What a pair.*

As if seeing my uncertainty, he stood and stripped out of his jeans and the navy blue boxer briefs that apparently had held him in very tightly. My eyes bugged, and I tried to hide that fact. He was tall, and the correlation between that and size meant something…but damn.

He extended his hand to me and then scooted me off the bed. His lips found mine softly. "Calm down."

He placed my hand on his dick, and with a breath, I started gliding it up and down the length of him. A groan escaped him at my touch. I couldn't keep a smile from tugging on my lips.

"Like this," he whispered, his fingers tightening around my small hand.

I gripped him harder and kept pumping. As I watched him, I couldn't help licking my lips. He was so unabashedly sexual.

Grant ran a finger against my bottom lip. "You keep licking those lips, Ari, and I'm going to want them around my cock."

I took a deep breath and then sank to my knees. I thought he stopped breathing. *I could do this.* I'd done it before. I'd done it at times when I didn't even want to. But I wanted to do this for Grant.

My lips wrapped around the head, and then I slowly took more of him into my mouth. Grant pushed farther in, and I gagged as he hit the back of my throat. My eye instantly watered, and I closed them to blink the tears away as I quickly retreated. *Yeah, I pretty much feel like an idiot.*

"Sorry," he grunted. "You just feel so fucking good."

I started again, drawing him in and sucking him back to the head in a slow rhythm. My knees were already killing me, and dear Lord, my jaw was on fire. I wasn't going to be able to open my mouth in the morning. He'd probably like it that way.

I pulled back too fast and felt my teeth nick him. *Ugh!*

"Fuck!" Grant stopped me entirely and wrenched me to my feet. "No teeth."

"S-sorry," I stammered.

He breathed out heavily. "It's okay," he said through gritted teeth. "Just get on the bed."

Oh man, am I that bad?

"Hey," he said. "You're going to get my dick nice and wet, and then wrap your lips around him. The faster you go, the faster I go. Focus on the tip, and we're golden. No teeth."

"Okay," I whispered.

He kissed me solidly on the lips before lying back on the bed. I guessed I hadn't sucked that bad if he wanted me to keep going.

I did exactly what he'd said. I didn't care that my jaw was locking up or that I was pretty embarrassed by the entire interaction. Grant was moaning and groaning enough encouragement to keep me working him over until he was done. He started thrusting up into my mouth, and I tried not to fight him, but he was so big. I could tell that he was getting close before he even warned me.

"Oh fuck, Ari," he cried out as he hit the climax.

I pulled back and felt his warmth run down my hand where I was still gripping him.

"Fuck. Fuck. Fuck me. Fuck."

DATE TEN

This thing with Ari—I didn't even have words for it. It was just fucking good.

I wanted to fuck her more and more every single fucking day, but now that she was handing out blow jobs, I didn't feel like I was going to explode every time I saw her. I had my standard that the girl either sucked or fucked, and I'd been amazed at how truly bad she was to start out with. For a split second, I'd thought about fucking her mouth until I finished or throwing her on the bed and having her prove to me that she fucked better than that.

But she had looked so damn concerned when I stopped her that I just wanted to *show* her. I'd never fucking done that before. And fuck, once I'd told her what to do, she was a quick study. I'd be okay if she was studying all the time like *this.*

The strangest part of all was that as much as I wanted to push for more, I was having such a good time with her—dating her, laughing with her—that I wouldn't. Each time I thought she was going to turn me aside for asking for too much, she would give just a little bit more of herself. *Like the cupcakes. She had fucking baked me cupcakes. And the concert. I hadn't been sure what I was in for when we walked into the venue, but not only was the show surprisingly good, Ari was also totally into it, which just made it that much better.*

I'd been planning to take her out dancing on Halloween, but at the last minute, Miller had gotten news that ContraBand was being plugged in at the exact party I had been planning to attend with Ari.

We were scheduled for the eleven o'clock slot right before the club would switch to some techno DJ for the rest of the night. Ari and her friends showed up about fifteen minutes before our set. She was in a fitted white dress with long gloves, and she was holding an elaborate mask in her hand. I could see her from backstage, and it was fun to watch her search for me in the crowd.

"Bro," Vin said as he took the spot next to me. "Halloween is the best fucking night of the year. So many chicks, so little clothing. I think I want a French maid, a Playboy Bunny, and a nurse all tonight."

"Good luck with that," I said.

"What are you going to take home? I saw a really hot referee."

When Ari couldn't find me, she secured her mask back in place and turned to talk to her friends.

"I'm thinking a masked angel."

"That one?" Vin asked, pointing Ari out.

"Yeah."

"Good choice. I'd bang her."

"No chance in hell."

The production manager popped his head backstage. "You guys are up."

It was our first show in weeks, but we got right back into our rhythm without a hitch. I played the crowd the best way I knew how. Drunken girls in lingerie were throwing themselves toward the stage, and I even heard a few screaming for me to take my clothes off. I obliged them by shrugging out of the jacket of the military fatigues I'd worn for the occasion. The fans screamed even louder when I tugged up my shirt to expose my abs beneath. I laughed softly into the microphone, pulled the shirt back down, and continued on with the chorus.

"This is our last song, and I know that you'll all be so sad to see us go. This one's called 'Letting You.' Come out to our last show of the semester at The Ivy League on the Saturday after Thanksgiving."

The crowd cheered.

I found Ari swaying and dancing all by herself in the second row. Her friends were grinding against guys who they'd found in the crowd, but she only had eyes for me. Right as we moved into the instrumental break, I pointed her out to the crowd and motioned for her to come onstage.

Her mouth dropped open, and she shook her head. I could see her mouthing, *No*, over and over, but the crowd roared and pushed her forward. I had the masses on my side, and soon, she was up the stairs and walking straight toward me. When I reached her, I swung her around into a dip and kissed her in front of the sea of people.

To everyone in attendance, this was nothing more than the band putting some random girl on display for the drunken Halloween crowd. But for me, this was new territory. I hadn't picked Ari at random. It felt more like…I was claiming my girl.

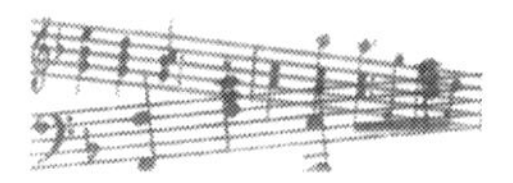

DATE ELEVEN

A week later, I picked up Ari from school. I'd dropped her off that morning after she stayed at my place. Ari was talking to some chick when she saw me pull up, and then she jogged over to my truck.

"Hey, Princess."

Ari hauled herself up and into the passenger seat. "Hey. My professor loaded us up on homework because he's worried we won't cover everything before Thanksgiving. I guess we got behind a week or something. Ugh! It's going to be terrible. I don't know if I'll be able to see you all weekend."

I didn't like the sound of that. "Do you want to cancel our date?" I asked anyway.

She chewed absentmindedly on her bottom lip. "No, it's already planned."

Good. She was going to go crazy for this one, and I didn't want to have to wait another week. The Weather Channel was predicting a drastic drop in temperatures over the next couple of weeks, so this might be the last chance we had.

I drove back to Ari's so that she could change before heading out.

"Do you want to come up?" she asked innocently.

"Babe, I don't think we have time for that," I said with a wink.

"I wasn't…" she began and then tilted her head and stared at me funny. "Who are you? And what have you done with Grant McDermott? Since when are you turning me down?"

I grabbed her chin hard in my hand and pulled her in close to me. Our eyes locked.

"You tell me you want to have sex with me, and all plans are forgotten."

"Maybe another time," she said casually as if her pupils hadn't dilated from the way I'd grabbed her.

One of these days, I was going to fucking take advantage of the situation, and then she wouldn't be the biggest cocktease I'd named her to be. But not today.

We walked inside, and as she darted into her bedroom, my phone started buzzing. Miller.

"What's up?"

"What are you doing the second weekend in December?"

"Nothing. Why?"

Miller sounded practically chipper. "Someone saw us at the Halloween show, and they want us to play a music festival at a ski resort in the Poconos."

"Dude, I barely know how to ski."

"Shut the fuck up! We're talking about getting picked up for a major event."

My smile grew. It sounded like a great opportunity, and since it was late enough in the semester, maybe I could steal Ari away with me.

Whoa, seriously, who the fuck am I? Two months ago, I would have been dying to go to a ski lodge to bang a bunch of snow bunnies. *Now…Ari.*

"Babe!" I called as soon as I got off the phone with Miller.

"My name is still Aribel!" she called right back as she stumbled into the living room.

Ari's roommates came out of their bedrooms when they heard my voice.

"You like to ski, snow bunny?"

"Is this a euphemism for something?"

"ContraBand got picked up for a music festival in the Poconos."

"That's great!" Ari cried.

I glanced at her friends, who were staring at us. "We'll have a couple of rooms the second weekend in December. Do you guys want to come to the show?"

"Oh my God!" Cheyenne piped up. "We were just talking about going on a ski trip. Weren't we, girls?"

"Ari?" I asked. All I could think about was spending three days with her in my room. I needed her in my bed. I needed to fuck that.

"I've only been skiing in Vermont and Colorado."

I gave her a pointed look. We didn't need to hear about her rich life right now.

"Yes, that sounds fun."

The other girls grabbed her and started jumping up and down. They were already planning out way more details than I was sure Miller had.

Once I got Ari back into the truck, it was a forty-five minute drive to where we were going. Ari seemed lost in thought, and I let the radio kill the silence. She perked up as soon as we entered the grounds.

"Hamilton Farm?" she gasped.

"You said you like horseback riding, right?"

She gaped at me. "I'm…wow, I'm a little speechless."

"That's a first, isn't it?"

"Grant, this means a lot." And then, she smiled one of those rare smiles reserved for me.

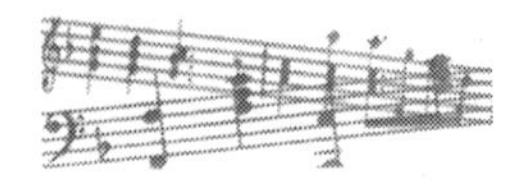

DATE THIRTEEN

A week later, I finally got Ari on the back of my motorcycle.

It didn't matter that I'd gotten on a half-ton animal for her or that she'd broken into a hotel swimming pool with me or that we'd made out onstage at a concert. She claimed to be utterly terrified of motorcycles.

"You won't go too fast, will you?"

"Nope." I didn't ask for clarification on what too fast meant to her.

Ready to feel the hum between my legs again, I slid my leg over.

Ari took a deep breath and then let it out slowly. "I can't believe I'm doing this."

"It'll be fun. Just get on."

She threw her leg over the bike, and her hands came tentatively to my waist. I grabbed them both in my hands and pulled her arms around me until her chest was flush against my back. I could feel the uptick in her heart rate. I knew mine was going to match it but not out of fear.

"Just follow my lead, Princess. Move with me."

"Okay," she whispered.

I started out slowly, but as soon as we hit the interstate, I kicked it into high gear. Soon, we were zipping past the other cars. At first, Ari would lean against me when I turned or switched lanes as if she could counterbalance the momentum of the bike, but once her fears had lessened, she did as I'd instructed. I thought I'd start her off easy the first time, so it wasn't a long ride.

When we reached our destination, she stood on shaky legs, handed me the helmet, and shook out her blonde hair. "That was…not so bad."

"I knew you'd like it."

"Don't get ahead of yourself."

"But I like to," I said, pulling her close and kissing her on the lips.

"I can't believe you convinced me to do that."

"And now, we're going to work on your aim."

Her eyes lifted to the sign. I expected her to groan, shoot me an angry look, or tell me off for the very thought of bringing her to a shooting range.

"You know…I've always wanted to fire a gun."

"What?" I asked incredulously. "You didn't want to get on a motorcycle, but you want to fire a *gun*?"

"A motorcycle could kill me! A gun in my hands would only kill someone else."

Excruciating pain cracked through my skull, and I squeezed my eyes shut to ward off the blinding torture. My hand dropped down onto my bike to hold myself steady. I couldn't keep the memories back.

"Are you okay?" Ari asked, resting her hand on mine and bringing me back to reality.

"Yeah. Sorry. Headache."

"Did you have one when you were driving? Do you need anything?"

"Nah. Just came on suddenly."

"I can get you some Tylenol."

"Ari, no. Let's just get you out of the cold."

I ushered her inside and paid for a rental gun and extra ammo for Ari, and then we entered our booth.

After I explained the mechanics to her, we took turns firing at the target across the room. She actually wasn't bad. I was pretty surprised since she had never held a gun before. She hadn't even seemed that freaked-out. It was hot.

I finished my last round of ammo and then set the gun down.

"You're kind of amazing at this," Ari said.

"Practice. You're damn good for a beginner."

She brightened and leaned forward for a kiss. I fucking loved when she initiated. It took all my control not to push her against the wall. She was so different from the girl I'd met who had dosed my drink, yet she was the same exact person who had intrigued me. She still intrigued me all the time.

Like she had grown accustomed to doing over the past couple of weeks, her fingers toyed with the dog tags around my neck. She softly kissed me once more. "Why do you always wear these?"

"Always have."

"I don't think I could picture you without them."

"I've had them since I was a kid." I wasn't sure why I'd told her that. I never talked about it with anyone, not even the guys. They thought, like Ari, that the dog tags were just a part of me.

"Is someone in your family military?" she asked curiously.

I tensed. "Yeah, my dad."

"It's so honorable to spend your life fighting for your country."

"Yeah," I said tightly. "The tags remind me of the man that I want to be."

DATE FIFTEEN

A few days later, I awoke to the sound of someone banging loudly on the front door. I blearily opened my eyes and took a look at the clock. Four forty-five in the morning. *Why is someone knocking on the door this early?*

Everyone else in my place slept like a rock. I doubted they'd even heard the knocking. *Ugh!* I hoped the person would go away already.

But I was out of luck. The knocking started again.

After hopping out of bed, I threw on a pair of sweats and trudged into the living room. The knocking started again just as I reached the door. I peered through the hole and sighed. *This feels familiar.*

"Grant, what are you doing here?" I asked with a yawn.

"I tried to call you."

"Not sure you checked the time right. It's almost five a.m., not five p.m."

"I know. Get dressed. We have places to be," he said, stepping through the door, uninvited.

"I'm not going anywhere this early. Are you out of your mind?"

He shook his head and started dragging me to my bedroom. "Bundle up. It's cold outside."

When he turned his back, I crawled into bed and closed my eyes. Grant noticed me and chuckled. He lay down beside me, and I rested my head on his arm.

"You're going to be difficult, aren't you?" he asked.

"I like having you here," I said softly.

"So, early mornings are when I can get you to tell me these kinds of things?"

I yawned again. "You're comfortable. Don't leave."

"Ari, we have places to be."

"Yep. Asleep. In your arms."

Grant sighed and wrapped an arm around me. I snuggled closer into him and felt myself drifting off so easily.

His hand slipped under my T-shirt and ran along my skin. "God, Ari, I love your body," he whispered against my ear.

His thumb ran against my nipple, and then he pinched it between his fingertips. I groaned faintly, and he took my entire breast in his hand. As he massaged me, I let my lips find the sensitive spot on his neck, and I trailed light kisses up to his ear. Taking that as encouragement, his hand tucked into the waistband of my sweats, and he started circling around my clit.

I was now fully awake. "Grant," I whimpered, clutching his T-shirt. It wasn't fair that he could get me this riled up.

He didn't respond. He just rolled me onto my back and captured my lips in a searing kiss. His hands were everywhere at once, sending butterflies through my stomach. His dick was pressing up against the thin material of my pants. *Oh God, that feels good.*

A tremor ran through me. My legs slid to either side of his and squeezed against his hips. One of his hands grabbed my ass, thrusting us closer together.

I couldn't breathe. I couldn't think. This was happening. I could just…do this.

"I…I want to," I whispered, stalling Grant.

"You do?" The eagerness in his voice was evident.

Then, my brain stopped my body. "I just…I'm not sure right now."

"Ari," he groaned.

Embarrassment hit me. I wanted to be with Grant, yet I couldn't shut my brain off enough to just be with him. We'd been at this for more than two months, and it was absolutely nothing like any other relationship I'd been in. There was no power struggle, no checklist going off in my mind, and no daily reminder to enjoy myself. I just *did* with Grant. It made no sense to me, and I was strangely okay with that.

When I didn't say anything else, Grant rolled off of me and out of bed. He adjusted himself in front of me, not covering up for an instant. He wanted me to see what I'd done to him.

"You're awake now, so let's go. We have places to be," he said stiffly.

I swung my legs over the side of the bed. "Where are we going this early?"

"You'll see, Princess. You know how much I like surprises."

Once I was bundled up enough for Grant's approval, we piled into his truck, and he started driving us away.

Grant shook me some time later, and I woke up, lying across the cab and resting my head on his lap.

"Hey, sleepyhead, time to get up."

I rubbed my eyes and groggily sat up. "Where are we?"

He just smirked and hopped out of his truck. Tucking a handful of blankets under his arm, he helped me out of the truck and took my hand. As we left the parking lot behind, I took in my surroundings—squat buildings, sea salt in the air, sand peppering the ground under my feet. Then, we turned a corner, and all I could see stretched out before me was the dark blue water of the Atlantic Ocean.

"The shore?"

"I used to come out here when I was in high school and watch the sunrise from the beach. I still drive out here sometimes when I need to think. It's always been my place of solace. I thought it could be yours, too."

I just stared at him. *Who is this man?* When I had first met him, all I'd seen was what was on the outside—playboy, manwhore, drunk, asshole, misogynist, rocker.

But this Grant, the one he didn't show to the rest of the world, was so much more than that.

"You hate it?"

"No! I love it," I said quickly. "You're just…not what you seem."

"I would generally disagree with that."

"How many people have you brought to the beach?"

Grant kissed me softly. "One."

"Why are you sharing this with me?" I couldn't help asking.

He shrugged and looked sincerely concerned about the question. It was clear that he hadn't really thought about it, and now that he was, he wasn't sure about the answer. "You make me want to share everything with you, Ari."

"I didn't do anything."

He smiled down at me and led me out into the sand without a reply. He spread out a blanket for us to sit on and then wrapped us up in a few more as we huddled together.

After a few minutes of silence, Grant spoke up again, "You did everything."

"What?"

"I don't know how to explain it. When I'm with you, I don't feel anything."

I turned to glare at him. *Is that supposed to be encouraging?*

"No, not like that. I'm bad at this. I'm not a good guy. I've never cared about anything. The only thing that made me feel was adrenaline—my motorcycle, the band, the girls. They were a temporary fix on my permanent lack of caring for anything and everything."

"You care about the band…and the guys."

"I know. I don't mean, I don't care about them. I guess I mean, I don't care about me—at least…I didn't until you."

Our fingers laced together, and we sat in the silence of his confession until the sun first broke the surface. Orange and pink rays cut across the early morning sky, and then we were kissing. My fingers tangled in his hair as his hands laid me back on the blanket. Our breaths came out short and frantic as we grappled with the rising emotions flooding our bodies.

"Ari, I want you," he groaned into my ear.

I responded by pressing myself against him. I wanted him, too. *Dear Lord, I'd never felt such fire coursing through me.*

Wasting no time, Grant found the waistline of my pants, and he began tugging them down my body. I heard the zipper on his jeans, and suddenly, he was free of the restricting material and pushing us together, skin-to-skin. My body arched as he slid up and down against me. His tip touched my opening, and I squirmed, wanting it so desperately but knowing deep down that I should tell him.

Grant felt me tense, and he retreated. "I have a condom," he said, assuming that was my concern.

"I'm sorry," I said, scooting backward, away from him. "I just…I, um…" *Fuck, I don't know how to do this.* "I'm sorry. I just never thought my first time would be outside…on the ground…in the freezing cold."

"First time?"

Fuck! Fuck! Fuck!

I quickly straightened myself up and took two steps back in the sand. *Why the fuck didn't I see this coming? Why the fuck didn't I see all the signs?* I'd assumed her innocence had something to do with bad experiences with other guys. I'd thought I could crack open the shell encasing her. I'd thought that she would see that it was okay to be with me.

But fuck…

Virgin?

That was a four-letter word in my vocabulary. Most dudes liked virgins. They got off on the idea of taking someone's purity, claiming her innocence. *Not me. Not ever.*

Ari's eyes were wide as she stared up at me expectantly. And I had no fucking clue what to do. Instincts told me to back away slowly and then get the hell out of here. This was a shitty situation. I'd fucked dozens and dozens of girls. I shouldn't be the one to take this from her.

"I should have told you earlier," she said, tugging her clothes back on. She stood and crossed her arms over her chest.

"Why didn't you?" I demanded.

Her hurricane eyes clouded over. "I wasn't going to tell you at first because I didn't think we would end up here. Then, the further and further we progressed in…whatever this is, I just couldn't force the words out."

"You should have told me." For some reason, it was the only thing I could think about. "Do you know how many times I've tried to have sex with you, and you could have easily told me?"

"Yes!" she cried. "Yes, I know. I know. I'm sorry, Grant."

I couldn't believe we were arguing about this. I couldn't believe this was happening. I should have been fucking ecstatic that Ari wanted to have sex with me and that she was being honest with me. It fucking meant that I could have her just like I'd been wanting since day one. But I kept pushing that thought away, and instead, I focused on the fact that I would have to start from square one.

It would be awkward, uncomfortable, and even painful for her. *Would she cry? Would I hurt her? Christ, I'd never once cared enough about a girl to wonder if I was going to hurt her.*

"I feel like an idiot…like I should have known."

"What? Should I have had *virgin* stamped on my forehead or something?"

I could tell she was getting irritated, but I couldn't get a grasp on it.

"Get it fucking tattooed to your forehead. That would have been a better indicator."

"Well, sorry!" she snapped. "I didn't think I'd be in this *condition* forever."

"How have you been in this condition for this long?"

"I'm nineteen!"

"I had sex at fifteen!"

"I'm not a whore!" she screamed back in my face.

"Babe, please, I prefer manwhore."

She angrily ground her teeth together. "You're such an asshole."

I couldn't keep it together. I was fucking it all up, but I couldn't stop. *Would I have continued to pursue her? In the beginning, no. After I'd gotten to know her…I didn't know.*

Yes.

I hadn't lied when I said Ari made me stop feeling. She made me stop feeling the pain. She helped push back the memories. She helped focus me. *Fuck, she makes me a better person.* And I thought, in turn, I fucking made her a better person. She might be perfect on the outside, but I'd expanded her universe.

I wanted to tell her all of this, to drop down to my knees in the sand and let her know everything I was feeling. Instead, I just stood there, letting my frustration get the better of me.

"And you know what? Since you're so set on being a manwhore," she spat the word back at me, "it's probably in my best interest *not* to sleep with you. It's not like *this* is anything like a relationship. I'm sure you've been fucking everything that walks when we haven't been together anyway!"

I fucking exploded. I couldn't let her think that. "Ari, I haven't been with anyone else since the day we fucking met!"

"What?" she asked, stunned.

"Yeah. You ruined me."

"But you were gone for a week, and the guys made it seem like—"

"I lied!" I blubbered on. "I fucking lied to them. I've been lying to them since we met because I didn't want to look like a pussy."

She stared at me in shock. "You really haven't been with anyone else…since *September*?"

"Damn, Ari, I'm not going to lie to you. I've wanted to get laid something fierce. Blue balls and I have gotten comfortable together. I haven't gone this long without sex since…ever."

"Well, that's reassuring."

I let the words tumble out of my mouth—everything I'd been holding back, everything I should have said to begin with instead of fucking freaking out on her for being a virgin.

"But that's the thing. Virgin or not, I've waited this long for you. I can keep waiting for you."

"Grant…" she said, releasing some of her anger with a sigh.

"I'm not going to fuck it up, Ari. I'm no fucking good at this. I've never done this before. I've never been a…boyfriend. But ever since the first time we met, I haven't been able to get you out of my head, and I'm not about to start now."

"Grant McDermott, did you just call yourself my boyfriend?" Ari whispered.

I tugged the dog tags over my head and then closed the distance between us. "Princess, you haven't figured that out by now?"

She took in a deep shuddering breath. "I didn't want to assume anything."

"Assume away."

I placed the dog tags around her neck. She fingered them loosely in her hand. Her mouth was open slightly in surprise.

"Now, everyone else will, too."

"Where the hell did you go this morning?" Cheyenne asked when I finally made it back to my place.

I still had an hour before my first class, but I knew there was no way I would be going back to sleep.

"Uh…" The words stalled on my tongue. I'd been so secretive about everything with Grant up until this point that it felt strange to be able to just freely divulge what had happened. It was kind of…exciting. "Grant picked me up."

"At five in the morning?"

"He drove us down the shore, and we watched the sunrise."

Cheyenne just stood there with her eyes narrowed. Her fiery red curls had been tamed, but she still always had this slightly manic appearance. Maybe it was just because I knew she was crazy.

"Grant McDermott?"

At that moment, Gabi walked in with a yawn. "Why are you guys so loud? Wasn't the five a.m. wake-up call enough?"

"Aribel is trying to tell me that Grant McDermott picked her up at five o'clock in the morning just to drive her down the shore to see the sunrise."

"That's so romantic!" Gabi gushed.

"It sounds like bullshit to me. That doesn't sound like Grant at all."

"Well, I've never been particularly romantic, so I don't think I'd make it up," I told her flatly.

"Cheyenne, the yelling," Shelby called, stumbling into the living room and collapsing on the couch.

"Did you hear?"

"How could I not?" Shelby grumbled.

I crossed my arms and waited for them to shut up. I knew it had been completely unlike Grant to do anything like that. He had been the first person to admit that, but it had still happened. "Are you through?" I asked, cutting off whatever Cheyenne was about to say to Shelby.

"Wait, you're serious?"

"Pretty serious." I held up the dog tags still hanging around my neck. "I'd say he's my boyfriend."

All three girls went silent, their eyes fixed on the dog tags. I was pretty sure I'd just shocked the shit out of them. Then again, the entire thing had surprised me. I definitely hadn't thought that this would happen after almost having sex, admitting I was a virgin, and then arguing about it almost to the point of no return.

Grant McDermott is my boyfriend. I had to mull it over for a bit to get used to that thought.

"You're dating Grant McDermott?" Gabi said to break the silence.

"Um…yeah. Well, we've been dating since September, but I guess it's official now." I shrugged.

Cheyenne blinked away her shock. "Girl, I'm excited for you. I'm just…wow. How did this happen?"

"We almost had sex."

"You haven't had sex?" Cheyenne gasped.

"Cheyenne," I said, rolling my eyes.

"To her credit, Aribel," Shelby said, "it has been *months*. Grant isn't known to keep it in his pants for more than a few hours."

"He hasn't been with anyone else since we started talking."

The disbelieving stares I received were enough to make my stomach flop. *He wouldn't lie to me about that, would he?*

Cheyenne glanced at the other girls and then back at me. "I don't want to be a Debbie Downer or anything. If Grant is your boyfriend and you want it, then I'm ecstatic…"

"But?"

"But he does have a reputation, Aribel."

Shelby jumped in, "We just don't want to see you get hurt."

Well, this is going great. "I know his reputation, considering *I* was the only one in this household who didn't fall head over heels every time he walked into the room. Maybe you remember that the first time I met him, I drugged him to try to get him to stay away from me. You were the ones pushing me toward him. I know you don't want me to get hurt, but you can't just get all concerned BFF when it actually works out."

Cheyenne sighed. "Well, I just have one question."

"What?"

"Does this mean I get to see more of Vin?"

We all broke down into giggles.

"Yes, I'm sure it means that."

We spent the rest of the time talking about the upcoming ski trip. I was really ready to just get through finals so that we could get away. I loved school, and I worked hard, but I'd never really had something like this to look forward to. I always just jetted off back to Boston to see my family.

Cheyenne, of course, was making it a much bigger event than just the four of us traveling up to the Poconos with Grant and the band. From the sounds of it, she had invited everyone that she knew whether they liked ContraBand's music or not. I didn't really care as long as Grant and the girls were going to be there.

I made it to calculus just in time. Grant's dog tags jangled as I found the last available seat. We had a pop quiz, and after hearing everyone's reactions, I seemed to be the only person prepared for it.

Soon, I was rushing to the chemistry building, ready to turn in my lab work before the final. I set my assignment down on the desk at the front of the room, and then I made my way to my regular seat.

Kristin took the seat next to me and then started messing around on her laptop. She had been acting strange toward me ever since I'd freaked out on her about Grant and I not having sex. Kristin and I weren't close to begin with, but we did have mutual friends, and I didn't want it to be awkward at the ski lodge.

"Cheyenne was telling me that you're coming to the ContraBand show in the Poconos!" I was terrible with false enthusiasm, but I was trying.

"Yep."

"Have you ever been skiing before?"

"Once."

Seriously? One word replies? I took a deep breath. "That's great. I'm rooming with the girls. Are you rooming with your friend Kimberly?"

Kristin shot me a disbelieving look. "You're not staying with Grant?"

I fiddled with his dog tags, and her eyes were instantly drawn to them.

"Oh, no, he's staying with the guys."

"Huh. Yeah, I'm staying with Kimberly, Tina, and Jodi. We're really looking forward to it actually. ContraBand has never played a venue this big before. Did you know that?"

I shook my head. *Well, now, she's talkative.*

"Yeah. They played a show in the city that was pretty big, but the music festival is by far the biggest lineup. They'll get to hang out with other celebrities. They could even get picked up there. It's a great opportunity. I mean, I'd be sad if they had to tour the country, but it would be worth it. They're so amazing."

Tour the country? Let's not get ahead of ourselves. They had been picked up on a whim for the Poconos music festival when someone saw them at the Halloween show, and that show had only happened because another band had dropped out of the lineup.

No need to jump too many steps forward. I'd just gotten Grant. I didn't want him to leave to tour the country. I knew what the groupies were like here. I couldn't imagine how much worse they'd be if ContraBand got signed.

Good Lord, Cheyenne's pity warnings are getting to me. Grant and I had been official for less than three hours, and I was already doubting everything.

25 GRANT

The week of Thanksgiving, Ari left to visit her family in Boston. I spent the time with my guitar.

Music lifted me up, tore me open, infused others with my very being, and then healed all our wounds. It had been for a very long time what made my world tick

But I'd never been a particularly good lyricist. I knew what I wanted to say, but that would never translate to what I actually wrote. When Miller wrote songs, they had a life force, a beating heart, an inherent energy. Yet, when I sat down to try to make that happen, I would end up tossing out more pieces of paper than were left in the notebook.

All of a sudden, I couldn't shut my brain off. The voices were there, incessantly calling for me to give them meaning. Every time I ignored them, they would come back full force until it was all I could do to get the words down.

When I handed the sheets of paper to Miller on our first day back to rehearsal, he looked at me like I was mental.

"Who'd you steal this from?"

"Your mother."

"And here I thought you reserved Mom jokes for Vin."

"I'm happy Grant is banging someone else's Mom for once," Vin chimed in.

"You know, I always give preference to Italian pussy." I smacked Vin on the arm and retreated to my guitar stand.

"Sounds like you're only giving preference to a certain pussy lately," Vin said.

I shrugged and slung my baby over my head. "And?"

"And…" Vin glanced at Miller and McAvoy for support.

Miller just ignored him, and McAvoy looked half-baked in the back of the garage.

"Bro, you're a fucking king, a fucking legend. You've bagged more chicks than anyone else. Your reputation is fucking off the charts. What the fuck are people going to say if you give all that up for some bitch?"

"Vin," Miller warned.

I didn't know what happened. I just reacted. I grabbed Vin by the front of his shirt and threw him into the nearest wall. "I'm going to fucking tell them to mind their own fucking business."

Miller and McAvoy were there in a split second. I hadn't even realized that McAvoy could move that fast in his state. Soon, they had my arms behind my back and were hauling me away from Vin. My own brother, and I had been ready to fucking destroy him over one dipshit comment.

I shrugged the guys off of me and ran a hand back through my hair. I needed to fucking get my shit under control.

"What the fuck is wrong with you?" Vin yelled.

"Why the fuck are you provoking him?" Miller asked. "You've known he's been with the same chick for a while."

"Stay out of this, Miller," Vin snapped. Vin took a step forward and got in my face. "You think she's changed you? I've known you since you were twelve fucking years old. You've been scamming girls into fucking your dumbass for nearly as long. And now, you're getting up in my face for pointing that shit out?"

I wanted to punch him. I wanted to fucking lay him on his guido ass. I wanted to bury him with his words. He lived in my fucking house. He played in my fucking band. He could learn how to fucking treat a brother.

"I don't need to hear this shit." I turned and walked toward the door.

"You're just going to fucking back down and walk away?" Vin taunted me.

"I'm going to fucking get out of here before I beat the shit out of you."

"All of this over one chick?"

I stopped with my hand on the doorknob. "Just think, Vin, more pussy for you."

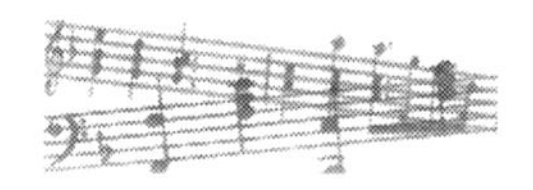

Shit was still tense between Vin and me backstage at the next ContraBand show. We'd rehearsed during the last week, but there had been no chance of us trying my new song when neither of us could see eye-to-eye on anything. It was our last show before the Poconos music festival, and we couldn't even agree on a set for tonight.

A part of me refused to see reason in what Vin had said. I could do whatever the fuck I wanted with whoever I wanted. If that meant I was spending all my time with Aribel and not fucking dumb useless chicks, then I was entitled to that choice. But the other part of me saw exactly what Vin had spouted. *Could someone do a one-eighty in a couple of months?* I hadn't gotten my dick wet because of her. *Is it even worth that?*

It was fucking Ari. I wanted to say yes. I'd told her she was worth waiting for. But just hearing Vin talk about it had made me second-guess everything I'd offered her at the beach. I was some uneducated jackass with no future and more than a few skeletons in my past. My reputation was warranted because the line of girls I'd fucked stretched from one end of the state to the other. Had I actually changed? Or did I just want to believe I had for her?

And just thinking about all of that fucked with my mind.

I should have been preparing myself to go onstage for our show. Instead, I was drinking like a fish backstage, trying not to think about how much of a fuck-up I was. I'd gone onstage wasted before, but my heart had been into it. Right now, the only thing my heart was into was the bottle in my hands.

"Hey, babe, you got a light?" I asked a chick standing near me.

Her big brown eyes stared up at me with reverence, and all I saw were her tits.

She fished in her purse and produced a lighter. "Let me do that for you." She cupped her hand around the cigarette hanging between my lips and then flicked the Zippo to light it.

"Thanks, darlin'."

I pulled a drag on the cigarette and then breathed the smoke out into her face. I preferred to smoke weed, but I hadn't gone to see my guy in, like, a fucking month, so this would have to do.

"Anytime," she said.

She wasn't even offended that I'd just fucking blown smoke into her face. She was actually leaning into me. *Damn, chicks are so easy.*

"What are you doing later?" she asked.

Not her—that's for damn sure. "You know, you have a familiar face."

The girl scrunched up her nose. "I've been to all your shows."

"Oh, yeah?" I breathed in and puffed out the smoke into her familiar face again.

She nodded slowly and placed her hand on my chest. *Yeah, so not happening.* There was brown hair where there should have been blonde, and brown eyes where there should have been hurricane blue.

"Huh. You know Aribel Graham by any chance?"

The girl straightened, flustered. "Aribel?" she snapped. "I think we have classes together," she said with a shrug.

"Blonde, kind of weird, always with some guy. Benjamin, I think?"

I stumbled a step backward. *What the fuck? No way. No fucking way. Not my Ari.* A pang of jealousy shot through my chest. I hadn't been with anyone else since fucking September, and Ari had still been seeing her ex-boyfriend? I thought I'd gotten rid of Benny on day one.

"Are you okay?" she asked, her tits pressing into my arm.

"Fine. Just got a show tonight," I said, passing her my beer without thinking.

I walked away to find Miller. Ari wasn't supposed to be at the show until we started performing, so I couldn't even fucking ask her what was going on. That wasn't something I could do through a text message.

"You ready to go?" Miller asked when I finally found him outside.

"Yeah."

"You look completely fucked-up. Are you even going to be able to play?" He sounded furious.

"Bro, lay off. I can fucking play this set blindfolded, high as a kite."

Miller shook his head. "Well, you can't sing with this in your mouth." He took the cigarette from me and stubbed it out under his foot. "And if you don't get your head out of your ass about the shit Vin said, then I'm going to fucking cancel tonight."

"You can't fucking cancel!"

"I can do whatever the fuck I want! I book the shows. I write the songs. I keep your dumbasses in line. You have feelings for Aribel. She's fucking knocked some humanity into you. Don't let Vin convince you that's a bad thing. That would make you even more of a fucking idiot than you already are, and I don't want to see what that would do to my best friend."

"I think she's seeing someone else," I confided.

"Fuck. You sure? You talked to her about this?"

"Nah, man."

Miller glared at me. "You fuck this up for no good reason, and you'll regret it. Play our set, and then talk to your fucking girl."

I was running late. Gah! I hated being late to anything. I'd barely even seen Grant this week since I'd been back in town. Now, I was showing up late to the last ContraBand show of the semester. Sure, I would get to see him perform again in a week, but this felt different.

Cheyenne, Shelby, and Gabi had left for the show an hour ago, but I'd *had* to finish my calculus assignment that was due on Monday, so I could spend all day tomorrow studying for chemistry. I was clearly a shit girlfriend.

Grant's dog tags clattered around my neck as I jogged across the parking lot and into The Ivy League. Just by catching a few chords, I knew that they were already on the third or fourth song. I eased my way through the crowd, using Cheyenne's bright red hair as a guide.

"Sorry," I said when I finally reached her.

"You missed 'Hemorrhage,'" she shouted over the cheers.

I shrugged apologetically. "But at least the homework is done."

"You're insane."

Like Cheyenne is one to talk.

I turned my attention away from my friends. There were more important things to look at. When I glanced up at Grant, he was staring right at me. His gaze burned through me like a firecracker igniting every inch of my body. I flushed at the intensity, but I didn't dare look away. There was something in his posture, in his stare, that was stripping me bare.

Being without him for a week had been a bit like suffocating. Going home to see my family had made me realize that I'd been living in a bubble. I loved my parents and my brother, Aaron, but the world was more than the kind of job I had, the kind of car I drove, and how big my house was. I'd felt stuffy and restricted in the world I'd always felt most comfortable in.

Maybe I wasn't part of Grant's world—a world run by how high someone could get on the next adrenaline rush—but I wasn't part of mine either. I'd never thought I'd be comfortable in a middle ground, not that I'd ever even given myself an option.

Grant ended the set, and then without a backward glance, he stormed offstage with his guitar still slung over his shoulder. *Odd.* He was never careless with equipment and certainly not his baby.

"What's up with him?" Shelby asked. "He didn't seem into that at all."

"What?"

He'd seemed into me, but now that I was thinking about it, Grant hadn't been invested in the crowd like he normally was.

"Your boy looked fucked out of his mind," Cheyenne said. "I wonder what he's on."

"He's probably just had a few drinks."

"More like a bottle to drink, if not something harder," Cheyenne said.

Hmm…well, only one way to find out. "I'll meet up with you guys later," I told them before making my way to the stairs on the side of the stage.

I hopped up to the top and then was stopped by solid muscle.

"Band only, sweetheart," Vin said.

"Oh, Vin, it's just me, Aribel," I said with a smile.

Vin shrugged, ignoring me. *What the…*

"Vin, let her through," Miller said, shaking his head.

"Fine."

Vin stepped aside, and I darted past him. I didn't know what that had been all about, but I was too focused on Grant to care.

No one was standing around in the backstage hallway.

I walked down to the break room and knocked on the closed door. "Grant, are you in there?"

No answer. Huh. Maybe he'd had to go to the restroom or he'd gone outside for some cool air. I knocked again just to be sure. "Grant!"

The door swung open. "Get in here," he growled.

I jerked at his tone. *What the hell is wrong with him? And why did he look so angry? Did I misinterpret what he had been feeling while onstage?*

"Ari, now."

The way he'd said that made me want to plant my feet on the ground, grit my teeth, and act as stubborn as possible. "Don't order me around."

"I don't have time for your shit right now, Ari. Get inside. We need to talk."

My heart sank, and my stomach dropped out of my body. Every thought I'd had up until this moment flitted out of my head. *We need to talk*. I'd heard that before. *Is he going to break up with me? Had our time apart been the time he needed to see that this was a mistake?* I'd always been strangely detached from my relationships, especially from my breakups, but just the thought of Grant leaving me made me feel like I was being fed through a meat grinder.

I struggled for that neutrality, for a shred of my indifference. I wanted that desperately because when he broke my heart, I wouldn't be able to walk away with a feeling of disappointment that he'd looked good on paper or filled a checklist. I would walk away shattered, destroyed, and empty, knowing I'd given him a piece of myself that I'd never known I could give. In turn, I'd let him fucking own me in every way that I ever found important. My body was just a vessel, but my mind, my soul…he'd taken over those, and frankly, I didn't want them back.

Somehow, I made it into the cramped break room, and Grant closed the door.

"What do we need to talk about?" I knew I sounded anxious. I *was* anxious.

Grant was staring at me with that same power he'd had onstage, but now, I saw what the girls had been saying. He was definitely drunk, if not high, and he looked pissed.

"You know what this is about."

"Don't play games with me, Grant. Say what you have to say." *If you want to break up with me, do it already.*

"You've been seeing someone else, Princess? You been with that ex of yours?" he growled.

I was so blindsided by his comment that I just laughed. I shouldn't have. It clearly just made him angrier, but it was such a ludicrous suggestion that there was nothing else for me to do.

"This isn't fucking funny!"

"You think I'm *cheating* on you?" I covered my mouth with my hand to keep from laughing again. "Dear Lord, please explain to me how it makes sense that I would be cheating on you, the self-proclaimed manwhore."

"What? Because you're a virgin, you can't be seeing someone else?" he asked.

"God, how drunk are you?"

"Just answer me straight, Princess."

"No, Grant. I don't remember the last time I saw my ex. Actually, I might have been with you. Why do you think I'm seeing someone else? Have I ever made you think that?"

Grant rubbed his hands over his eyes. "I don't know."

"You don't know? Or no?" I prompted. *He better be messing with me.*

"I don't fucking know, Ari! Someone told me that she sees you with your ex all the time. What am I supposed to think?"

"Who told you that?"

"I don't know. Some girl."

"So, you just believe some strange girl who is probably trying to get in your pants instead of me?" I asked in disbelief. "Did I miss the part where I became your girlfriend?"

Grant cleared the distance between us in a second. He grabbed my shoulders roughly and stared down into my eyes as if he was trying to find the truth buried within. I'd never lied to him, and I didn't want anyone else. I knew it was crazy. I knew we didn't really make sense, but I wouldn't have it any other way.

"You're mine?"

"I'm your girlfriend."

"No, Ari, you're fucking mine."

It wasn't a question, and I didn't have to respond. Nothing else was truer in that moment.

27 GRANT

The next week was hell for Ari during finals. I barely saw her, but at least I had the ski trip to look forward to. Vin and I worked out everything that had happened between us. He'd admitted that he wasn't actually pissed that I'd found a girl, but it kind of sucked that he no longer had a wingman. If I wasn't chasing ass, then he was kind of fucked over in that department. There wasn't much I could do there, but it helped knowing what was up. And maybe I hadn't changed, but the thought of Ari with someone else had knocked the nonsense out of me.

With Vin on board again, we started on my new song. The guys liked it enough that they wanted to use it in the lineup for the music festival. Miller thought it might draw some attention from label scouts. I wasn't holding my breath after the last incident.

I was just happy to get away with my girl and my friends.

Two days before we were supposed to leave, I received a call from Sydney.

"Hey, cuz. Pick me up from Newark on Thursday."

"Find your own way. I've got plans."

"Cancel them. I'm going to come visit before I go home for break."

Apparently, her Jersey accent had only gotten thicker when she moved to the South. It seemed contradictory to me.

"I can't cancel, Syd. We're playing the Poconos music festival."

"Poconos, eh? Vin going with you?" she asked with a giggle.

"He's still in the band, last I checked," I said dryly.

"Change of plans. Pick me up, and take me with you."

"You are *not* coming with me to the Poconos."

"So, my flight gets in around eleven in the morning. Don't park. I'll just meet you outside. Are you going to be in your big, black, jacked-up truck?" she singsonged.

"It's blue."

"Whatever. Eleven o'clock. See you then." And she hung up on me.

I told Ari that Sydney was coming with us, and Ari was excited to meet her. I didn't know how to prepare Ari for my cousin. Sydney was really one of a kind.

I stopped by Ari's place Thursday morning on my way out of town. The guys were driving the van out around noon, and Ari's group of friends was leaving around the same time. I'd meet them there after I stopped in Newark.

"Come in!" someone called after I knocked on the door.

"I could have been a burglar or a murderer," I said. "You just letting anyone inside without seeing who it is?"

"We let you in," Ari said, walking out of her bedroom.

Her blonde hair was tied up into a tight ponytail that I was looking forward to using as leverage this weekend—or at least, that was the goal.

"Darlin', I'm no stranger."

"You're going to be if you keep calling me that." She closed the distance between us.

I bent down like I was going to kiss her, but instead, I grabbed her legs and wrapped them around my waist. She latched on to me as I carried her into her bedroom.

"What are you doing?" she demanded, sounding only half-irritated.

"You keep talking back to me, woman, and I'll have to put you in your place."

Ari laughed at me. "Put me in my place? And where exactly would that be?"

"Do you want me to show you?" I asked, sliding my hand down her thigh.

She squirmed and tried to get out of my grasp, but I had her secured against me. Her eyes fluttered closed, and I chuckled softly at how easy she was to rile up. Her reaction was only turning me on. I'd be happy to show her *exactly* where her place was.

Lowering her until she was resting right over my dick, I bounced her up and down over it.

Her eyes flew open. "Grant—"

I kissed her lips to hold back whatever comment she had been about to throw my way. "That's your place, Princess."

Her pupils were dilated, and I could tell she was fighting with herself for the right reaction. She bit down on her lip to stop herself from spitting out whatever she was thinking.

"Come on, just admit it. You want my dick, and you want it bad."

She flushed at my vulgarity, but she didn't deny it.

I smirked and leaned forward to speak huskily into her ear, "Don't worry. I'm going to give you what you want."

Ari cleared her throat and hopped down from where I'd been holding her. Her body was on fire, and all I wanted to do was fuel the flames. She turned her cute, little ass toward me to try to compose herself. I took the opportunity to admire her soft body. *Fuck me, I want to bury myself in that.*

"You seem pretty confident in yourself."

"When am I not?"

She finally faced me again, a mask of composure. "That's a fantastic question."

"I've got to go soon," I said, inching toward her again.

"Oh, right, Sydney."

"I just have one question." I hooked my fingers into the loops of her jeans.

"What's that?"

"Are you bringing something sexy for me?"

"*That's* your question?" she asked, dumbfounded.

"Yeah, babe, I want to see you in some lingerie. Fuck, I'd die happy."

"Even if I brought some with me, how do you know you'd even get to see it?" she asked, teasing me.

"Who else would you show it off to?"

"I thought I'd wear it to the show and see if I got any attention."

The glint in her eye was fucking hot as hell. The very thought of someone else seeing my girl in lingerie got my blood boiling.

"Oh, you'd get some attention all right," I said, yanking on her belt loops. "You'd be getting my dick spreading you open. I'd let every one of those fuckers who paid you any attention see who you belonged to."

She rolled her pretty blue eyes at me. "Voyeur much?"

"I just want to be inside you."

"I know." Her tough-girl routine wavered, and she smiled up at me innocently. "I…I want you, too."

"So forward, Princess. If we had more time, I'd let you have your way with me. Unfortunately, I have to pick up my crazy-ass cousin. You'll have to wait to ravage my body."

"Whatever will I do with myself in the mean time."

"Masturbate while you think about me. It helps," I said with a wink.

"Oh my God, why do I even like you?" She pushed away from my chest, but only made it two steps back before I had my arms around her again.

"Because you can't resist my charm."

"Is that what you call this obnoxious, persistent Neanderthal routine?"

"It worked on you."

Ari shook her head and shoved me toward the door. "Go see your cousin. We'll discuss your charm later."

I arrived at the Newark airport at exactly eleven o'clock. Sydney's plane was late, and I had to idle while she picked up her three enormous bags from baggage claim. She suckered some poor guy into carting everything out to my truck. He practically salivated when she smiled at him. I knew chicks had reacted to me like this, but seeing a dude act this way was fucking pathetic. *Grow some balls.*

After hauling all three bags into the bed of my truck, the guy nervously asked for her number.

"Oh, sorry. I'm here with my boyfriend," Sydney said with a smile, pointing at my truck.

That was her go-to excuse. Sydney had had as many boyfriends as I'd had girlfriends. Well, I guessed I had one more than her now.

She hopped into my truck in the shortest fucking skirt I'd ever seen, not giving two shits if anyone could see what was underneath. Her chest was on full display in some tiny top, and she was in fucking cowboy boots. *My born-and-bred Jersey cousin in motherfucking cowboy boots.*

"Hey, cuz," she said.

"Are you shopping in the kids' section again, Syd?"

"Yeah, do you like it?" She uncrossed and crossed her legs.

"You look like a tramp."

Sydney rolled her brown eyes to the ceiling. "Don't start this shit with me again," she said dismissively. "If one of your slutbag groupies wore this outfit, you'd fucking cream your panties."

"*You* are not one of my slutbag groupies though. You're my cousin—my younger, not-even-legal-to-drink, don't-want-to-know-what-you're-fucking cousin." I shook my head. "I can't take you to the Poconos wearing that. You'll give every guy within a mile radius a hard-on."

"Ever think that might be the point?"

"Oh, I fucking know that's the point."

"Then, shut the fuck up," she said, jabbing me in the ribs.

"Will you just *try* to behave this weekend?"

I knew it was a lost cause to even ask, but I had to do it. She was still my baby cousin.

"Oh, Grant, I'll try. I'll try *really*, really hard, but sometimes, guys come on to me, and I just want to blow them. What's a girl to do?" She batted her eyelashes at me.

There was no reasoning with her. We were two peas in a pod. We always had been while growing up. That meant I needed to let her know about Ari before she heard it from someone else. Sydney needed to get the jokes out on me. I didn't want them getting back to Ari. Even though I was close with Sydney, I wasn't sure how to tell her that I had a girlfriend. It had never happened before.

"Syd, before we get there, I need to talk to you about something."

Her ears perked up. "Has Vin been asking about me?"

"What? Well, yeah, he has, but this isn't about him." I blew out a quick breath and just went for it. "I have a girlfriend."

Sydney burst out laughing. She kicked her feet up onto the dash and leaned back. "Funny. That'll be the day."

"No, Syd, I'm serious." I ventured forward. "Her name is Aribel, and she's going to be at the resort this weekend."

"A girlfriend?" she said the word as if it were new to her vocabulary. "But…you don't *do* girlfriends."

"Nah, I don't, but she's different."

"Who the fuck are you? Are you sure that you're my cousin?" she asked. "Where did we grow up? What street did you find me on when I fell off my bike in the sixth grade? How many doughnuts did we eat that one time before we both thought we were going to throw up?"

"Point Pleasant. Carter. Lucky number thirteen," I fired back. "Still me."

"Okay. So…what's she like?" Sydney sat up and then tucked her feet underneath her like she used to do as a kid.

So, I told her about Ari. Sydney was most amazed that Ari wasn't some dumb slut—as Sydney put it. I didn't tell her that Ari was a virgin because Sydney probably would have just laughed at me and told me that I was only still with Ari because she hadn't given it up. I wanted to fuck Ari more than I'd wanted to fuck anyone in my life, but that wasn't why I was interested in her.

"Does she know about…" Sydney trailed off.

"No," I said gruffly.

"Well, are you going to tell her?"

"I don't know." I clenched the steering wheel tightly in my hands until my knuckles turned white.

"Maybe you should."

"That's my business, Sydney."

"I know. I just thought since this is the first time you've had a girlfriend—"

"Drop it," I growled.

"Okay," she whispered. She fluffed her brown hair and changed the topic. "You know I get the final stamp of approval, right?"

"Since when?" I asked, relaxing after that last part of the conversation.

"Ever. I'm your cousin," she said as if that settled it all. "I can't wait to meet her."

I had the strong sense that this was going to be a disaster.

The girls and I arrived at the ski resort about an hour behind Grant and Sydney. He'd texted me to let me know that they'd already gotten their ski rentals and to meet him on the slopes. I'd gone skiing with my parents two or three times a year since I was little, but this was the first time I was going with friends.

After we dropped our stuff off in our rooms, the girls and I went to get our rental equipment. I had my own skis at home, but there hadn't been enough time to get them shipped to me. My parents hadn't been thrilled that I wasn't coming straight home for the holidays, but I'd insisted that this was something I wanted to do. Even though they were strict, they had trouble denying me anything.

We spent the afternoon on the slopes, and after about an hour, we ran into Grant and Sydney. I wasn't sure what Grant had told her about us, but she had this humorous glint in her eye every time she looked at me. She and Cheyenne hit it off right away, which was just fine with me. They seemed like kindred spirits.

Sydney disappeared halfway through the day. When I asked Grant where she had run off to, he just laughed and told me not to worry about it. I shrugged and followed him to a Black Diamond trail while Cheyenne, Shelby, and Gabi met up with Kristin and her friends.

I didn't mind being alone with Grant in the quiet, looking over the precipice to the world below. Actually, being up here at the top of a mountain felt about the same as it had the night when we sat on the shore, watching the sunrise.

"You ready for this, Princess?" he asked, leaning precariously over the edge.

"I've been skiing since I was four. Are *you* ready?"

He leaned over and kissed my frozen red nose. "Race you to the bottom."

I laughed when he jumped down the slope without warning, taking a head start. *He would need it.* About halfway down the trail, I glided across a particularly icy patch on the ground to take the lead. I heard Grant hit the snow behind me. I came to an abrupt halt and turned to see him sprawled out with one ski sliding down the slope toward me and the other sticking straight up out of the snow in the woods about ten feet away from him. I couldn't help myself. I just started laughing hysterically.

"Oh my God, are you okay?" I asked through my laughter.

"Bitch, are you laughing at me?" His head popped up to glare at me.

"You look ridiculous." I grabbed his spare ski when it reached me and stuck it in the ground.

"Well, are you going to just stand there? Or are you going to help me?" he asked, dropping his head back into the snow.

"You keep calling me a bitch, and I'll just leave you there."

"Babe…"

I kicked off my skis and made sure they were secure. I jogged awkwardly in my snow boots back up the mountain while carrying his ski with me. I dropped it down next to him and then went in search of the other. Once I had it in my hand, I placed it next to its mate.

Grant was still lying, unmoving, on the slope.

"Are you going to be okay?" I asked him.

He slowly eased up into a sitting position and rested his snow-covered arms on his knees. "I'm going to be fine," he said. Then, he reached forward, grabbed me by the backs of my legs, and pulled me down on top of him.

I shrieked and my knees landing hard in the snow. He just laughed, rolled me over, and covered my body with his. His mouth was on mine in a second, and any thoughts about the snow vanished. I wrapped my arms around him, pulling him closer.

We stayed like that, lost in each other's touch, until a group came by to make sure we were okay. Grant seemed completely unperturbed by them watching us, but I laughed nervously and told them we were fine. After dusting the snow off our bodies and snapping on our skis, we made our way down the mountain.

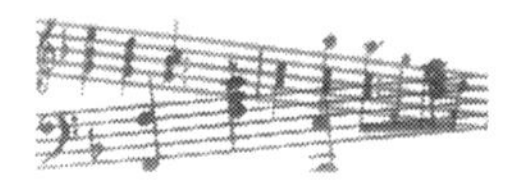

After a much-needed shower, I changed into a pair of skinny jeans, a tight black undershirt, and my baby-blue cardigan. I draped Grant's dog tags over my head. It didn't really go with my outfit, but I never went anywhere without them anymore. I grabbed a peach scarf and my peacoat, and then I headed down to the lodge with Cheyenne, Shelby, and Gabi in tow.

The opening bands were playing tonight to kick off the music festival. There would be shows the rest of the weekend, culminating in a giant final performance with The Drift. Their song "Tell It Like It Is" was playing nonstop on the radio.

The lodge was a massive open room that had been completely renovated for the music festival. The main area was a built-in stage that was used year-round for local events, and rooms branched off of it with stages for smaller bands. A second main stage along with two other slightly smaller ones were set up outside in tents with heaters for day performances.

At the door, we slipped on highlighter-green wristbands that gave us an all-access pass to the concerts all weekend. I stepped into the room, and I admired the mass of people gearing up for the opening act of the evening. The room setup was like a log cabin with high ceilings, exposed beams, and giant fireplaces that blazed brightly. I spotted the band near one of the fireplaces, and for once, I took the lead and walked my girls over to them.

"I'm so going to hook up with Vin this weekend," Cheyenne whispered into my ear as we walked over.

I just laughed, feeling happy and carefree. It was a nice change of pace for me. "Have fun with that, Cheyenne."

Two girls I didn't recognize were talking animatedly to Grant when I approached him. He hadn't seen me yet.

One leaned up to whisper something in his ear and then her friend slipped something into his hand before they walked away.

I arched an eyebrow as I approached. "What was that about?"

Grant shrugged. "Just groupies."

"What did they give you?" I asked curiously.

He unfolded the note and passed it to me. I glanced down and saw that a room number was scrawled on it. *Lovely.*

"Is it always like this?"

"Nah, Princess. Normally, I take them home," he said, pulling me close to him. "But the only person I'm taking home with me tonight is you."

I hadn't doubted that for a second—okay, maybe a second—but hearing that helped.

"Oh fuck!" Grant groaned.

"What?"

I glanced over in the direction where he was looking, and I saw *exactly* what he'd meant.

Sydney had just shown up in the most outrageous outfit for a ski lodge. She was in a teeny-tiny skirt that showed off a large rose tattoo on the outside of her right thigh. She was shrugging out of a parka, and underneath was an insanely low black tank top, displaying her half sleeve. She was wearing some god-awful cowboy boots that made it look a bit like she was trying to be Daisy Duke. Eyes followed her as she approached us. She was all smiles while her boobs bounced with her wavy brown hair trailing behind her. If this was her normal clothing choice, I suddenly understood where she had disappeared to this afternoon.

"Hey, cuz," she said in greeting.

"Didn't I tell you to behave?"

"Didn't I say I'd *try*?" She gestured down. "I tried…but failed. Now, where is Vin?"

My eyebrows shot up at that. *Sydney is interested in Vin?* Cheyenne was gorgeous and forward, but she didn't dress like *that.*

Grant sighed and pointed Vin out. He was standing only a few feet away from us by the fire, chatting up some girl.

"Thanks," she said with a wink. "Oh, Aribel…"

"Hey, Sydney," I said softly.

I didn't know what it was about her, but at that moment, she made me feel about two feet tall. I'd never be comfortable in an outfit like that, not that I needed that kind of outfit or anything. *Wow. When did I turn into such a girl?*

She flicked the dog tags hanging down between my breasts. "Nice necklace."

"Thanks," I said as she sauntered away. "She's, uh…something."

"Ignore her. She's trouble."

"Sounds like someone I know."

"You have no idea," he said, slapping me hard on the ass.

I squeaked, and that only made his insufferable smirk widen.

"Watch this," he said, gesturing to Sydney. "It'll be entertaining."

My eyes returned to Sydney, who had since pushed the girl Vin had been talking with out of her way.

"Vin, baby," she cooed, slithering into his grasp and running her hand temptingly down his chest.

"Sydney, I've fucking missed you." His hands ran down her sides to grab her ass. He looked like he'd just won the jackpot.

"Oh God, it's so good to see you. I've missed these huge muscles." She grabbed his biceps and squeezed. Her eyes fluttered closed, like she was going to orgasm.

I almost felt rude for intruding.

I glanced over to Cheyenne. She was standing not too far off, and she was watching the whole scene, like everyone else. She was fuming, and her face was as red as her hair.

"Syd, you know you can have these…muscles anytime you want," Vin said, thrusting her hips against him to emphasize exactly what he'd meant.

Her hand slipped between them, and his eyes widened further.

"I've been dreaming about your dick. Actually, I've been dreaming about you drilling it into me."

"Let me take you upstairs right now and give it to you, baby," he groaned. "I got all the dick you'll ever need."

"All four inches?" she asked with a devilish smirk. "Or is it five now?"

The watching crowd started laughing at her insult. I covered my mouth and shot Grant a look. He nodded his head back to them as if to say, *It gets better.*

"You know I'm a solid eight inches. Don't even mess around."

"Eight inches? What are you measuring with?" Her hands made quick work with his belt and then went for the zipper next. "Let me get a good look just to make sure."

"You've fucking seen it before. The next time you see it, we'll measure it inside your pussy where it belongs."

"Oh, Vinny," she cooed, "we all know you're an ass man." She winked.

"I'd fuck your ass, too."

Sydney turned and shimmied her body down his and then back up, gripping his hips. Then, she wrapped her arms around his neck, tilted her head back, and planted a soft kiss on his cheek. "Maybe next time, lover," she said before walking away from him.

"Is it just a game?" I asked, trying to comprehend what I'd just witnessed.

"One they've been playing since she got tits," Grant told me. "Vin always made fun of her when she was a kid, and then she turned out…well, like Sydney. He's wanted all over that ever since. I think she gets more amusement out of torturing him."

"So, she's not even interested in him?"

"Last I checked, no."

"Still no," Sydney said, coming up behind me. "No Vin for me, but I think your friend digs him."

I turned back to Vin and saw that he had Cheyenne pressed against the side of the brick fireplace. Their lips were locked, and hands were roaming all over the place.

"So, are you going to come home for the holidays?" Sydney asked Grant. She seemed completely unperturbed by what had happened. "Randy was pissed that you missed Thanksgiving."

Randy—that name sounds familiar. "Wait, Randy from the pizza place?"

"Uh…yeah," Sydney said, eyeing me suspiciously. "Duffie's."

"Syd…" Grant said softly.

"Why would he be pissed that you missed Thanksgiving?" I asked hesitantly.

Grant just looked down.

Sydney answered for him, "Because Randy's my dad. Sydney Duffie. Nice to meet you."

My mouth dropped open as it all came together. Randy was Sydney's dad. That made Randy…Grant's uncle. No wonder they had been so accommodating when we were there. We'd had the best seat in the place. Randy had been so happy to see Grant and to see that he had brought a girl to the restaurant. I didn't know why he hadn't told me that it was his uncle's place before this moment.

"You took me to Duffie's and didn't tell me that it was your uncle's place?"

"Whoa! You took the chick home?" Sydney asked.

"Sydney," Grant snapped, shaking his head.

"Um…what am I missing?" I asked.

"I know you said she didn't know, Grant, but—"

"Sydney!" he practically shouted. He pointed away from him. "Go."

Sydney rolled her big brown eyes. "Whatever. I'm going to go find Miller."

I waited until he had calmed down a bit before speaking. "What don't I know?"

"Ari, I can't…" He took a deep breath. "There are some things that you don't know about me."

I nodded. There was a lot that he didn't know about me. "I want to know though."

"You might have a different impression about me." He looked completely torn.

I wasn't sure if it was because he didn't want to tell me or because he really wanted to tell me.

"How could I have a different impression about you?"

He shook his head and glanced away from me. "I don't really talk about it. The guys don't even know. Well, they know some of it but not all of it."

"The *guys* don't know?" I was shocked.

They were his best friends. He'd known them since middle school. *What could he tell me that he hadn't even told them?*

"Yeah."

"Does this have something to do with your family?"

The last time he'd brought up his dad, he had completely clammed up, and now, Sydney had just been talking about his uncle. I didn't know what it was, but I could piece together some context clues.

His eyes stared down at me in utter shock. "How…"

"Good guess." I gently laced our fingers together.

His brow furrowed, and he looked like he was warring with himself. I'd never seen him look so…vulnerable.

"You can trust me," I whispered.

His lips fell on top of mine, and the noise from the lodge and all the people in it disappeared.

"You know there's never been anyone else like you in my life, Ari."

My heart thudded in my chest. "I feel the same way."

At that moment, the first band of the night started up onstage, and the crowd gravitated toward them.

"Come with me," he said.

Then, he led me out of the ski lodge.

I didn't know what the fuck I was doing. I'd never fucking told anyone about this. I never fucking talked about it. I never even discussed it with the people who knew, like Sydney.

I didn't touch those memories. They were the motherfucking crux of my emotionless existence. They ate at my very being and reminded me how much of a worthless piece of shit I was.

So, I tried everything to get rid of them.

I tried to outrun them.

I tried to drown them in booze, music, and sex.

I use any and everything to force them down deeper and deeper within me.

When that stuff had stopped working, I would fucking knock the memories upside the head with the flat side of a shovel, dig the memories' graves with it, and bury them six feet under.

Ari was the only thing that had ever made me simply forget without trying, without self-medicating, without riding out a high. Now, I was going to take my only hope of forgetting and tell her what had happened?

She was the last person I wanted to know about it. I didn't want to see the fear or pity or sorrow in her eyes. I didn't want to get that from *her*. Maybe I should turn it around and just try to fuck her.

No. Fuck.

I didn't fucking know.

So, I just kept my damn mouth shut as I guided her back to my room. We'd splurged on a suite so that we would all have more space and our own rooms. I left Ari in the living room to find some liquor in the mini bar. I poured myself whiskey on the rocks and her a glass of wine. She took it graciously, but I could tell that curiosity was burning a hole through her.

Even though she didn't touch her drink, I took a long sip of the whiskey, letting the burning sensation spread through my stomach. I nodded my head toward the far wall, walked her over to the door, and opened it into the master suite. Her eyes widened, taking in the luxurious surroundings. I'd claimed the best room. It was lush with a massive bed, Jacuzzi tub, walk-in shower, and the best view of the mountains.

I'd thought I'd be fucking her here tonight, not telling her about my past. I guessed she deserved to know the kind of person she was going to give herself to—that was, if she even wanted me afterward.

"Grant," she whispered.

I glanced up at her and tried to push down my rising desire at seeing her gorgeous body here in my suite, standing by my bed. It was a defense mechanism. I just wanted to bury myself in her and forget everything.

"You don't have to tell me if you don't want to."

I sighed and made up my mind. "Yes, I do."

"I can tell that you're beating yourself up about it. I just didn't want you to think that you had to do anything just because Sydney had slipped and mentioned it."

Fuck. This woman. She was too good to me

"Just take a seat," I told her. *If I'm going to do this, then I need to do it now.*

"Okay," she said softly, hoisting herself up onto the bed with her feet dangling.

I paced back and forth, not sure where to start.

Here goes nothing.

"I grew up as a military brat. Born in Knoxville and moved all over the country for the next eight years before we landed at Fort Benning in Columbus, Georgia."

"I thought you grew up down the shore?" Ari asked.

"I'll get to that." I ran a hand back through my hair and started pacing again. "My dad…well, I'm still not sure what he did for the Army. He was gone a lot, so my mom basically raised me. He had been deployed overseas and one day, when he came back, and he was different. I was only nine years old, so my mom didn't give me any details."

Ari wrung her hands in her lap. Her face was a mask of concern. "Did something happen to him overseas that made him different?"

"Yeah. He set a house on fire, but they hadn't gotten all the civilians out. He could still hear their screams when he went to sleep."

Ari's hands flew to her mouth. Her face was stricken. "I'm sorry."

"Don't be sorry yet," I said grimly. "My dad insisted that he didn't need to see any doctors. He just needed some fresh air to clear his head. He retired from the Army, moved us back to Knoxville, and spent the next year skinning squirrels alive in the woods."

She flinched at my brusque tone.

I wished there were another way to tell this story. I wished there wasn't a story.

My hands were trembling, and I fought for control. I was going to need it. I gulped and continued, "I regularly woke up to my dad's screams in the middle of the night. Even though my mom was working two jobs to try to make ends meet while taking care of me, she told me not to worry about the screams and to just stay in my room."

I turned my back on Ari, breathing heavily. My heart felt like I'd dropped it into a blender and set it on high. I couldn't keep it together, and I remembered exactly why I'd never told anyone else. I had to peel back layer after layer just to force the story out.

"Grant," Ari said, hopping off the bed and wrapping her arms around me from behind. "You don't have to tell me the rest."

She was trying to protect me from my own memories.

But I had to continue.

"One night, I awoke to my mom's screams. I didn't have any rules against checking on my mom, so I made my way down the hall. My dad had pulled a gun on her, and she was begging him to come back to her. She just kept yelling, 'Come back to me, Mike.'"

My throat seized as a vision of my mother cowering on the opposite wall hit me like an arrow to the heart. I could still see my father standing threateningly next to the dresser, telling her that he couldn't save her, that he hadn't been able to get her out. I imagined my ten-year-old eyes growing wider and wider, knowing what I was seeing but not believing that it was happening.

"I ran out to cover my mom, not wanting anyone to get hurt, but all I did was startle my dad. He freaked and fired without warning. I ducked, trying to pull my mom down with me, but she was already gone."

Ari gasped behind me, and in that second, I was glad that she couldn't see the tears welling up my eyes.

"He shot her in the chest twice."

"Oh, Grant, I'm so sorry," she whispered, coming around to my front and holding me tight to her.

"The gunshots broke my dad out of his stupor. He saw my mom dead, and he blamed me."

"What?" Ari asked, pulling back to look at me.

"If I hadn't jumped in the way, it would have been like every other nightmare. Nothing would have happened."

"You don't know that!"

"She's gone! It doesn't matter!" I roared.

She shrank back, and I immediately regretted taking my anger out on her.

"I'm sorry, Ari."

"It's okay. What happened to your dad?"

"He pistol-whipped me, and I blacked out. The neighbors had heard the gunshots though, and they called the cops. I was taken to the hospital, and my dad was taken to jail. He got an attorney to claim that he had PTSD, so instead of first-degree murder, his sentence was reduced to manslaughter with the option for parole. I moved in with my aunt and uncle on my mom's side, the Duffies."

"So, the dog tags," Ari said, holding them out from herself. "They belonged to your dad?"

"Yeah."

"How could you wear them all the time?" she asked.

"I told you once, they remind me of the man I want to be. And I want to be nothing like my father."

"You're nothing like him," she told me simply.

"How do you know?"

"I've seen the man you hide from the rest of the world. You would never be careless with your family. You love them fiercely, even the ones who aren't blood."

I said the words that I'd been holding back for years, the words I believed to my very core, "I could have saved her."

"You were ten years old. You should have never been in the position to have to save her. It's not your fault."

I wanted to believe those words so badly. But thirteen years of convincing myself of the opposite just wouldn't go away.

I could have saved her. I'd never forgive myself. I'd never forgive him.

Whatever I'd thought Grant was going to tell me…was nothing compared to what he'd just revealed. We all had skeletons in our closet, but this wasn't a skeleton. This was a body bag and a twenty-plus-year jail sentence. This was uprooting his entire existence to move in with his aunt and uncle. This was thirteen years of guilt weighing down on his shoulders.

No wonder he had hidden this from the rest of the world. Yet, I couldn't imagine hiding this, being all alone in my grief, not having anyone to lean on. The fact that he was as normal and stable as he appeared was a miracle. Experiencing something like this could have done a lot worse to him than turning him into a callous playboy.

I felt a newfound respect for Grant blossoming. He'd survived so much, and while it was clear he was still in pain from it, he had risen above what had happened to him. He had friends who would kill for him, a younger cousin who adored him, and legions of adoring fans.

And he was here…with me.

"So, that's my story," he said. His eyes looked off in the distance as if he was still lost in that tragic night.

"You made it through a lot and without any help. I mean, you didn't even go to therapy or anything, right?"

Grant scoffed. "Therapy was the bottom of a bottle and a warm pussy."

"That sounds like you. How did you survive when you were a kid though?"

"My guitar. It saw me through all the hard times," he told me. "My guitar and the tags."

I sighed as he mentioned the dog tags that were still hanging around my neck.

I slowly pulled them over my head. "Grant, I don't know if I can keep wearing these."

"What?" He looked astonished that I would even think of taking them off after he'd given them to me.

"I don't think you or I should have a constant reminder of what happened. I think you should just…let it go."

I knew it was easy for me to say. I hadn't been there thirteen years ago. I hadn't experienced what he had gone through. I had no idea what it would be like to see my mother die right before me, to see my father sent to jail, to feel the guilt that had clearly sunk into Grant at an early age.

"I can't *let it go*," he said the words like an insult. "I…you don't understand."

"No, I don't," I said, not letting him rile me up for once. "I could never understand. I'm sure few people could understand what you've gone through, Grant. But I want to." I ran my hand up his arm.

"The tags…I know that they should hold the opposite feeling, that I should hate them…hate everything about them. But I don't. It doesn't make any sense. It's a complete contradiction. One part of me knows that they're not enough to keep me from ending up like him. The other part knows they're the only link I still have to the only life I've ever been happy in. I lost both my parents in the same day. All I can remember is the bad—the memories, the inexplicable fucking horror of what occurred—but sometimes, when I look at them and when I look at you wearing them…I remember those earlier days. I remember when I didn't feel the pain."

Grant took the tags I still held in my hands and eased them back over my head. "Every time I see you, Princess, I feel better. Every single day, you push away the pain and the memories. You're my life raft in an endless ocean. You saved me from drowning. You saved me from myself."

I stopped breathing and just stared up into the depths of his chocolate orbs. Gold flecks at the center reflected back at me. In that moment, I saw every ounce of sorrow consuming him, but I also felt the warmth directed at me. Grant McDermott was baring his soul.

And the scariest part of it all was that I felt the exact same way. I hadn't gone through what he had gone through, but Grant had still saved me. I'd thought I was happy becoming the person my parents had always wanted, but I'd never felt passion until Grant. And I'd never forget it.

My lips found his softly. He held me against him and took comfort in what I was giving him. I knew then, trapped in his arms and lost in his kisses, that I wanted this to move forward. I'd held back, wanting to give myself to someone I truly cared about, waiting for the right moment, waiting to *feel* ready. I could never be more ready than at this moment.

I took Grant's hand and gingerly led him back toward the bed. My heart was hammering in my chest in anticipation, and words were stuck in my throat. He read the questions in my eyes and returned them with a kiss. He effortlessly lifted me onto the bed, and I slid backward while I unbuttoned my cardigan. He smiled as I tossed it to the ground.

Everywhere he touched me was igniting a fire on my skin. I couldn't get enough of him, yet I was terrified of exposing myself like this. His fingers ran along my stomach, pushing the shirt aside, as he lay kisses across my milky skin. I sucked in at his touches, at his utter adoration of every inch of my imperfect body.

"You're so beautiful," he murmured. His tongue teased the edge of my belly button.

"You make me feel beautiful."

He smiled knowingly up at me and unsnapped the button on my jeans. "You should always feel that way, inside and out."

I flushed at his compliments. He wasn't teasing me. He truly thought I was as beautiful as he'd said. Under that gaze, I couldn't disagree with him.

My jeans followed my cardigan, and Grant's shirt came off next. I admired his body in a way that I'd never really appreciated. I'd seen it before. I'd run my hands over it, but here in the light…God, he was gorgeous. He was tall and tanned with strong arms and six-pack abs. His tattoos were bold and prominent against his skin. He had those V lines that made girls go crazy, and I suddenly understood why.

His lips traveled to the hem of the lace thong I'd worn especially for this evening. I didn't have any lingerie—I'd never had use for it before—so this was as good as it would get. Grant didn't seem to mind. I yelped softly as he nipped at the tender skin before dragging the thong down my hip with his teeth.

My legs trembled softly in anticipation as he eased my legs apart and fluttered his fingers lightly along my inner thighs. I gasped at his warm breath before he experimentally flicked his tongue on my clit. I was so lost in all the emotions swirling between us that I already felt like I was feverish with need for him.

There was no hesitation. There was no holding back. There was only Grant and me. This was what it was supposed to be like.

I'd spent so much time thinking about what it would all be like and whether I'd be comfortable moving forward that I'd never let myself just be in the moment. But none of that anxiety plagued me tonight.

His tongue continued its work, making me squirm, and then I felt him ease two fingers inside me.

"Mmm," he groaned. "You're so wet."

My cheeks heated at the admission. Everything about us being together right now was turning me on. I shouldn't have been surprised, but it made me tense anyway.

"It's a good thing."

He started moving his fingers in a come-hither motion inside me. That released all the tension I'd been holding.

"You know another good thing, Princess?"

Whatever his tongue is doing?

He swept his tongue across my lips again, and I whimpered.

"The way you taste."

"Mmm?"

He repeated the motion. "You taste so fucking good."

I felt the beginning buildup register in my core and radiate out through my body. No one else but Grant had ever made me feel this good. Or maybe I'd never dropped my defenses long enough to open myself up to this. Well, my body was open now, and it was all I could do to hold on to the covers before an orgasm arched my back right off the bed. I moaned as I rode out the wave of euphoria that followed.

"Nothing sexier than your face when you come."

I smiled hesitantly and inched closer. "I think you should take these off," I said, snapping the waistband of his boxer briefs. I fought for the confidence I always had outside the bedroom.

Grant was out of the rest of his clothes and pushing me back onto the bed again within a minute. Our bodies pressed tight, our lips melded together, my fingers digging into his hair, his grasping my hips desperately. I could feel the need rolling off of him in waves. And it was rolling off of me, too.

I could feel him ready between my legs, and Lord knows Grant had completely warmed me up.

"Ari," he breathed into my neck before planting a soft kiss on the skin. "I want you tonight, love."

My heart beat wildly at the pet name. He used a million-and-a-half different names as if they were commonplace but never that one.

"You always want me."

He kissed me again. "That's right. I do."

I wanted to tell him to continue, but I didn't know how.

As if sensing my unease, he spoke up, "Can I take you tonight?"

I swallowed hard, and after only a moment's hesitation, I nodded. I wanted Grant McDermott like I'd wanted nothing else in my life. I definitely wanted him more than I wanted to keep my virginity.

Grant slipped on a condom he'd retrieved from the nightstand and then moved to cover my body again. He managed to look completely confident and hesitant at the same time. I wished I knew what he was thinking, but all I could concentrate on was what was about to happen. Fear pricked at the back of my mind, and I bit down on my bottom lip to try to dispel it.

This was Grant. This was what I wanted.

Our lips met softly, and then I felt his dick press up against me. My apprehension was palpable at this point. I swallowed, and he smiled softly.

"Ari, I don't want to hurt you," he whispered.

I met his gaze. "Then, don't."

He kissed me again. "Don't be afraid to tell me if I am."

I nodded because I was too worried about what would come out of my mouth. Grant leaned over and tenderly kissed me once more. He eased forward slowly…so slowly in fact that I felt a slight tremble in his arms as he held himself back. He pressed farther into me, and it took everything I had not to clench up at the pressure.

"Fuck, you're tight," he growled.

A tremor tore through my body as he pulled back an inch and then pushed forward all the way into me. I fit around him like a glove. Despite the pressure and stretching, I felt complete, whole. It wasn't exactly uncomfortable but not entirely comfortable either. In that moment, I realized my entire body was shaking.

"Are you okay?" he asked, his brown eyes full of concern.

I managed a smile and nodded. I was fine, just momentarily freaking out. At least it didn't hurt like I'd thought it would.

"I'm going to move now."

He gradually pulled out of me and then back in. The slow buildup was torturous. He was so gentle, so perfectly controlled, that I wondered if he was feeling anything at all.

One look at his face told me that he was feeling *everything* just fine.

I reached out and touched his arm. "You don't have to be so gentle."

Grant smirked at me and shook his head. "Yeah, I do, Princess."

"Would it be that bad?"

"Bad?" He chuckled and then pushed into me harder.

I gasped at the feeling. My eyes bulged.

"Amazing." He nibbled on my earlobe and then kissed his way down my throat. "If I took you how I wanted, I'd end up tearing you in half. We have time to get to that."

My fear spiked through the roof, but I was tinged with a sense of curiosity. And then all thoughts were lost. Grant grabbed both of my hands in one of his, and he held them above my head as he continued to slide in and out of me. He picked up his pace and moved his other hand to grasp my hip. I was breathless at the feel of him.

My whole being shook. It felt so good, better than anything else I'd ever felt, yet it was also painful. It was a mixture of the two. It was both hot and cold. Down was up, and up was down. The world tilted. My body ached and pleaded and retreated and demanded. It was so many things all at once that my thoughts, feelings, senses mingled together into an indescribable sensation. It was a bit like reaching the top of a roller coaster right before I felt like I was going to plummet to my death and a bit like the first time I'd gotten tipsy and still more like riding with the top down in the convertible. It was all of those things and none of those things and so much more that I could never even think of.

"Fuck," Grant grunted under his breath. His body shuddered against mine, and then he was still.

My breathing was ragged, and I was shaking from head to toe—not just light shaking, but uncontrollable trembling.

Grant seemed to recover himself, and he pulled back to look at me. "Hey, are you okay?"

"Um…just shaking," I stated the obvious.

He took a few seconds to get rid of the condom. Then, he yanked the covers back and rolled me toward him. "Was I too rough? Did I hurt you?"

"I think I'm fine. It was…it was good. Overwhelming," I breathed.

"You felt amazing."

I giggled and leaned against his chest. "You sound like you want to go again."

"Babe, I don't think you're going to be able to walk tomorrow."

"Oh." I hadn't thought about that. "What about skiing?"

He grabbed my chin in his hand and kissed me roughly on the mouth. "You think I'm letting you out of my bed now that I've got you in it?"

"Seriously, you can't keep me in here all day," Ari said, flopping back on my bed. "I'm going to need to eat."

"I'll order us something." I shot her a devilish smirk.

We'd spent the rest of the night tangled up in my sheets. I'd wanted to go again, but I was too afraid of hurting her. She was fragile enough, and while I'd been gentle, I could tell that she was sore by how much she winced when she walked. I would give her a day and see how she was feeling then.

It had been more than three months since I'd had sex. It had to be a record. Now that I'd tasted it again, I was dying for more. I couldn't believe I'd held out for twelve hours straight already. If it were up to me, I would have been riding her all night.

"Can't we just go downstairs and get breakfast?"

I leaned against one of the bedposts and arched an eyebrow. "I'd be happy to show everyone what we were doing last night."

Her cheeks colored pink. "I think you're exaggerating."

"Go ahead and try walking around the room then."

Determined, she stood and started toddling around the room.

I couldn't hold back my laughter. "Babe, you're all wobbly and waddling around like a penguin."

She glared at me. "What did you do to me?"

I strode over to her and pulled her against me. "I fucked you."

"So crude."

"Are you saying you don't want me to fuck you again?" I asked, pushing a hand up into her hair.

"I didn't say that."

"I didn't think so."

"Maybe we could do it again," she whispered hesitantly. Her hand landed on my chest.

"Are you asking me to fuck you?"

"Maybe."

My hand slid down between her legs and gently rubbed against her. She winced and retreated from me just as I'd expected.

"I think I'm going to have to save you for dessert."

"I think I'll be better after your show tonight."

I loved her enthusiasm. I kissed her on the mouth. "We'll see. But first…breakfast."

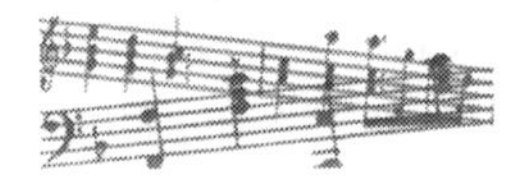

Room service arrived sometime later, and I threw some clothes on to go answer the door. Vin was lounging around in his boxers, watching some CrossFit championship on ESPN. I shook my head and opened the door. The guy wheeled the tray into the room, and then he was gone after I tipped him.

"What'd you get me?" Vin asked, hopping off the couch to examine the food.

"Nothing. Fuck off." I pushed the food toward my room.

"You've been in there all night and morning. Do you guys even come up to breathe?"

"Nope." No use telling Vin any details.

"I ended up fucking her ginger friend last night."

"Cheyenne?" I asked. It was still shocking that I'd managed to remember other girls' names longer than a couple of seconds.

"Yeah, bro. She's a total freak in the sheets. We should swap, and you should try that out."

I stopped walking and tried to keep my temper on lock. The last time I'd reacted on Vin, it had fucked up our rehearsals for the next week. I gritted my teeth. "I don't think so."

"Yeah, you never were into redheads."

"Did I discriminate?" I didn't remember it that way.

"You didn't used to."

I could hear the annoyance in his voice but chose to ignore it. We had a huge show tonight. If Vin had something to say, he could fucking say it after the show.

"I wish I'd seen where Sydney went off to though. Think I could get her into a threesome with the ginger?"

"I'd assume it wouldn't be Syd's first, but she's my cousin, so shut the fuck up about her."

"She's a goddamn cocktease. You should say something to her, Grant. I've been wanting in that ever since I took her virginity. I'm fucking obsessed with her."

To my credit, I didn't throw Vin across the room like I wanted to. I had beat the shit out of him when I first found out. Luckily, Sydney had enough sense not to actually be interested in my dipshit friend for a repeat performance. Her teasing was pretty entertaining, but fuck, I still wanted to kick his ass for ruining my little cousin.

"I'm not saying a word to her, and you should just fucking leave her alone. Concentrate on Cheyenne. She's crazy about you."

Vin cocked his head back like I'd just said the most shocking thing. "Since when are you the fucking voice of reason? You been hanging out with Miller too much, bro."

Speak of the devil, Miller's door cracked open, and he walked out in a clean pair of jeans and a band T-shirt. Sauntering out right behind him was Sydney, still in the clothes she'd been wearing the night before. *Fuck!*

"What the motherfucking fuck?!" Vin roared.

"Oh, Vin, baby," Sydney said in a chipper voice. "It's so good to see you."

"Bro, are you fucking my girl?"

Miller leaned against the doorframe, crossed his arms, and gave Vin the best eat-shit-and-die look I'd ever seen from him. He didn't need to say a word. That look had done the trick.

"Whoa!" I said, slamming my hand down onto Vin's chest. "Fucking chill out. You were fucking someone else last night."

"He fucking knew I was into Sydney!" Vin cried, trying to push past me.

He had more bulk than I did, but I wasn't going to let my brothers kill each other. Miller was tall and lanky, but I knew firsthand that he packed a punch. He had been taking jiu-jitsu and various other martial arts classes since he was a kid.

Sydney rolled her eyes. "Vin, baby, calm down."

"Don't fucking tell me what to do!"

I shoved Vin backward. "Don't talk to my fucking cousin like that, jackass."

The other doors to the suite opened, and Aribel and McAvoy appeared out of nowhere. McAvoy came over to help block Vin's path to Miller.

"What's going on?" Aribel asked.

"We got it covered, Ari. Just go back into the room."

She gave me a look that said, *No chance in hell.*

"You motherfucker!" Vin yelled at Miller, ignoring the bodies standing between them. "You broke code."

"What code?" Miller was completely calm. "Did you claim her? Is she sharing your bed? Has she been there since high school? No. And last I checked, Sydney is perfectly free to decide where she wants to spend her nights."

Sydney turned and smiled at Miller. *Oh fuck!* This hadn't been just some scheme on her part, like normal. She actually liked Miller. *Well, just fucking great. Way to split up the group, Ono.*

"Vin is just overreacting. I don't have time for this," Sydney said with an exaggerated eye roll. She turned, grabbed her parka, and walked out of the suite.

I fucking knew she was going to be a disaster.

"We have a show in ten hours," I said. My eyes darted between the two guys. "Are you going to fucking get over this shit before then?"

"There are going to be scouts," McAvoy said, surprisingly coherent. His eyes weren't even bloodshot. He nodded his head at me when he saw me notice.

"This is huge for us," I repeated Miller's words back to him.

"He fucking slept with Sydney."

"Yeah, we all got that," Miller said.

"Enough!" I yelled at both of them. "You should just go find your ginger and fuck her the rest of the afternoon to get over this."

"Hey! That's my friend!" Aribel called.

"You want to go for a spin, honey?" Vin asked with a wink.

Aribel narrowed her eyes.

I was ready to knock that shit look off his face, but McAvoy jumped between us.

"He's just pissed. He doesn't need a broken nose, too."

"Maybe he does," I growled.

"Look," McAvoy said, raising his voice.

That caught our attention. He never raised his voice.

"We have a fucking show tonight. We shouldn't be arguing over some fucking girls. It's about the music. It's always been about the fucking music. Why have I been the only one who seems to remember that lately?"

Miller stood up and dropped his arms. Vin looked away from McAvoy's gaze. I shrugged my shoulders and sighed. These were my brothers. We didn't need to be arguing like this.

"He's right."

"Yeah," Miller said.

Vin continued to look off toward the TV.

"Vin?" McAvoy prompted.

"Yeah. It's about the fucking music."

"So, go get laid, blow off some steam, whatever you need. But when we step onto that stage, this shit never happened."

Grant stormed back into the room like a thundercloud. Our breakfast had been forgotten in the midst of Vin and Miller's fight. He slammed the door closed behind him, scooped me up like I weighed nothing, and tossed me back onto the bed. I bounced once and then lay flat.

"Are you turning into a caveman on me?"

"Is this some new thing?" he asked, yanking his shirt over his head.

"I suppose not. Are you pissed about Sydney?" I could tell he was, but I wanted him to talk to me about it.

"I knew she'd fucking be trouble on this trip the moment she called and asked me to take her with me. She's a fucking mess—bed-hopping, wearing those ridiculous clothes, acting like a dumb slut." He shook his head in frustration. "She's actually a really smart girl. Full scholarship to the University of Tennessee, straight A's, on the fucking Dean's list. She's just a fuck-up in her personal life."

"Doesn't sound like anyone else I know."

Grant turned his dark eyes on me, and his whole body softened. "Nah. I'm not as smart as Sydney."

"You wouldn't say you fucked up your personal life?"

"Last I checked, you're in my bed, Ari. I'm a fuck-up, that's for fucking sure, but I must have done something right because you're here. Or maybe I'm a real fuck-up, and you deserve someone better than me." The words tumbled out of his mouth before he even realized what he'd said.

A part of me knew that he felt that way, but still, I didn't think he'd actually meant it.

"I think you're spouting off stuff that you don't mean," I whispered, grabbing his hand.

"How do you know I don't mean that?"

"Because you don't."

He didn't say anything. Up until we'd gotten involved, I would have thought the very same thing. Actually, I'd spit that at him when he first pursued me.

"You're just worked up about the argument. I can think of better things to take your frustration out on other than yourself."

His eyebrows shot up, and a small smirk crept onto his face. "I have a feeling I like where this is going." He crawled onto the bed after me.

"If Vin was instructed to fuck Cheyenne all afternoon to get over the argument, I think it's only fair that you take your own advice."

"You want me to fuck your friend?" he asked with that mischievous glint in his eye.

"Yes, I want you to ruin your relationship and the band all in one swoop," I said sarcastically.

Grant just laughed and then rolled me underneath him. "I believe you're asking me to fuck you."

"I didn't—"

"Ask me."

"Ask you what?" I played coy.

"Ask me to fuck you." He leaned over and nipped at my ear. "Talk dirty to me. Tell me what you want."

I squirmed underneath him. There was no way I could do that. I was…not that kind of person. Now, I didn't mind it when he would talk dirty to me while we were in the middle of our escapades. Actually, it usually really turned me on.

I tried to force them out, but the words stuck in my mouth from embarrassment.

"I'm sorry. I didn't hear you," Grant teased. "Do you want me to eat you out, suck on your clit, finger-fuck your pussy?"

My whole body flushed at that word. His lips trailed down my throat.

"Do you want me to spread you wide? Do you want me to slide my cock deep inside you? Tell me what you want, love."

My breathing was heavy as he started circling his hips against me. God, even through his jeans, I could feel him getting turned on.

"I want you," I whispered.

"To fuck you."

I swallowed hard. "I want you to fuck me, Grant."

There was no hesitation on his end. He didn't even ask me if I was still sore, which I was, but at this point, I just didn't care. I was pretty sure I'd suffer for this later, but damn, I wanted him.

Grant grabbed my head, and our lips met with an intensity and ferocity that had been missing in our gentle embrace last night. He kissed me like a starving man with his first morsel of food, like a heroine addict getting his next hit, like a reigning boxing champion clamoring for his next fight. I was his drug of choice, and he was using me to feed his addiction.

Our lips moved against each other, tongues twisting and massaging. His teeth latched onto my bottom lip and dragged it back toward him.

I couldn't get enough. I needed his touch. I needed him pressed against me. I needed us to be connected like this.

We quickly removed the remainder of our clothing, and Grant slipped on a condom. His hands found the backs of my legs, and he dragged me out flat on the bed. Our bodies were aching for each other.

He went in easier this time even if it hurt like a bitch. I bit my bottom lip hard and tried to push the pain back. *Oh God, nope.* It still felt like he was tearing me open. I took a few deep breaths as he filled me all the way.

He started moving sooner than he had last time, and I found that the more he slid in and out of me, the less I noticed the pain. Actually, all I was starting to notice was the pleasure rushing up my body and spreading to my fingertips, causing me to clench the covers and curl my toes.

"Fuck, Ari," Grant groaned, leaning his body over me.

"Oh my God," I whispered.

"I should slow down," he said reluctantly.

I shook my head. Yes, he should slow down, but no, I didn't want him to. I didn't have to tell him twice about that either. Grant pulled one of my legs up and leaned forward into it. My eyes widened. I hadn't thought that he would be able to get deeper, but clearly, that was not the case.

My head tilted back into the pillow. My world was spinning. Pain mixed with pleasure in a way I'd never experienced and had no way of explaining. Grant was moving not too fast but not slow either, and all I could feel was the energy building inside me.

"Grant," I moaned.

My walls tightened all around him, and I couldn't hold back the release rocking my body. I dug my fingers into the duvet and felt like I was ripping through the material.

A moment later, Grant gasped and then shuddered as he finished just after me.

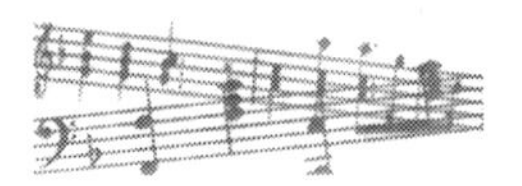

Exhaustion pulled me under, and when I finally woke up again, it was already early afternoon. I'd practically missed the whole day with Grant, and I was starving. But when I woke up, Grant was missing. *Where did he go?*

I stretched out my aching muscles and then made the mistake of trying to stand up. *Holy fire and brimstone!* My body was down for the count. Besides the tenderness between my legs that felt like I'd just run a mile, I was so weak with hunger that it took real effort to keep the dizziness at bay.

My skinny jeans were somewhere on the floor, and I winced as I pulled them on. This was not going to be fun. After throwing my shirt and cardigan back on, I went looking for Grant. The bathroom was empty, but the shower seemed to beckon me. I would die for a shower and a hamburger right about now, not at the same time. Maybe. I peeked my head out of the room to make sure I wouldn't get caught in any crossfire this time, and I found the room mostly empty.

Grant was sitting on the couch with his guitar in his lap. He expertly picked at a few chords and repeated one line over and over again. I recognized it from their song "Letting You." They liked to close with that song, and it was one of my favorites.

"I like that one," I whispered, coming out of the bedroom and taking a seat next to him.

"Yeah. It's one of Miller's best. How did you sleep?"

"Like a rock. You couldn't sleep?"

"Too pumped about the show."

He strummed out a melody I hadn't heard before, and I stretched out as he played it on repeat.

"You'll be great."

"All I know how to do, Princess."

"What's this song? I haven't heard it."

"Something new."

"I didn't know Miller had written something new for the show."

Grant stopped what he was playing and ran his fingers back through my loose hair. I sighed and closed my eyes.

"I wrote this one," he finally murmured.

"Oh," I said, surprised. I hadn't known that he wrote music. "Will you play it again?"

He picked up on the rhythm he had been playing, and I let the music soothe me. Now that I was listening, I could tell that it had a different quality than what Miller usually came up with. It was softer, yes, but it was almost more emotional with more heart.

"Are you going to sing for me?"

"Tonight."

"You're singing for the whole lodge tonight."

"I'll only be thinking about you."

I giggled and sat up. "I bet you say that to all the girls."

"You're accusing *me* of charming girls with music?" he asked with his distinctive smirk.

"Oh no, not you. Certainly not you."

I knew that he'd used his music hundreds of times to pick up women, but I wished that this song were just for me and that I really was the only girl he would be singing for. Maybe I was being petty. He was my boyfriend. Just because we were together and had sex didn't mean that I erased everything that had ever happened before that. And I didn't need to. We were together, and that was what mattered.

"You know," I said, letting the music take me away, "we work well together."

"You think?" he asked, amused.

"Against all logic…yes."

"Yeah, you've got the world at your feet, and you're with a guy like me," he said offhand.

I knew it affected him.

And he was right in a way. We had come from two different worlds, had grown up in two shockingly different ways, and had coped with our lifestyles in completely different fashions. My parents were high society, and his father was in jail. It didn't make sense.

But it did.

"Even though we grew up differently, we've come out very similar."

That *did* surprise Grant. "What? You're a boozing manwhore? Did I miss that?"

I laughed. "No! I just mean that up until you, I'd never let anyone close enough to really get to know who I am. My parents aren't exactly emotional, and my education was my escape."

He nodded in understanding. "Before you, there was no one. Just the next high."

"Yeah. It's easier to be emotionless even if that means trying to come off as a carefree playboy."

"Hey, that's not an act!"

I rolled my eyes. "Sure. But do you get what I mean? I kind of bring you back down to earth, and I think you open up my world a bit."

"Just a bit," he said with a wink. His hand traveled down my thigh.

I laughed and shook him off. "I'm being serious."

We were shockingly different yet perfectly in sync. It was a harmony, a yin and a yang. In that moment, as I lay there listening to him play his music, I felt like things were right where they were supposed to be.

"That's why I keep you around."

"To be serious?"

"Someone has to be," he said, reaching for me again.

"And here I thought it was for the sex," I joked.

"When you put it like that…"

I shook my head at him, and he captured my lips again.

"Definitely more than the sex," he said.

I liked that answer.

"We could always go again."

"Whoa there!" I held up my hand to stop his advance. "I should go back to my room. I bet my friends are freaking out. Plus, I really need a shower."

"I can arrange a shower."

He reached for me, but I slipped out of his grasp.

"I'm not sure I'm capable of showering with you."

"Might get tempted?"

"Might break in half."

"I don't see a problem," he said, looking at me hungrily.

"I'll see you at the show."

"Hey, Ari," Grant called when I reached for the door. "Come early. I want to show you a real backstage."

33 GRANT

When Ari left, I took a quick shower, threw on some jeans and a dark blue T-shirt, and left for the lodge with my leather jacket and guitar. Our set started in a few hours, but I figured it would be a good idea to get there early and see what was going on. Maybe I could meet a few people. I had no interest in all the talk about labels looking at us, but it still tickled at the back of my mind.

What would it be like if a label liked us and wanted to sign us on? Would we record an album in L.A., tour with another band, make a living on the road? Would I see Ari?

I stopped that whole train of thought. It didn't fucking matter because we weren't fucking signed. We had no prospects. We were just here for the fucking music, just like McAvoy had said. I loved my guitar, my brothers, the band, everything. I wanted it to fucking stay that way.

The lodge was teeming with people for the music festival, so I cut around to the side entrance for employees, bands, and staff only. Since there were so many acts, our equipment was still waiting in the back of our van. We would set it up once we got closer to showtime.

With my guitar slung across my back, I walked through a door backstage. I didn't recognize anyone, and that didn't bother me one bit. I'd always been a bit of a floater, meeting people along the way.

As I'd expected, there were twice as many girls back here as bands. A few were eyeing me suggestively. A few were really fucking hot, like off-the-charts hot. One had tits that were huge and perky and still fucking real. Another girl bent over to whisper to talk someone else, and I could see half her ass in her short skirt. *Fuck me.* The girls didn't look like that in Princeton.

And I had a hot piece of ass all to myself, and she had been in my bed all day. Self-control had never been my strong suit. I could look but not touch or kiss or fuck. Just look. That was possible. With some difficulty, I averted my gaze entirely and kept walking.

I was about halfway through the backstage area when a guy stopped in front of me. He didn't look familiar, but I was bad with faces anyway. He was dressed casually in dark jeans and a polo, yet I could tell he had some authority to him.

"Grant McDermott, right?" the guy asked, pointing his finger at me.

"Depends who's asking."

"Hollis Tift."

We shook hands.

"I've heard a lot about you, Grant."

"That so?" His tone made me cautious. *Who is this guy?*

"Mostly good things."

"Sounds accurate."

The guy cracked a smile, and he looked younger than I'd thought he was. "Did you really tell Frank Boseley to go fuck himself?"

Frank Boseley—well, that was a name I never thought I'd hear again and also one I wasn't going to soon forget. He was the asshole label scout from BankHead Records who had treated me like a chump.

"More or less. I think I actually said that he was a fucking piece of shit, and I wasn't some fucking dick he could jack off with."

Hollis laughed and nodded his head. "Yeah, that's better than when he told the story."

"You know the guy?"

"We have mutual friends."

Ah, he was a label scout or at the very least someone in the industry. I should have been ecstatic to talk to this guy. Miller would go nuts if I didn't follow through with this in some way.

"Surprised you're even talking to me after I shot down your friend."

"Friend is such a loose term. Frank is more of an acquaintance. And I couldn't be happier with how things turned out."

"Why's that?"

"Because I was the one who brought you here. Didn't Miller tell you?"

I shrugged. "He didn't go into specifics."

"Well, I didn't really go into all that many specifics with him. I was waiting to see your show here. I was at the Halloween performance. You sold me when you pulled that girl onstage. Clever. It didn't even look like you were faking it."

I hadn't been, because I'd pulled Ari onstage. This guy had been there. I was reeling.

"So, are you a scout?" I asked flat-out.

"A scout of sorts. I represent a number of artists for Pacific Entertainment."

Fucking Pacific Entertainment. They were top-notch. Right up there with some of the best labels from Sony and Universal.

"Nice gig."

"It has its benefits. Do you have a minute? Perhaps I could introduce you to one of my clients?" Hollis offered.

I glanced around backstage as if someone might snap me out of what was happening and tell me it was all a joke, but no one appeared. Miller, McAvoy, and Vin hadn't shown up yet. I was here to meet people from the label all on my own.

"Sure. Why not?"

Hollis spoke to the people he recognized as we passed them. Some, he even stopped to introduce me. I wasn't going to remember them for shit, but it was a nice gesture. Some of the bands I knew. I couldn't remember faces, but music, that was a different story.

We rounded a corner, and Hollis stopped in front of a black door.

He knocked twice and then entered. "Hey, guys!"

"Hollis!" two guys cheered.

Another one yelled out, "Hey, man!"

The room smelled like booze and pot. A myriad of girls were sitting on different guys' laps. People were lounging on the furniture and taking shots at the bar. It seemed like the exact place I would have wanted to be just a few months ago. Maybe I still did.

Hollis walked around as if he were everyone's best friend. A handshake here, a fist bump there, and a few snide remarks until he'd made a full circuit.

"Guys, this is Grant McDermott. He's the lead singer of ContraBand."

"Stellar," one guy said. He looked completely obliterated.

"Dude, nice Gibson," another guy said.

I really wanted to say that these guys looked familiar. There was a nagging feeling at the back of my mind, but I just couldn't place them. And maybe I should care more, but I didn't.

"Grant, this is Donovan, Ridley, Joey, Nic, and Trevor."

Oh fuck!

"The Drift."

As soon as I opened the door to my room, everyone started speaking at once. I hadn't expected to be bombarded, and I jumped clear out of my skin. I groaned at the sudden movement, and I couldn't keep from wincing at the soreness between my legs.

"Ah!" Cheyenne shrieked. "I know that face."

"What face?" I asked defiantly.

"You did it, didn't you?"

"Did what?"

I knew I wasn't going to keep this from them. Cheyenne, Shelby, and Gabi had been trying to get me to lose my virginity in the year and a half since I started living with them. It had been downright shocking to them that I still had my V-card after all this time. Well, I guessed I didn't have it anymore.

A smile touched my lips.

"You did! That smile!" Cheyenne continued.

"Cheyenne, leave her be," Shelby said.

"But did you?" Gabi asked in her soft voice.

"You guys are so nosy." I tried to walk around them to my luggage. I seriously was in need of a shower and change of clothes.

Cheyenne started giggling. "You can't even walk straight."

"I'm *fine.*"

"We're just excited for you," Shelby said, smacking Cheyenne on the arm.

I flounced down on the bed and sighed. As much as I wanted to remain stoic about the whole thing and keep so much of it private, just the thought of what had occurred brought another smile to my lips. *God, that man!*

"Yeah, so spill the details!" Cheyenne cried.

I opened my mouth to tell them what had happened, but instead, I said the first thing that came to mind, "I heard you were with Vin last night."

"Um…yeah! It was fucking amazing."

"Yeah, actually, she won't shut up about it," Shelby said.

"I could probably give you a play-by-play," Gabi confirmed.

A part of me wanted to tell Cheyenne what had happened between Vin, Miller, and Sydney. She should know what she was getting into, but as she started yammering on about dick size, how rough he had been, and a whole slew of other things I didn't want to know, I just couldn't break it to her. She was too happy about what had happened. Plus, Sydney lived in Tennessee. It wasn't like that was going anywhere. As far as I could tell, Sydney was more interested in Miller, and Vin had just overreacted. *No need to bring it up unnecessarily.*

Shelby snapped her fingers in front of my face. "Earth to Aribel. Was Grant really that good?"

"What?" I asked in a daze.

"We were talking, and you were off in la-la land," Gabi said.

"Oh my God, would you *please* just tell us that you slept with him?" Cheyenne pleaded. "I mean, we all assume, especially with the way you're walking like you've been riding a horse all day—i.e., Grant's dick. Plus, you never came back last night!"

"I'm just going to completely ignore the horse reference," I said with a shake of my head, "but Grant and I did sleep together."

I would have thought that I'd just won a million dollars in the lottery with the enthusiasm from my roommates. In the society I came from, virginity was lauded and encouraged. I wasn't especially religious, but I'd attended church with my parents. Even if I had never purposely avoided sex for religious reasons, holding on to my virtue was still ingrained in me in a way. Getting praised for having sex was such a bizarre thing to me.

"I can't believe it took you guys this long, but I'm so happy for you," Cheyenne said. "Was it amazing? Is he huge? Was it rough? Did you orgasm like ten times? Did he make you come on command? You know that actually works."

"What *are* you talking about? It was my first time! I think he would have killed me if he'd been rough or whatever else you were saying," I said, exasperated.

"Yeah, but…was he, like, gentle then? Did you go back to back? I bet he's been dying for this. I bet he went again right away."

My face flushed. I did *not* want to talk about this. *Did these things actually happen? I thought I was pushing it by having sex again the next afternoon!*

"Cheyenne, you're freaking her out again," Shelby said.

"I'm not freaked out!"

"Your face is super red," Gabi murmured. She flipped a strand of hair out of her face and smiled at me.

Thanks for pointing out the obvious.

"It could be because I'm getting drilled on my sex life!"

"That's not the only thing that's drilling you," Cheyenne said with a giggle.

I laughed along with my friends. *What else could I do?* I'd walked right into that one.

"So…seriously," Shelby said, glaring at Cheyenne who had opened her mouth to say something that would likely be crude, "worth the wait?"

My mind wandered off to the feel of Grant's arms around me, his mouth against mine, him sliding in and out of me. It had been painful, uncomfortable, and even a little awkward, but it had also been incredible, emotional, overwhelming, and all-consuming.

"Totally worth the wait."

After my shower, the girls insisted that I wear something nice for the ContraBand show, so I decided on a V-cut blue sweater tucked into a high-waisted Aztec-print skirt with my knee-high black riding boots. I had plans to meet with Grant ahead of time, but the girls decided to walk down to the lodge with me.

Grant had given me vague directions on how to get backstage, so I waved good-bye to my friends and walked around to the back of the building. There was a side entrance with a guy standing nearby, absentmindedly texting on his phone. I wasn't sure if I should check in with him or not. Grant hadn't mentioned it. I decided to throw caution to the wind and just pretend like I was supposed to be here. I was sure there were going to be other girls backstage. As little as I wanted to look like some groupie whore, it would probably be easier than explaining myself.

The guy barely glanced up at me as he muttered under his breath, "Who are you here with?"

"ContraBand," I said stiffly.

"Okay," he said with a shrug.

Top-notch security. Seriously, top-notch.

I walked through the employee-only door to backstage. Grant had been right. This was nothing like being backstage at The League. The room was massive with enough space for a medium-sized theater production. Band equipment was everywhere from drum sets being assembled to keyboards being wheeled into position to several thousand-dollar guitars lying haphazardly across couches. I knew Grant would never treat his baby so carelessly.

Amidst all the chaos of bands, groupies, and staff, I was somehow supposed to find Grant. My eyes roamed the room, but there were simply too many people for me to pick him out. I shot off a text asking him where he was and then started to wander around the room.

I'd made it halfway when I spotted Miller and McAvoy off in a corner. McAvoy was in a short-sleeved shirt showing off the intricate tattoos that ran up his arm and across his chest. He was flipping his drumstick in one hand and smoking. Miller, as usual, was dressed nicer in a clean polo with his brown hair pushed off his face.

"Hey, guys. Have you seen Grant?" I asked as I approached.

They both turned to look at me.

"We thought he was with you," Miller said.

"Nope. I left a while ago, and he said he'd meet me here. I haven't heard from him."

"Strange," McAvoy said, looking surprisingly with it today.

"Yeah, he's supposed to be here already. Vin...well, we expected him to be late but not Grant."

"Try giving him a ring," I told them. "I'm going to do another sweep, and I'll meet you back over here."

I was lost in thought about Grant being late for the band's assigned meeting time. He wasn't a forgetful person. *What had held him up?*

As these thoughts swirled in my head, a hand reached out to stop me. I turned around and shook the guy off of me.

The last thing I would consider myself was someone who got muddled by a pretty face. I'd held Grant off long enough after all. This guy was rough around the edges with a soul-searching look that made want to do what he asked. He...was beautiful. Straight-out-of-a-magazine, model-worthy beautiful. One look in his green eyes told me he knew it, too. Tall, trim but muscular, perfect skin—probably better skin than me—with flawless tousled hair and full lips. A guy like this made me feel flat and dull.

At least I still had my charming personality.

"Can I help you?" I snapped.

"I think you can." His eyes shifted to my chest.

I'd worn a low-cut top for Grant, and I suddenly felt exposed. "I really don't think so."

I started to walk away, and he cut me off. "You are truly striking with the most incredible lips."

"Is this a walking Little Red Riding Hood joke?"

That startled him. "No joke. You're beautiful. Did you want to come meet the rest of my band? I'm certain you've heard of us."

Doubtful. "Nope. Just looking for my *boyfriend*."

"Perhaps he shouldn't have left you unattended."

"What is this? The seventeenth century?"

The guy laughed again and then stuck out his hand. "I'm Donovan Jenkins. I sing lead in The Drift."

Oh. Well, damn. I actually did know who they were. Worse yet, I actually *liked* their latest single.

"Ah…so you have heard of us."

"I think everyone has heard of you. As nice as it is to meet you, I am really just looking for my boyfriend, Grant McDermott."

"Oh, Grant?" Donovan asked. "Yeah, he's cool. He's hanging out with us."

"What?" I asked, surprised.

"Yeah. Come with me," Donovan said, slinging an arm across my shoulders.

I shrugged him off again but followed. *What would Grant be doing with The Drift?*

We rounded a corner, and then Donovan opened a door to a private room. It was like walking into a crowded nightclub. Music was blasting, booze was everywhere, and smoke coated the air, making it nearly impossible to see in the dim lighting. A few girls were dancing on the center table while others were draped across every available space in the room, and a couple was making out in the back corner. I was pretty sure I saw someone snorting a line of coke on the bar.

I coughed to clear the smoke from my lungs, and Donovan closed the door behind me. He draped his arm across my shoulders again, but there wasn't enough room to wiggle away, and he was already walking us away from the door. I hoped this wasn't some stunt, and he actually knew Grant, or I was going to be pissed.

Donovan easily maneuvered me through the crowd. Everyone knew him, and people seemed to part like the Red Sea in his wake.

Then, he stopped and whispered in my ear, "That your boy?"

There was Grant—sitting on a couch, drinking whiskey straight out of the bottle, a cigarette hanging between his lips, chatting and laughing with two guys sitting across from him. His arms were resting across the back of the couch, and two girls were cozied up beside him.

One of them I even recognized. *Kristin. What the fuck?*

"Hey, Grant!"

Disoriented in the smoke-filled room, I glanced up to try to see who had called my name. *Jesus fuck, the room is fucking spinning. How much of this did I drink?* I glanced at the bottle and saw it was more than half gone. I couldn't have killed that all by myself.

I slammed the bottle back down on the table, pulled a drag on my cigarette, and then stubbed it out in the ashtray. A girl pulled on my arm, but I shrugged her off and stood. Then, I caught sight of who had spoken—Donovan.

And he had his arm around my girl.

Then, I got a glimpse of Ari. *Oh fuck!* She looked smoking hot. She was wearing a short fucking skirt that hugged her body, her tits were on full display, and she had on sexy black boots that I wouldn't mind her just leaving on as I fucked her. *Fuck, I'd been inside that.*

Why the fuck is Donovan touching my girl?

My anger fueled me forward, and I managed to surge toward them without stumbling. "What the fuck is this?" I growled.

Ari's eyes smoldered. I knew what that look meant. Even in my haze, I knew that the girl I'd fallen for, the one who had drugged me and then laughed in my face at the suggestion of ever seeing me again, was about to rear her head. My mouthy little thing looked about two seconds away from punching me in the face. Instead of infuriating me, it only fucking turned me on. *Is there a dark corner around here?*

"Hey, man. I found your *girlfriend*," Donovan said the word like he didn't understand what it meant. And the way his hand slid down her arm to her waist made it seem like he might actually not believe in the word.

I hadn't believed in that word before Ari. And if he didn't back the fuck off, I was going to lay his ass on the floor. I didn't give a shit that his loyal and dedicated fans and bandmates surrounded me. I was going to knock his ass into tomorrow. But I didn't get a chance because Ari was already squirming away from him.

"Cut it out," she said, slapping at his hand. "I'm not a groupie. Go grope someone else."

I grabbed her wrist and pulled her into my chest. "Yeah, she's not a fucking groupie. You lay one more hand on her, and I'll fucking destroy you."

The people around us were getting wind of what was happening, and the noise was dying out.

Ari smacked me on the arm. "You don't touch me either!"

"Princess…"

"Don't even start that shit with me," she growled.

"You've got a live one, McDermott," Donovan said.

Ari shot him a death glare, but her anger was really directed at me. "What the fuck do you think you're doing?"

"Having a good time," I offered lightly.

Apparently, that had been the wrong answer.

"Having a good time? Because it's a great time to get wasted and high with a bunch of girls who have probably fucked every guy in the room."

"Babe, it's normal to be jealous," Donovan said with laughter in his voice. "This is just the life."

"Why don't you stay out of this?" she asked. She turned back to me. "You left Miller and McAvoy out there without a word right before your set. You're trashed. How are you supposed to perform?"

I just shook my head. She didn't need to be laying this shit on me right now. "I've fucking performed blitzed out of my mind before."

"You're acting like an idiot. You're not *this* person. These guys are feeding into your personality, and you're just sitting idly by and letting it happen."

"I'm just having a good time, Princess."

I was starting to get irritated. I wasn't a child. She didn't need to lecture me. *Why shouldn't I get to hang out with another band? Another very successful band?* I wasn't ditching my boys. I wasn't ditching her. I was just meeting new people and getting drunk.

"Yeah," Donovan said. He was practically giddy. "Why don't you have a good time with us, too?"

He reached for her again, like she was a toy he wanted to play with.

Ari deflected his advance. "Do I look like I'm here for your amusement, pretty boy?"

"You're pretty amusing. Everyone else thinks so."

Ari glanced around, and it seemed to dawn on her that we had an audience. Her cheeks colored. I could see her withdraw from the world around her. She hated crowds, and she hated being noticed. I saw the same panic in her eyes now that I had seen the time we'd been on the quad when she'd flipped her shit on me.

"Whatever. Have your fun then," she said.

She was silently pleading with me, but I was pissed, too. *Who does she think she is to come in here and bitch me out in front of all these people?*

I crossed my arms over my chest. "All right."

She shook her head at me in disbelief and then turned and started walking out of the room. Donovan started walking after her, but Hollis got in his way at the exit. *Good.* I wouldn't have to go beat the shit out of him. I kind of liked the guy. But he couldn't touch Ari.

At her exit, everyone started talking again, and the room quickly returned back to its earlier state of debauchery. My thoughts were swirling in my head, telling me that I should fucking go after her. I was an idiot. I should make this right. She was too good for me. I was just a drunk loser who had managed to win a girl I didn't deserve. If I wanted to keep her, I needed to go—right now.

But I remained rooted to my spot. I wasn't going to go after her. She had embarrassed both of us. They weren't just some band. They were also my future colleagues. These were people I needed to know if I wanted to get picked up. Having a girlfriend chastise me in front of everyone wasn't exactly a way to endear myself to them.

I'm not going to cry. I'm not going to cry. I'm not going to cry.

Tears welled in my eyes, and I took several healing breaths to try to keep them at bay. I couldn't believe what had just happened. I couldn't believe I'd just seen Grant in that state. I couldn't believe how that argument had just gone down. I couldn't fucking believe that all he had said was that he was having a good time.

God, he's being so careless. It wasn't just the girls. Though, the whole Kristin thing was irritating. *Is that what all that shit had been about in class? Is she interested in Grant? Ugh, I didn't want to think about it.*

Either way, while the girls had irritated me, I didn't actually think he would do anything. He'd had his chance for months, and he'd said that he hadn't. He could have been lying, but I didn't want to believe that.

The truth of the matter was that I was more worried about him throwing away everything he'd worked for. It had been clear he thought The Drift could help them get signed. But he obviously hadn't thought about the fact that none of the *other* guys had gotten an invite to the private party. To me, that meant they wanted him, not the band, and that was something he absolutely would not agree to. *Would he agree to that if he were obliterated like he was?*

No. No way.

Gah! Even when I was pissed at him, I was more concerned for his well-being than anything. *Stupid. Stupid. Stupid. Why should I bother being concerned about his future when he isn't?*

Then, I thought back to the way he had treated me. One second, he had manhandled me and said he was going to destroy Donovan if he touched me, and the next second, he hadn't said a damn word when I was being humiliated. After what had happened last night and this afternoon, I just couldn't fathom what the fuck his problem was.

I found Miller and McAvoy almost as soon as I'd exited the private room. They looked at me and then at each other with worry between their eyebrows. I hadn't hung out with them all that much, but I must have looked like a wreck to get that much concern from them.

"What happened?" Miller asked.

I swept my hands under my eyes and shook my head. I never got like this. I'd been broken up with countless times, and I had never shed a tear. Grant and I were just arguing, and I was crying.

To my surprise, it was McAvoy who comforted me. "Grant's kind of an ass. He probably didn't mean whatever he said."

"That's comforting," I said sarcastically.

"We've known him for a long time. He doesn't exactly have a way with words."

They were probably right, but I just wanted to walk back into the room and punch Grant in the face. When I could speak without a shuddering breath, I finally told them. "He's with The Drift."

"What?" Miller gasped.

McAvoy looked just as shocked.

"I don't have any idea what he's doing, but he's all fucked-up."

"Christ! And we have to go on soon," Miller said.

"No Grant and no Vin," McAvoy said, looking at Miller accusingly. "This is going to be a great show."

"Vin will fucking be here," Miller grumbled.

"I'm just going to go back inside and hang out with my friends. Grant was going to show me around backstage, but obviously, that isn't happening."

"Do we need to go get Grant?" Miller asked.

I shrugged. Honestly, I didn't know. Grant was pissed, but I didn't know what that meant. I couldn't imagine him not playing the show. Music was his passion. It had gotten him through much worse times than this. I didn't care how fucked-up he was. He would never ditch a show.

"I think he'll show."

McAvoy nodded. "He's never ditched us before."

A flicker of worry passed across Miller's face. *Did he know that it's a very real possibility that record labels are interested in Grant, but not necessarily ContraBand? Is he worried that the more time Grant spent with other bands, the more likely he might sell out?* It was my worry…my fear. I hated seeing it reflected back to me.

"No, he wouldn't," Miller finally agreed.

Just as I was turning to leave, I saw Vin stalking across the room.

"Looks like you're only one short," I said.

I didn't want to be here to see this confrontation. Hopefully, Vin had taken McAvoy's advice, calmed down, and left that shit behind him. By the fury on his Italian face though, I was starting to think he didn't do calm.

"So, I'm fucking here," Vin said.

"And I'm leaving," I said.

"Hey, where's Grant?"

"Occupied."

Vin raised his eyebrows at me. "Well, if he is, you want to be?"

McAvoy smacked him on the chest. "Not right now, bro."

"What? If Grant is fucking some other girl, then I can fuck his girl. That's how it works, right?"

Vin and Miller glared at each other.

"Fucking drop it, Vin," Miller snapped.

I heard McAvoy say something else, but I was already walking away. The band went on in thirty minutes, and I didn't want to be backstage when Grant surfaced. I was having a hard enough time keeping my emotions under control around his friends. I wasn't sure what I would do when I came face-to-face with Grant again.

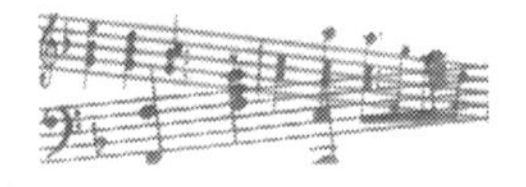

Cheyenne, Shelby, and Gabi had staked out a spot near the front of the stage. Drinks in hand, they were discussing the last band who had performed. Apparently, the lead singer had been dressed in drag, and the band had played "Piano Man" to close their set. They said that it had been a sight to behold.

"What was backstage like?" Shelby asked me.

The crew was onstage setting up ContraBand's equipment.

I wrinkled my nose. "Full of sluts and booze."

Cheyenne laughed. "Isn't that everywhere?"

"Did you get to meet other bands?" Gabi asked.

"Yeah," I said, grinding my teeth together.

"Which ones?"

I sighed. "The Drift."

The girls all just stared at me.

"Oh. Ha-ha. That's cute," Cheyenne said, rolling her green eyes.

They didn't believe me. *Good.* I didn't want to talk about it.

"I think she's being serious, Chey," Shelby said.

"Who did you meet?" Gabi asked, wide-eyed.

I didn't miss a beat. "Donovan Jenkins."

"Holy shit!" Cheyenne whispered. "He's gorgeous."

"Yep," I said stiffly. "He tried to get me to become his groupie. I turned him down." I sent her a scathing smile.

"You know, when you do that, I really can't tell if you're serious or being a sarcastic bitch like normal."

I laughed and gave Cheyenne a hug. She looked positively stunned by the display of affection.

"I'm glad you're my friend, Cheyenne, or else I'd probably hate you."

"I feel like that all the time."

The lights flickered, announcing the start of the next band, and my heart raced in anticipation. We were jostled forward as the crowd pressed in on the stage. I was moved closer and closer, and all I could think about was my argument with Grant. I was so angry with him, but at the same time, I just wanted it to be right.

Things felt…complete when we were together. Despite our differences, we clicked. But then, I remembered the way he had drunkenly looked at me, like I was an embarrassment to him, and it solidified my anger. I'd rather make him beg than give in to that girlie feeling of helplessness over a man.

The band walked onstage. First, McAvoy took a seat at his drum set, then Miller walked to the far side of the stage, then Vin followed his typical charisma returning with the start of the show…then Grant. The crowd whooped as he strode confidently onstage. Only I could notice the swagger in his walk was from liquor.

Grant gripped the microphone in his hand, and I couldn't help it. My heart skipped a beat. *Damn him for making me feel this way!*

"What's up Poconos music festival?" he called into the microphone. "We're ContraBand. Here tonight from Princeton, New Jersey. Any people from Jersey in the house?"

A huge crowd cheered, my friends among them.

"We're opening tonight with a song written for Jersey about getting the fuck out of there. Every now and then, you just want to leave your home and be somewhere else. This song is 'Hemorrhage.'"

Our eyes locked right before he started in on the first verse, and then he was just a presence taking over the ski lodge. I was compelled to him as much as I was repulsed by his shit behavior.

"We have a few more songs for you tonight, but this one…this one is new."

I narrowed my eyes at the stutter in his voice. Grant didn't stutter. His gaze shifted to mine, and then his eyes didn't move.

He was staring right at me. "We call this one 'Life Raft.'"

Vin started up on the melody, and then McAvoy chimed in with a slower down beat. Miller brought in the bass, and then Grant started strumming his guitar. My mouth dropped open slightly. He seemed to nod at me as if telling me that I did know this one. It was what he had been playing earlier today in his suite.

I let the sounds of the strings wash over me just as Grant's voice came in through the speakers. I didn't want this. He wasn't supposed to charm me onstage while I was angry at him. I deserved an apology.

But then, I heard the chorus.

Every time I see you. You make me feel better.
Every single day. You push away the pain.
You push away the memories.
You're my life raft. In an endless ocean.
You saved me from drowning.
You saved me from myself.
You're my life raft. In an endless ocean.

I'd heard those words. He'd said them to me last night…right before we'd had sex. This song was for me. It was about us.

I fought back tears and remembered what we had said earlier.

Are you going to sing for me?

Tonight.

37 GRANT

Ari was crying.

Shit! I kind of hoped that was a good thing. I hadn't intended on making her cry. I'd poured everything into this song when I wrote it while she'd been gone over Thanksgiving break. I couldn't believe I'd actually spoken the lyrics to her right before we had sex last night. But the words were for her. I'd written them to express how I felt when I was around her.

Even drunk and angry, I couldn't deny that the words were true. I had been pissed, and I'd let her walk away. I hadn't even gone after her. Maybe I was never meant to be a boyfriend. I should have stood up for her, or at the very least, I should have taken our conversation to a private location. I'd known what she was feeling, but instead, I'd just stood there.

Donovan and Hollis had spoken to me afterward to make sure everything was all right. It had felt strange having this conversation with them. I didn't even fucking know them. They seemed cool, and damn was the life incredible. It was like living in a dream—a dream that hovered just on the edge of reality.

I could have this. All I had to do was reach out and take it. Hollis wanted to talk after the show. I'd given him a dismissive answer, but I really fucking wanted to find out what he wanted. He'd be stupid to give me the same offer that Frank had tried to spell out for me, but Hollis seemed to have a bit more sense than Frank.

I didn't know. All I really knew was that, I would talk to him. I'd never been one to deny myself anything, and I wasn't going to start ignoring the curiosity that sprang up.

That didn't mean I was going to walk out on the guys or Ari. *It just meant…well, what the fuck did it mean? That I'm keeping my options open?* I wasn't. I wouldn't compromise what I believed in. I just wasn't stupid enough to ignore the opportunity to get everything I wanted.

We closed out the set with "Letting You." The crowd cheered loudly with the success of our show. My eyes were locked on Ari's. I needed to talk to her. I wanted to tell her to meet me now, that we needed to talk, that we needed to make this right between us. But I couldn't. I'd talk to her later. By then, maybe my anger wouldn't be simmering so close to the surface.

Hollis was waiting just offstage when we exited. He clapped me on the back like we were old friends. "Fucking great show, Grant!"

"Thanks."

I tried to keep my enthusiasm to a minimum, but Hollis had a certain charisma about him that made something simple sound amazing. I could understand how he'd gotten so far in the business.

"So, we good to talk? I got us a room."

Miller, McAvoy, and Vin looked at me expectantly. *Yeah, shit.* I hadn't told them about this. I hadn't even told them that I was with The Drift when I'd joined up with them earlier. "The guys can come with us, right?"

"Of course! Hollis Tift. Nice to meet you," he said, shaking the guys' hands.

Miller's face relaxed. "We've spoken on the phone. Great to finally meet you in person."

In hushed whispers, I filled the guys in on what I knew and why Hollis wanted to speak with me…us. Though I wasn't sure exactly what he would say, I slung my guitar over my chest and talked confidently about it to the guys. This was our opportunity, just like they had all been saying.

We walked into a small room that was strangely reminiscent of our meeting with Frank—except Hollis lounged casually against the wall with his arms crossed and a big smile on his face.

"ContraBand," Hollis said like he was testing the weight of the word. "Glad you guys are here. I was lucky enough to see your Halloween performance while I was in town, and after seeing what I just saw, I think you have a pretty marketable look and sound."

Everyone tensed, anticipating the letdown.

"What are your plans for New Year's Eve?"

I glanced over at Miller. Our eyes met, and he shrugged. *Nothing.* I'd been planning to go down the shore with Sydney while Ari was out of town, but I could cancel. It seemed like the same thing passed over everyone's faces.

"No plans," Miller said.

"How would you like to open for The Drift in New York City?"

It took a split second for reality to set in. *Holy shit!* We were being invited to play a *huge* show in the city. The Drift played sold-out shows all across the country. Opening for them could be our in.

"Are we signing a contract? Or is it just for the one show?" Miller asked, always getting straight to business.

"No official label contracts just yet," Hollis said. "We're looking for you guys for this show, and then based on how everything turns out, we'll discuss terms from there."

Another audition. Well, this one already seemed like a better opportunity than the show that Frank had shown up for. Hollis had said *yet.* That had sounded promising. I knew we'd rock out any show we performed, and this time, there was no mention of me ditching the band.

"So, are you in?"

"Definitely!" I said.

All the guys agreed.

Hollis handed us paperwork to fill out to confirm that we would be in attendance on New Year's Eve. I scribbled down my information and then handed it off to Hollis.

"McDermott!" he called, stopping me at the door. "Are you going to be around the rest of the night? I'd love for you to introduce the rest of the band to The Drift."

I smiled, feeling as light as air. "Yeah. Let me just put my guitar back in my room, and I'll come back."

"Perfect."

I exited with the guys, and despite the high I was on, I could tell Miller and McAvoy wanted to say something. I wasn't going to push them to initiate a conversation though. If they wanted to talk to me about hanging with the band, they could, but I'd helped get us this gig, so they couldn't be pissed with me.

"I'll meet you back here later," I said.

Miller opened his mouth to say something but then shook his head. McAvoy nudged him, but Miller just grumbled something under his breath.

"Man, you going to talk to Ari?" McAvoy asked.

I was taken aback. "Why?"

"She just walked out of here pretty upset earlier," Miller offered.

"She was crying," McAvoy added.

Shit! I'd made her cry? I felt a part of me die. *Yeah, fuck, I need to talk to her. But what the fuck am I supposed to say?*

"I don't know," I finally said.

"Just remember what I said about her," Miller said, giving me a knowing look.

How could I ever forget that Miller had said Ari had knocked humanity into me? What kind of person would I be at this point without her? I for sure would have fucked one of those chicks in the back room, if not more than one. I would have pushed the limits. All right, I'd fucking talk to her when I got back.

I told them as much before walking out of the venue with my guitar strapped to my back, leaving the rest of the guys to hang out backstage.

It was fucking cold outside, and the temperatures sobered me up further. I'd been a dick to Ari. She'd been out of line, but I'd acted like…well, like me. I'd done what I always did. And she was better than that.

My thoughts were broken when I heard what sounded like someone falling behind me. I turned around and saw a girl sitting heavily on the ice. She was wincing and holding her hand against her chest.

"Hey, are you okay?"

"Um…yeah. I just hit the ground pretty hard."

"How's your hand?"

She grimaced. "It's bleeding a bit."

"Need help getting back inside or anything?"

I wasn't exactly chivalrous, but she was kind of pretty. I would feel like a dick just leaving her out here. After how I'd treated Ari this afternoon, I felt like maybe I owed it to this girl to be nice.

"Oh, no, thanks. My cabin is just ahead. I'll just go clean it up there." She struggled to her feet and started walking uneasily again.

"I'm this way, too."

She finally looked up into my face, and I swore I'd seen her somewhere. *Damn my bad memory!*

She smiled, and we walked together in silence. Before Ari, I probably would have taken this girl up to my room for a quickie or something.

We reached the ski resort hotel, and she started rifling through the small purse in her hand. I nodded to her and started to walk in the opposite direction. I let the feeling of giving up easy game pass over me. I'd have Ari alone later, and I'd convince her to have pretty epic make-up sex.

"Hey!" the girl called, jogging up to me. "Sorry to bother you again, but, um…I don't have my key. Do you think I could wash my hand in your place before braving the cold again?" She suggestively fluttered her eyelashes at me.

I wondered briefly if she was telling the truth or just trying to get a step closer to my bed.

I could have sent her back to the lodge. It wouldn't be the worst thing I'd ever done to a chick before, but it wasn't like it would really hurt anything. I was heading right back out anyway.

"Sure. I'm going back to the lodge after I put my guitar up. I'm Grant."

She smiled a knowing, maybe even triumphant smile. "I'm Kristin."

As much as I'd wanted to rush backstage to talk to Grant, I'd forced myself to chat with my friends for a few minutes. A knot formed in my stomach over what had happened, and I just wanted to scream.

How could he go from having sex with me to getting drunk with some girls to acting like a total jackass to serenading me onstage all in the span of an afternoon?

I didn't care how wasted he was. I knew that I needed to talk to him. Grant was just being stupid and stubborn. I might have been in the wrong by going on the defensive when I'd found him backstage, but he would have flipped his shit if he had found me in a similar state. I wanted him to have his space to be the person he wanted to be, but I didn't want that to jeopardize who he really was.

My mind was all clouded. I was going to agonize about this all night if I didn't go and find Grant.

When I made it backstage, the room was even more packed than it had been before. The later shows were supposed to be completely full, and bands were getting their equipment together. On instinct, I returned to the spot where I'd seen Miller and McAvoy earlier, but they weren't there.

Unfortunately, Donovan Jenkins was.

"You following me, beautiful?" he asked with a wink.

"Hardly. I was just looking for Grant."

"Again?"

"Yes, again," I said irritably.

"You should reconsider your seventeenth-century assumptions and keep a closer eye on him."

Okay. I didn't care how much I liked The Drift's music. Donovan Jenkins was officially on my shitlist.

"I don't *need* to keep a closer eye on him. Now, if you haven't seen him, then I'm going to continue looking."

He reached out and grabbed my arm as I started to walk away.

I stared down at it in disgust. "Don't touch me."

He slowly released me. "You're not like most other girls."

"I've heard that before."

"Well, I haven't seen your boy. He probably went off to celebrate."

My stomach fluttered. This didn't sound good. "Celebrate what?" I knew my voice sounded lighter than normal, but I couldn't control it.

"ContraBand is opening for us. New Year's Eve in New York City. They just signed the paperwork after the show. Are you going to be there, too?" He gave me his most dazzling smile.

And yeah, damn, he was attractive, but he wasn't Grant.

Right now, that was all I could focus on. Grant was opening for The Drift in the city. I was happy for him. This was what he'd wanted, but still…the news scared me. It made my stomach twist, and I felt a bit nauseous.

Grant hadn't told me about this. As far as I could tell, he hadn't even come looking for me. And now, I didn't know where he was, except for hearing Donovan's vague notion of *celebrating*. That didn't sit right with me either.

"Hey, Ari," Miller said, walking up to us.

Sydney had finally reappeared after the blowout with Vin, and she was standing awfully close to Miller.

"Hey. Have you seen Grant?" I felt a sense of déjà vu wash over me at the question.

"Yeah. He went up to put his guitar away. He should be back any minute."

I released the breath I hadn't even realized I'd been holding. *Just putting his guitar away. Totally normal. No reason for me to worry.*

"Thanks," I said appreciatively.

"Hey, Ari," Donovan said.

Ugh, he knows my name now.

"Think about New Year's."

I rolled my eyes and kept walking. I couldn't even dignify that with a response. If I was going to be in New York City for New Year's, then I was going to be with Grant. Donovan Jenkins wasn't even on my radar.

Jogging up the path to the rooms, I felt a burst of adrenaline rush through me. I'd been basically holding my breath since I walked out of the private room. I didn't like fighting with Grant. We were both too stubborn and strong-willed for it. All it did was make me emotional and irritable.

Once I reached the door to his suite, I took a deep breath. I wasn't looking forward to this conversation, but it was necessary. I pushed open the door and froze. My stomach lurched, and I felt all the air push out of my lungs. Grant was standing there, just outside of his bedroom, kissing a naked woman.

My gasp must have brought him out of his stupor, and he forcefully shoved the woman away from him. That was when I recognized her—Kristin.

My world spun, and I latched on to the doorframe. Grant turned abruptly, and our eyes met across the distance.

"Ari," he whispered, his face aghast.

I thought I might be sick. Bile touched my throat, and I had to push it down to keep from throwing up. I'd never doubted him. I'd thought he had been sleeping with other women before we were serious, but even then, he'd claimed that he hadn't. Even in a compromising position back in the private room, I'd never once suspected that he was cheating on me. And now…with the proof before my eyes, I just felt disgusted with him, with myself, with everything. *How had I believed him?*

"This isn't what it looks like," he said. His hands were splayed out in front of him.

"What does it look like, Grant?" My voice was shaking.

"Bad. It looks bad."

"Oh, Aribel," Kristin said sweetly. She didn't even bother covering up. "Are you guys still together? Grant never said—"

"Shut your fucking mouth!" he roared. "Go put some fucking clothes on and get the fuck out of my room."

"That's not what you were saying earlier."

"Are you out of your fucking mind?" he yelled.

Kristin jumped at his harsh tone and darted into the bathroom.

I just stood there, unable to move forward or to run away. There were so many things I wanted to say, but I just watched as Grant screamed at Kristin. She knew that we were together. Even if she had been in the room when we argued earlier, we hadn't broken up.

Grant's attention returned to me. He quickly walked across the room and tried to reach for me.

"Don't," I said menacingly.

"Ari," he pleaded.

The tears hit me without notice. Full-on hysterical tears that made my chest shake and my whole body tremble. This couldn't be happening to me. I'd given up so much for him. I'd concentrated less on school. I'd gone to all of this shows. I'd spent weekends with him instead of doing homework. I'd fucking given him my body, mind, and soul.

He had told me about his family, and then he'd crushed me under the weight of his callous, abrasive nature. He'd let himself get drawn into things that fed his addictive personality. And after he'd had sex with me, he'd just pushed me aside without batting his eyes. I felt like a total idiot. I threw my hands over my face, sank to a crouch, and just let the tears fall.

"Ari, come on. Please let me try to explain."

I just shook my head. I couldn't do this. That was all I could get out, "I can't do this."

"Do what?" he asked carefully.

I stood stiffly and wiped the tears away with the backs of my hands. They still flowed easily, but I couldn't stop them. My voice wavered as I said, "This. I can't do this, Grant."

"Us?"

"I don't know." And I didn't. I wanted him desperately, but I hurt everywhere.

He'd ripped out the very part of my body that he completed.

Kristin took that moment to scurry out of the room. Luckily, she was fully dressed. She looked sullen that she was getting kicked out, but maybe a bit too cheerful when she caught a glimpse of my face. She strode over to the door where Grant and I were standing and gave me a smug look.

I couldn't help it. I just lashed out. My hand connected with her face with a satisfying crack that whipped her head back. She gasped, and her hand flew to her face. A big red handprint was already forming on her cheek.

"You bitch!" she shrieked.

"Fuck you!" I spat. "You're a dirty fucking whore. You'll never be better than a groupie slut who gets passed around like the disgusting piece of shit you are. No one will ever take you seriously! You're a fucking disgrace."

Kristin lunged for me, but Grant was there first. He knocked her back into the door.

"Don't even fucking think about it," he growled. "Get the fuck out of here!"

"You just think you're fucking better than everyone else, Aribel. But you're no better than I am. You think he won't drop you for someone else just as fast?"

"Get out!" Grant roared, shoving her out the door and slamming it in her face.

And just like that, my walls broke down. I couldn't do this. It was the only thing ringing through. I was still crying, but my strength was returning. "I can't believe you. I can't believe you sang that song for me and then went off with another girl. I wasn't even worried about this shit! You couldn't have…I don't know…shopped around for someone who wasn't in my circle of friends? Someone I hadn't come on this trip with? Someone who I didn't have classes with? Someone I wouldn't have to see all the time after you fucking ripped out my heart and tossed it aside like it was nothing?"

"Ari, please listen to me. I did absolutely nothing with her!" Grant said. "She slipped on the ice, and then I thought she accidentally lost her key. I was just letting her clean her hand before coming back downstairs. She came out of the bathroom naked and, like, attacked me."

"I don't want to hear your story!" I cried. "I'm sure you have a million explanations for why you had a naked girl in your room."

"No. There is only one explanation."

"I don't care. I just…I can't believe I thought you would change."

"Ari, come on. I'm not the same person I was when we first met. The only person I want to be with is you."

"I just…find that hard to believe, considering you had a naked woman in your room."

"Just because I had a naked woman in my room doesn't mean I'm cheating on you!"

"The fact that you have a naked woman in your room at all should be a red flag! Don't you see how serious all this is?"

"I can't fucking help what other people do."

"You had your hands on her!"

"I was shoving her out of the room!"

I shook my head. We could argue this in circles all night.

"Ari, just listen to me."

"I was stupid. Stupid, stupid, stupid. I got played so perfectly."

Grant ran his hands back through his hair and shook his head. "I'm not playing you. Ari, you're the one that I want. Can't you see that?"

"No!" I said, losing it completely. "All I see is a very confused person who has a lot of emotional baggage but no idea how to treat people he cares about. You went with Drift earlier without a thought for your friends. You humiliated me in front of a group of people. You just let me walk away, and you never came looking for me again. Then, I find you *kissing* someone else! That does not sound like someone who wants to be with me! That sounds like someone who is congratulating himself on taking my virginity and moving on!"

Grant openly glared at me. "Who the fuck do you think you are, talking to me like that? You think I would treat you like that?"

"I think you would say anything to get a girl into bed," I said in my frustration. I wanted him to feel what was coursing through me in that moment. "You freaked the fuck out when you just thought that I'd been talking to my ex-boyfriend. You told Donovan that you'd fucking destroy him if he came near me. But where were you? Off with some other girl? There's an insane double standard to everything happening right now, and you don't even see it!"

"What do you want me to do? I'm trying. I've turned my world upside down for you!"

"What have you turned upside down?" I nearly screamed at him. "You're still playing your guitar, boozing, smoking, hanging around groupies. The only thing that's different is that you're *supposedly* not sleeping around with everything that walks by."

"You have no idea what's changed in me…"

"That's the point! I don't know because you won't tell me. You confided in me about your parents. You gave me these dog tags. But for what? So, you could take my virginity and then fuck someone else? Well, congratulations! That's the only thing you're getting out of this whole trip. You have absolutely nothing to offer me. You're not educated, motivated, or ambitious," I said, ticking off all the characteristics I'd thrown to the wind when I became enamored with Grant. "How could I *ever* want someone like that?"

Grant lost all semblance of control after that. I was feeding into his belief that he wasn't good enough for me. I knew his inadequacies, and I was pushing his buttons in my anger.

"What? You think you're perfect? You talk about your family like you're picture-fucking-perfect, but they're controlling. You live in a motherfucking bubble. You've never experienced anything because you're too fucking scared of your shadow. You might be educated, motivated, and ambitious, Princess, but you have no common sense when it comes to the real world. Not to mention, you never fucking shut up, and you think you're smarter than everyone else in the room."

"I *am* smarter than everyone else in the room!" I screamed back in his face. I couldn't control my temper at this point.

I'd given everything to Grant, and now, we were just digging our heels in. We were being mean on purpose. Every single thing he'd said felt like a knife wound to my chest.

"I can't do this, Grant."

He ground his teeth and took a deep breath. "Ari…I'm sorry."

"No…" I said, backing up toward the closed door.

"We shouldn't have said those things."

"But you meant them. I meant them. That's all that matters."

"Ari, please," he pleaded.

Too little, too late.

"I just need some space, some time to think," I whispered, the tears hitting my eyes again.

"Don't do this."

I shook my head. "Just give me some time," I said before grabbing the door handle and rushing out of Grant's suite.

Holy fucking shit!

What the fuck had just happened? What had I just said to her? The entire argument was a blur. It had been ugly, really fucking ugly. The tears in her eyes still stung, and all I wanted to do was run out of this godforsaken room and make things right. But I knew that wouldn't help. Something deep down inside me told me that no matter what I said or did to try to fix this, it wouldn't work.

I'd broken her—just like I'd feared that I would. And in doing that…she'd broken me.

I'd never felt this kind of hurt before. Pain, yes, pain I was used to. Pain and guilt and agonizing repressed memories and torture. But this…goddamn, this was like someone had taken a razor blade to my chest and started slicing through everything important.

How could I have been stupid enough to let Kristin into my place? I hadn't been sober enough, or maybe I hadn't cared enough to put the pieces together. I'd seen her on more than one occasion, and I'd just never given two shits who she was because she wasn't Ari. Now, that was kicking me in the ass. She was the fucking chick who had told me that Ari was seeing her ex. She had been in The Drift's backstage room. She had probably fucking slipped on the ice on purpose, just to get me to walk with her.

I was starting to feel like I had gotten played. I'd set my guitar down and shown her where the bathroom was. She'd gone in there, and I'd sat on the couch to wait her out. When she'd called my name, I hadn't even *thought* she would put the moves on me. There simply wasn't anyone but Ari anymore. Then, the chick had stepped out of the bathroom naked. And yeah, I'd looked. *What the hell was I supposed to do?* I'd just shaken my head and told her she needed to leave. Then, she'd literally forced herself on me. I wasn't usually caught off guard, but I hadn't been prepared for that.

It was my fault for letting her in, and I was paying for it. I wanted to throw something or put my fist through the wall, but that wouldn't bring Ari back. Feeling defeated and even more fucking angry, I stormed out of the suite and down to the lodge.

"Hey, man. What took you so long?" Miller asked when he saw me approaching.

Sydney was sitting on his lap, and Vin was nowhere to be found.

"Whoa! What's wrong? What happened?" He scooted Sydney to the side and stood.

"Alcohol. Now. Lots of it."

Sydney jumped up. "Cuz, you all right? You look murderous."

I just glared at her. "You got alcohol, Syd? Or are you not understanding?"

"Whoa there, motherfucker! I'm your fucking cousin, not some groupie whore."

"Then, get out of my way because I think I need one."

Sydney gave me a disgusted look. Coming from the dirty slut that she was, it should have sent off warnings, but I just ignored it. Miller, however, I couldn't ignore.

"No way. No can do. Ari would kill you and me both if I let that happen."

"Well, she's not here, is she?"

"What's wrong with you?" Sydney snapped. "You're normally this disgusting pig but not with her."

"Are you done wasting my time?" I asked, pushing her out of my way and back onto the couch.

Miller grabbed my arm, threw it behind me, and gave a small shove upward. I grimaced. *Shit, that hurt!*

"You going to stop acting like an idiot?" Miller asked.

He had the upper hand, and I just wanted to pummel him, but I wasn't mad at him. I was mad at Ari. Or myself. Or Kristin. But mostly myself.

Finally, I nodded. Miller released me and then strongly encouraged me to take a seat.

"What's going on?"

"Yeah, cuz. What the fuck has gotten into you?"

I ground my teeth together and ignored Sydney as she crawled back onto Miller's lap. *Great. One big fucking reminder of what I'd just completely trashed.*

"I don't want to talk about it, so just lay off. I should go find Donovan since you two seem to be a bit lost in your own world, and all my other brothers are gone," I said bitterly.

"Something happen with Ari?" Sydney probed.

"Did you not just hear me say that I didn't want to fucking talk about it?" I bit back.

"All right," Miller said.

He dropped his hand on Sydney's knee, and she sighed back into his chest. *Fuck that!*

"Are we done with the interrogation now?" I had other things on my mind, like booze and pot and women and incoherence and blacking out and forgetting that this shit day ever happened.

Miller was giving me a sympathetic look, like he'd already guessed what was going on without me telling him. "Are you sure you want to go hang out with The Drift right now? Being around Donovan and the rest of the band might not be in your best interest."

I stood abruptly. "The only person who made me care about my best interest just fucking walked out on me, so I don't think it fucking matters what else I do."

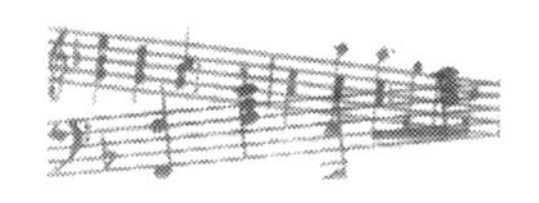

I woke up at the crack of dawn, feeling like absolute shit, and it wasn't just from the bottle of whiskey last night. *Aribel. Oh shit! No, this could* not *be happening to my life.*

I needed her. I couldn't go on without her. She was my breath of fresh air. She reminded me what it was like to live. She was the only person I'd ever cared enough about to invest time into. I couldn't just let her get away.

Throwing my legs over the bed, I immediately regretted my decision. I had a splitting headache and the sudden need to vomit. I braced myself on the side table and then stood up. Drinking with Donovan last night had been a terrible idea. The guy could fucking drink me under the table, and I had no clue how. He'd tried to throw groupies at me, but luckily, I hadn't been a total shithead. My bed was mercifully empty. I would have regretted that for the rest of my life.

Clothes were a struggle, but I eventually managed to throw something suitable on. Then, I was out of the room and out the front door before the sun had cleared the horizon.

I needed to talk to Ari. I needed to make this right.

That conversation should have never happened. I'd been fucking wasted, and nothing I'd said had come out right. I should have told her that I would never even touch another girl if it meant we were together. I should have told her that Kristin was nobody and that it was wrong for her to be in my suite and that I did understand how serious the situation was. I should have begged Ari to stay. I should have followed her. A heavy cloud of regret settled in the pit of my stomach, and it did nothing for my hangover.

I was still shrugging into my leather jacket in the freezing cold when I reached her door. I banged on it as hard as I could until I felt like my hand was going to fall off from the cold.

"Ari! Are you in there?" I yelled. "I need to talk to you about last night! Please, please talk to me. Aribel! Come on! I'm freezing out here. Can we please just talk this out? I was an idiot. A motherfucking idiot. Look, I don't care how cold it is out here. I'll stand out here all day if you won't let me—"

McAvoy opened the door. "Bro, I think we got that."

"What the fuck is this?" I asked, bewildered.

"I stayed the night." He shrugged like it was no big deal.

"With who?"

I wasn't sure why it even mattered. McAvoy had had his fair share of women, but he wasn't like Vin and me. He would pick chicks for a purpose, and usually dated them casually. We'd had a number of girls McAvoy dated like that hang around the band for a few weeks, but none of that really mattered right now.

"Gabi."

Huh, the little pixie. I would have never guessed. "Is Ari in there? I need to talk to her."

McAvoy looked confused. "She left early this morning."

"Left for where?" My blood ran cold. *No. I need to fix this. She had to let me fix this.*

"Bro, I thought you knew. I would have told you."

"Where did she go?"

"Back to Jersey. I heard her tell Gabi something about an early flight to Boston, but I guess I assumed she meant Sunday."

"Thanks, man."

I dashed away back to my room. I heard McAvoy yell something after me, but I didn't bother listening. I had to get back to Jersey. I had to see her. She could not leave for Boston before we talked.

I packed quickly and grabbed my guitar. I banged on Sydney's door. When nothing happened, I moved to Miller's door. "Where the fuck is Sydney?"

Sydney's head popped out. "Can I help you, resident asshole?"

"We've got to go. Get your shit together."

"What? I'm not going."

"I need to leave now! So, let's go." I was getting hysterical. I needed to get to Ari as fast as I could.

"Bro," Miller said, "she can come back with us."

"Take care of her."

"I'm not a doll."

"See you later, cuz," I said, mimicking her nickname.

Then, I was out the door.

The drive back to Princeton felt like it was taking forever. The roads were shit from a snowstorm that had blown in recently. It had been awesome on the slopes, but it wasn't so great to drive in. I was thankful for my truck because I drove recklessly back to Ari. I just had to get to her. I had to make it right. No matter what it took.

I heard the beating on the door before Cheyenne did. I dashed to her room and flung the door open wide. "Chey, you have to answer the door."

"Ari, are you sure about this? I've never known you to back away from confrontation," Cheyenne said, her voice sympathetic.

"I'm not backing down from confrontation. We had our confrontation last night, and it was horrible! I can't talk to him today. Please, I've never asked you for anything like this."

"Besides driving you back from the ski resort a day early when I was getting together with Vin?"

I shuddered. *Vin. Gross.* "Thank you. You're the best friend ever."

"All right, but I'm only doing this because I love you," Cheyenne said.

She walked to the door, and I huddled on the floor within earshot of the conversation that was about to go down.

I hadn't thought that Grant would follow me. I'd made a split second decision this morning to come back to Jersey. I'd even called my parents and asked if we could move up the flight to Boston, so I could come home earlier. They'd been surprised since I'd insisted on going on the ski trip in the first place, but they hadn't complained. They missed me.

Now, Grant was here. *What do I do now that he's here?*

"Grant…hey," Cheyenne answered warily.

"Where is she, Cheyenne?"

My heart pounded from the sound of his voice. I just wanted some space. I needed time to think about whether or not this was what I wanted, but then hearing his voice…it just brought back all the memories.

"She left already."

"What? No way. Her car is still out there!"

"I dropped her off."

"In Newark?" he asked incredulously. "You would have never made it back by now."

I watched Cheyenne shrug. She was lying for me. I would squeeze her if I didn't feel like a total jerk for cowering behind the door while she fought my battles for me.

"Come on, I know she's in there. I need to talk to her."

"I already said she's not here. You should just go back home."

"Ari!" he yelled.

I heard his hand hit the door gently to keep Cheyenne from closing it.

"Ari, I know you're in there! Just come talk to me. Can't we talk about this?"

I closed my eyes and put my head between my knees. God, I just wanted to run to him. I wanted to see him and have that feeling of completion again. But I couldn't forget our argument, and I wasn't ready to have another one. I'd asked for time, and I still needed it.

"She's not in here!" Cheyenne yelled back. "And even if she were, do you think she would talk to you with all this yelling? Haven't you done enough damage?"

"I just want to fix this," he told Cheyenne. "She has to know how I feel about her."

Oh no, not the tears again.

"Well, if you really care about her, I think the best thing to do is to just back off. She's stressed. She's never been in this kind of situation. I told her you were going to break her heart, but she wouldn't listen."

I felt the tears trickle down my face at Cheyenne's words. There was the *I told you so* that Cheyenne had kept from her lips when I asked her to drive me home this morning.

"So, just give her some space. Maybe after the break, she'll want to talk to you."

"I can't wait that long. I can't risk losing her, Cheyenne."

"You already have."

Her words hit me like a ton of bricks, so I couldn't imagine what it had just done to Grant. I'd risked so much by getting involved with him, but it felt like I was risking more by giving him up. And this relationship purgatory we were currently hanging in made the agony of a decision even worse.

He hadn't lost me. I was still his.

My heart and my body called out to comfort him, but I didn't. My mind was still reminding me of how much he'd hurt me.

"Well, if you see her, then tell her I'm sorry. I shouldn't have said those things. I shouldn't have even let Kristin into my room. I understand how serious it all is, but there is *no one* else for me. No one. It wasn't even a thought in my mind. Ari is it. She's the only girl I've ever fallen for, and I'd really be worthless if I let her walk away without a fight. So…so, just tell her to talk to me. I want to make it right." Grant's voice was hoarse. I'd never heard him like this.

"I'll tell her, but I really think you should just leave her alone," Cheyenne said.

"I can't. I'll never be able to."

Cheyenne sighed. "At least for break. Just think about what *she* wants for a change. If she wanted to talk to you and make things right, wouldn't she be talking to you right now?"

"I'll give her whatever she wants. If she wants silence, I can give her that." He practically forced the words out. "But I'm here to stay, Cheyenne. You tell her that, too."

"I'll tell her," she said before closing the door. "Well, that went well."

I shook my head and let the tears fall freely. "I should have spoken to him. He sounded so distraught."

Cheyenne plopped down next to me and wrapped a comforting arm around my shoulder. "I know this is your first real relationship, Ari, but take it from someone who knows…it's better to let him suffer a little."

"I don't want him to suffer."

"Don't you? Just a little?"

I laughed, but it came out more like a hiccup. "I just want to put the pieces back together. I feel…God, I don't even know. I feel like he ripped my body in half."

"It'll be okay," she said softly.

I rested my head on her shoulder and cried.

"Just go away for break. Take some time to think about everything that happened. If you want him back, then it sounds like he's willing."

"What if I wait too long?" I whispered the fear that came to me.

"Then, he was never worth it to begin with."

The only thing I wanted for Christmas was hundreds of miles away and refusing to talk to me. Despite telling Cheyenne that I would remain silent if that was what Ari wanted, I was having a terrible time with it. I'd texted her constantly the first couple of days, and I'd called her more times than I even wanted to admit. She hadn't responded. I had to face facts that she actually wanted my silence.

I still texted her when I couldn't bear to let her think that she was off my mind. But even those, I let dwindle to once a day, then every other day, and then every third day.

Guilt infected everything. Guilt about how I'd treated Ari, how I'd talked to her, for not going after her, for not doing enough. Guilt about how I'd treated Sydney, how I'd treated the guys, how selfish I'd been in everything I'd been doing for months…years. I was no better than my old man. That much was becoming a pretty obvious fact. Self-sabotage was the name of the game, and I was the goddamn reigning champion.

Normally, in these situations…well, shit, I'd never been in this kind of situation. But when I got down, I usually overindulged in anything that would make me forget. Everything made me think about her though. I didn't want to drink. I didn't want to smoke. I didn't have the energy to think about anyone but her, so there was no way I was going near women. A fucking blizzard had ripped through Jersey, so I couldn't ride my bike. The only thing I still had was my guitar, and her song seemed to be the only one I remembered.

"Are you going to mope around all break?" Sydney asked a few days before Christmas.

I'd apologized to her as soon as she'd gotten back from the ski lodge. She'd brushed it off like it didn't matter and told me it just ranked right up there with my other bizarre behavior. *Really reassuring.*

"I'm not moping."

"You are *so* moping!"

I just shrugged. I didn't want to argue with her. I started strumming out "Life Raft" for the hundredth time, and Sydney groaned.

"Stop playing that song. Can't you just…I don't know…find someone else?"

My eyes shot daggers at her.

"All right, all right. Bad idea."

"She just needs time."

"Has she spoken to you *at all* since she left?"

I couldn't think about that. I couldn't consider that she had moved on. My life was hanging on the edge of disaster with those thoughts constantly swirling through them. I didn't need the push that would send it into a spiral of chaos.

"Look, cuz," she said, sinking into the seat next to me, "I know this is hard on you, but you need to do something else, something to get your mind off of her."

"Like what? Everything that I've ever done in the past just conjures up more memories."

"I don't know. Just do something productive. Go work out or go for a run or go work for Randy again. Sitting here and thinking about her all day is only going to make you depressed. You were never exactly chipper, but this…this isn't you."

I ran a hand back through my hair and tried to listen to reason. Sydney was right. Ari was on my mind 24/7 and if I didn't get myself together, her walking out of my life was going to destroy me.

"All right then."

Sydney and I drove to Duffie's, and I smiled at the old familiar feeling at seeing the building. A long line of people greeted us when we entered. The hostess recognized

Sydney. They hugged and started talking rapidly. That was my cue.

I wandered back to the kitchen and found my aunt and uncle where I'd always found them before. Randy was busy making pizza dough from scratch while young servers busied themselves around him. Carol was sitting at a cash register, ringing out customers and making change. It felt…homey.

"Grant!" Carol said with a big smile on her face. "How wonderful to see you, honey."

"Hey, Aunt Carol, Uncle Randy."

"Sydney get you out of the house?" Randy asked with a knowing glint.

So, he had been behind this.

"Yeah, she did."

"Well, what are you waiting for?"

A white apron was launched at my head, and I caught it easily with one hand. I laughed. It felt good to have something to laugh about.

"We have a lot of work to do."

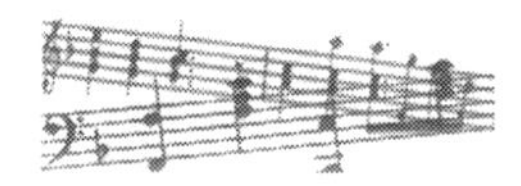

The pizza place closed at midnight. I stayed after to wipe down tables and refill Parmesan and red pepper flake containers. The steady motion of running the restaurant had kept my mind occupied and had given me a blissful reprieve from my thoughts. When I finished around one in the morning, I closed up shop. Instead of going straight home, I turned and walked out onto the beach.

I'd been avoiding the beach at all costs. It had once been my place of solitude—just me and the crashing waves, the sand between my toes, the salty air. Peaceful, serene, entrancing. But I'd brought Ari here. I'd shared my favorite place in the world with her, and now, it wasn't mine. It was ours.

I was exhausted from working hard all day, and I wanted to feel a piece of her when I couldn't be anywhere near her. The only time we'd ever been closer was when I'd told her about my parents. We'd connected on such a strong emotional level that she'd given me her body. I couldn't have either of those things right now, so I gave myself the beach as a small consolation.

I tramped out through the snow, letting the dry, cold air seep into my lungs. I finally reached a point where the ocean had washed away the snow, giving way to hard-packed sand. I stood there in icy silence, just watching the waves come in and then flow back out.

Working had never held any real interest to me. I had money, lots of money, from what had happened with my parents. And the band made good enough money to top that. But I suddenly wanted a job. I wanted to feel like I was doing something worthwhile. A secret part of me wanted to prove Ari wrong. I'd never been motivated or ambitious. I'd been treading water in my life for a long time. Maybe it was time to change that after all.

Going through the motions at home was surprisingly easy. My family had never been particularly emotional, so I could hide my feelings behind an expressionless mask. I'd never told my parents that I was dating anyone. Thus, they had no reason to suspect my sullen attitude was anything out of the ordinary. Only Aaron seemed to notice a shift in my moods, but he kept his thoughts to himself, just like my family always did.

I was upstairs, getting ready for my father's annual Christmas party, when Aaron appeared in the bathroom mirror.

"Are you about ready to go?"

Sometimes, I swore that Aaron and I could have been twins. He was much taller than me, but he had the same natural blond hair and matching dark blue eyes. He'd graduated from Princeton the year before I'd attended, and he was now working in business in Boston, like our father.

I swished the mascara across my lashes one more time, and then I put the tube away. "Sure."

"Have you been okay?" he asked, crossing his arms over the chest of his designer tuxedo.

"Fine."

"Aribel, I know you're not *fine*."

I ran my hands down the front of the black lace dress my mother had picked out for me when we'd gone shopping. It had an open V-cut with thick straps falling over my shoulders, a tiny empire waist, and an A-line skirt that fell to my knees. Grant's dog tags had been replaced with a simple gold chain with a little bow pendant. My parents had gotten it from Tiffany's for me for Christmas. It was simple yet extravagant.

I hated taking off Grant's dog tags almost as much as I hated wearing them. They were my reminder as much as his text messages were. I desperately wanted to pick up the phone and make it all right, but something had kept me from doing it. I missed him terribly, and honestly, I couldn't believe some of the things we'd said to each other, but I wanted to trust Cheyenne's advice. I *did* need time away from him to get my head on straight again.

"Are you daydreaming?" Aaron asked, waving his hand in front of my face.

"No," I said immediately. "What were you saying?"

"If I didn't know better, I'd say you are lovesick."

The color drained out of my face, and I was thankful for the rouge I'd just applied to my cheeks. "I'm just not feeling well." I took a step around him. I found a pair of black heels and slipped them on.

"Aribel," Aaron said softly, following me into the room. "Did something happen at school? Is that why you came home early?"

Oh, how I wanted to confide in my brother, but I knew exactly what he would think about Grant. Aaron would assume what I'd assumed when I first met Grant. But there was so much more to Grant than met the eye. I'd said that he hadn't changed, that he wasn't ambitious…and more terrible things, but none of them were true. His drive, and ambition just didn't fit the mold I'd been carefully cut from. That didn't mean it didn't exist.

"I don't want to talk about it."

"I'm your brother. You can trust me."

I sighed and relented. "I was dating someone. We got into a big fight when school ended. I'm just trying not to think about it."

"Well, as your brother, I can say that no guy is ever going to be good enough for you."

I cringed at his words.

"And if you're already fighting, then it's probably only going to get worse. But if you decide to see this guy, tell him your older brother will beat his ass if he hurts you again," Aaron said.

The thought of Aaron trying to beat up Grant was highly amusing, and I cracked a smile for the first time in what felt like forever.

"That's better. Come on, we have to get to the hotel. You'll get to meet Sarah."

In the limousine, my parents chatted aimlessly on the way to the Christmas party, and Aaron had his arm around his new girlfriend, Sarah. I gazed out the back window and prayed for the night to end quickly. We pulled up in front of the hotel and were escorted to the ballroom.

My mother took me aside at the entrance. "Aribel, please do try to smile while you're here tonight," she said with a wary look in her eye. "I've noticed that you seem sullen, but maybe the festivities will do you some good."

I managed a polite smile and nodded. "Of course."

"Also," she said, gesturing for me to follow her, "we have invited a delightful young man who works for your father."

I groaned. "Please don't do this."

"Just meet him!" she insisted. "His name is Henry. His parents are from the area. He graduated from Harvard three years ago, and he is already making his way seamlessly up the company."

Twenty-five. My mother was pitching me to a guy who was six years my senior and listing off his good qualities, like he was antique furniture being auctioned off to the highest bidder.

"I'm not interested."

My mother gave me a stern look. "It's good and well that you've been focused on your schoolwork, but it doesn't hurt to look around. You never know. You might like him."

Grant. I liked Grant. No do-gooder Harvard grad from high-society was going to compare to Grant. I almost couldn't believe those thoughts had just crossed my mind. *Hadn't I thought the same as my mother only four months earlier?*

"Henry!" my mother said, fluttering her fingers.

Oh God, she had just been walking me right to him.

"Diana, so good to see you," Henry said. His eyes swept past my mother and landed on me. "And you must be Aribel. I'm Henry Arbor."

I handed him my hand to shake, but he brought it to his lips. His blue eyes stared straight through me. I managed not to squirm uncomfortably, but I quickly retrieved my hand.

"Nice to meet you," I said.

I got my first real glance at Henry, and he was everything I'd suspected—tall, blond, blue-eyed with a suit to rival my brother's, and a smile that could charm a snake.

My mother smiled brightly at our introduction and then went back to find my father in the crowd. I avoided Henry's curious glances and scurried after her. I spent the remainder of the evening tucked into a corner of the room, wasting time on my cell phone. A text pinged on the screen from Grant, and my heart raced.

Merry Christmas, Princess. Hope you get everything you want. Unless you manage to get a ticket into Jersey, I'm afraid I'll be without the only thing I want. Stay warm, and come back soon. I miss you.

Tears swam in my eyes. *Damn him! How did he bring out this much emotion in me from a simple text message? Ugh!* I felt positively dreadful. There was no other way to put it. I missed him, and I wanted to make things right. I'd have to find a way to talk to him.

"Are you all right?" Henry asked, materializing out of thin air.

"Oh!" I blinked the tears away. "Sorry. I'm fine."

"Do you want to take a stroll around the hotel?"

"Did my mother send you?" I asked before I could stop myself.

Henry looked taken aback, and I wasn't sure if it was an act or not.

"No, of course not. I just saw that you looked sad and wanted to get you out of here in case other people noticed."

"So…this is about appearances?" *God, my stupid mouth.*

"Have I done something to offend you?" Henry asked plainly. "You looked like you needed an escape. I can provide one."

"All right," I said softly.

I wanted to push Grant's text out of my mind anyway. Henry walked me to the nearest door, and we started wandering leisurely around the hotel. He didn't say much, which was a relief. The silence was better anyway.

"Want to see something?" Henry asked.

"Um…sure."

He pushed open a door and led me into an empty ballroom. It was dark, the only light coming in from the panel of windows along the far wall. Henry shrugged out of his tuxedo jacket and walked me out to the balcony overlooking the city.

"Here," he said, slipping his jacket over my slim shoulders.

I felt a touch of guilt for taking it, but I was glad I had it.

"God, it's freezing."

"Yeah," he admitted. "It looks better in the summer. You'd like it."

I shrugged. "So, how do you like working for the company?"

"It suits me. How are you enjoying Princeton?"

I turned my face back out toward the city. "It's nice."

"Will you be in town much longer?" he pried.

"Through the rest of break. I don't have school again until the second week of January." That meant I would be away from Grant for a couple more weeks. *Could I wait that long?*

"Do you have plans for New Year's?"

New Year's. Oh my God! Why didn't I think of that before? My whole face lit up. Grant would be in New York for New Year's. He still had to be opening for The Drift. I could go there. We could talk then before I came back to school.

Realizing I hadn't responded to Henry, I spoke up, "I'm going to be in New York City with one of my friends."

He looked disappointed but managed to cover it up. "What about after that? I'm leaving on vacation with my family to Paris for a week, but I get back on New Year's Eve. I'd love to take you out."

Oh…

Oh!

"Um…I really appreciate the offer, but I'm not sure what I'll be doing."

"Well, just think about it. I'd like to see you again," he said, turning me to face him.

He looked completely one hundred percent sincere. I guessed I'd somehow charmed him in our short time together, or it was the parental influence behind the whole exchange. He was rather handsome. Before Grant, I would have totally been into this. But now, all I saw was a life I didn't want to fit into because it was one without Grant.

Henry's eyes dropped down to my lips, and I saw his intention a split second before he leaned down to kiss me. I turned my face at the last second, and he chastely kissed me on the cheek. Henry cleared his throat. I'd embarrassed him. That much was clear to me.

"Perhaps we should get you back inside. You're shaking."

"I think that's a good idea," I whispered.

I was certainly shaking but not from the cold. It was from what had almost happened.

Grant and I were on a break.
We needed space.
We needed time.
We weren't broken up.

"Not a drop to drink?" Vin asked me, holding the bottle of tequila out in front me. "I bet we could get someone over here to do body shots."

"Not interested," I said.

I leaned back against the bar and surveyed the crowd hovering backstage at The Drift's New Year's show. We were low profile compared to them, and while girls still gravitated toward us, most of the attention was on the other band—mostly Donovan to be honest.

I'd driven into the city a few days early to meet with Hollis. He'd hooked me up with Donovan, and we got along so well that he'd ended up inviting me to some exclusive party last night. I'd had a few drinks there but nothing to throw me over the edge. I wasn't looking to do that tonight before the show—not after what had happened before our last show with The Drift. Not after what had happened with Ari.

I still hadn't heard from her since she left the ski lodge. I hadn't messaged her since Christmas, and I was going to try to keep that up until she got back to school. I wasn't sure I'd be able to stop myself from rushing over to her place as soon as she was supposed to be home.

"Bro, when are you going to stop this shit? I've only been back around you for a fucking week, and already, I'm tired of you sober," Vin complained.

"I just don't feel like drinking tonight. You drink enough for both of us anyway."

"Is it still about that chick?"

"I don't want to talk about it," I said quickly. My standard answer.

"Good. Don't talk about it. Just fucking get over it."

"I'm not just getting over her either, so just drop it." My voice lowered dangerously.

Vin knew this was a bad topic, yet he wouldn't let it go. One day, he was seriously going to get his ass handed to him.

"I know what you should do."

"What's that?"

"*That*," he said, pointing out a banging brunette who had been eye-fucking me all night.

"No."

"Fuck, man, look at those tits. She's got them on full display for you. And that ass. I know you're an ass man, bro. When she leans over, I can straight-up see ass cheeks. That chick wants your dick. She wants to blow it, suck it, fuck it, ride it. You name it. She wants it. Why the fuck would you stay sober and mope around about your ex-girlfriend when that ass is begging you to shove your cock in it?"

I clenched my fists at my sides. I would not blow up on my brother. I would not throw my fist in his face. "She's not my ex-girlfriend," I said as calmly as I could.

"She walked out on you. Sounds like a free-for-all to me. Just get over it."

"Are you over Sydney?" I asked just to shut him up.

Vin glared at me. "Don't even bring that shit up. Miller's on my fucking shitlist."

"You weren't even together. You haven't been since high school. I'll get over Ari as soon as you're over Sydney, all right?"

"Only one difference—I'm fucking other chicks, and you aren't."

I shrugged. I wasn't Vin, and this wasn't Sydney. This was Ari. I only had about two weeks left before I would see her, and I wasn't going to fuck up between now and then.

Hollis walked up to us with a big smile and clapped his hands together. "You guys ready for the biggest performance you've ever experienced?"

"Fuck yeah!" Vin cried.

"Grant?" Hollis asked.

"Course I'm ready."

"Hollis, bro, you need to convince Grant to get over his ex. He won't listen to me anymore."

I glared at Vin and crossed my arms over my chest. I wasn't going to talk about this shit with Hollis.

"Ah, relationship trouble? This about the girl who walked in at the ski lodge?"

I ground my teeth and nodded.

"Not the first time I've seen that happen unfortunately. That's just the life, the way it is. Girls don't stick around long in this environment."

"See, bro?" Vin said, slapping my arm. "Go fuck that girl."

Hollis glanced over in the direction where Vin was pointing. "Ah, Jaci. I bet you'd like her, Grant. She floats around with the band."

Groupie. Fucking groupie slut. That was all I could think. Suddenly, I was repulsed by the thought instead of encouraged like I always had been.

"That's the kind of girl you should be hanging around with anyway. No real attachments. She understands the life, and when you guys become famous, she won't make a scene," Hollis said with a laugh.

Shit, he's fucking serious.

"This is the shit I've been telling him," Vin agreed as if what Hollis had said made perfect fucking sense.

"I'll introduce you after the show. Come to think of it, you'd probably like her friend Jennifer, too. In the meantime, you guys are up." Hollis gestured to a side door where Miller and McAvoy were already standing, waiting to go onstage.

I could tell they were a bit nervous by the look on Miller's face and the habitual way McAvoy flipped his drumstick.

I didn't even have time to tell Hollis I had no interest in Jaci or Jennifer whether or not they were friends who would probably let me take them home together.

We were ushered to the side of the stage. Someone announced us, and the crowd erupted into applause as we walked onstage. To my credit, I kept my emotions in check, but this was, without a doubt, the biggest venue we'd ever played. The pit was teeming with people on their feet, screaming our name.

Once I was onstage, there was nothing else in the world. This was where I belonged, where I'd always wanted to be. I grasped the microphone in my hand and took over. "Happy New Year, New York City!"

The screams were deafening, even without earpieces for the show.

"We're ContraBand, coming to you from Princeton, New Jersey. While you might not know us yet, I'm sure you're going to be screaming our name all night long."

I launched into "Hemorrhage" at McAvoy's lead, and I lost myself in the performance. Feeding off of the crowd's energy, we played phenomenally.

I wished Aribel could be here to experience it, but she was in Boston, probably going to fancy parties and trying to forget about me.

But I was goddamn certain that no one at the venue was going to forget about us tonight. We blew through our set like it was the easiest thing we'd ever done. I tossed a guitar pick into the crowd, and girls screamed as they literally clawed at each other to get it. I expected this behavior for The Drift…but for us? We were nobody. But maybe…maybe we were becoming somebody tonight.

Then, we hit "Life Raft." I'd insisted that we keep it on the set list. It tethered me to Ari, and even though I knew I was emotionally unstable, I'd wanted to sing it for her. I'd wanted to imagine her in the crowd and remind her of what she meant to me.

Except now that I was here, it was the last song I wanted to sing. The truth was…Ari wasn't here. She couldn't hear me sing to her. She wouldn't get to listen to me reminding her how she had saved me.

Pain pierced my heart as Vin picked at the melody I'd been strumming all winter break.

"This next song is our latest." I looked out across the thousands of people screaming for us, waiting expectantly. My breath caught in my throat, and then I envisioned Ari out there, listening. It made it easier to say, "This one is for every time you've ever fallen in love. We call it 'Life Raft.'"

I gasped.

Straight-up gasped.

If everyone else around me wasn't screaming at the top of their lungs, then someone other than Cheyenne might have noticed my shock. *Did Grant McDermott just confess his love for me onstage in front of thousands of people?*

I reached out and grabbed Cheyenne's arm to steady myself. I couldn't breathe. This was the most unreal moment of my life. I'd come here to make amends, and he'd gone and done *that.* Whatever I had been planning to say was sure to pale in comparison.

Love.

Well…fuck. That was all I had. He'd knocked me down to four-letter expletives.

"Are you going to be okay?" Cheyenne asked.

I shook my head. "No. I don't know."

Whatever Cheyenne said next was lost on me as Grant sang our song. Despite the gentle quality of his voice, I could tell he was struggling to get the words out.

You're my life raft in an endless ocean.

They ate at him. They showed every single emotion that he'd been sending through those text messages over break. He missed me, and he was hurting.

You saved me from drowning.
You saved me from myself.

And everything about him in that moment showed me how much the words affected him. He was drowning, and

I wasn't there to pull him out of it. I felt my heart breaking all over again.

The song ended, and without another word, Grant stormed offstage. The other guys stared after him in shock. This clearly had not been part of their plan. Grant had just disappeared. I needed to get to him.

Miller recovered himself enough to grab the microphone and thank the crowd for coming out to see them. It cut their show off by at least three songs. They always closed with "Letting You." Something was wrong.

"We need to get backstage," I told Cheyenne frantically.

"What the fuck was that about?" she asked as she gestured for us to break through the crowd.

"I don't know, but it wasn't good. He wrote that song for me."

"He wrote 'Life Raft' for *you*?" Cheyenne asked in disbelief. "Holy shit! That's their best fucking song."

"Yeah, and he kind of looked like he was going to go off the deep end when he was singing it."

"Well, no shit! What do you think he's going to do?"

"I don't know. Nothing. He was probably just pissed."

"Then, why are we running?" Cheyenne asked.

I didn't justify that with an answer. I didn't know what Grant was thinking. He'd never stormed offstage before. He loved his music. But he missed me. I knew he did. I didn't think the combination of all that pent-up anger and frustration along with the reminder of me was going to do anything *good* for him in his mental state.

We rounded a corner that took us to the backstage entrance. A bunch of girls were standing around. Some were talking to the bouncer, and it looked like they were trying to sweet talk their way backstage. Other girls were just hanging around, hoping someone would let them inside. Cheyenne confidently elbowed her way past all the annoying girls and walked right up to the bouncer. One of the girls gave her a death glare.

"Name?" he asked, giving us a look that said he was thankful not to be talking to the other girl now.

"Cheyenne Redding and guest."

The man ran his hand down the list and then checked us off. "Good to go, ladies."

"How—"

"Vin," Cheyenne said dismissively.

Of course.

We got backstage and saw that it was not just a large area, but it was packed. I sighed. I didn't know where Grant would be and what state I'd find him in.

"Split up?" Cheyenne suggested.

"Sure."

Not knowing where to start, I turned to the right went in search of Grant. I figured he'd be surrounded by people, but there was the possibility that he was off somewhere alone. I was also looking for the other guys, hoping to catch a glimpse of them coming offstage, but I had no such luck.

I was thinking about circling back to the entrance to find Cheyenne when I nearly ran into a guy. He looked like he was in a hurry and *pissed.*

I squeaked and got out of his way. "Sorry."

His gaze fell on me, and his anger disappeared. It was replaced with curiosity, and then he smiled. "No problem at all. I wasn't looking where I was going."

"No harm, no foul," I said.

"Can I help you with anything?"

"I'm just looking for Grant McDermott," I said with a sigh.

I always felt like I was looking for him at these kinds of things. They needed to make the backstage smaller.

"Oh, Grant? Yeah, sure. I just saw him walk out."

"Really?" I asked, surprised. "Where did he go?"

The guy shot me an amused look, and my stomach dropped.

"I think he had a girl with him, so I can only imagine."

No. I wouldn't believe what he was telling me. That just didn't make any sense.

"Um…are you sure? I mean…he looked pretty upset when he got offstage."

"He *was* pretty upset. I don't know if we've met, but I'm Hollis Tift. I manage The Drift. I've been working pretty closely with Grant since Halloween. I have a feeling you're this Ari who everyone keeps talking about."

I blushed. "Um…yeah, I am."

"Well, I hate to break it to you, Ari, but this is just how it is. This is the life." He spread his arms wide, indicating all the groupies. "I'm sure he liked you. But why would he wait around? He realized his mistake, and he's reconciling that problem."

My mouth hung open, and for once, I was rendered completely speechless. I couldn't listen to this. I couldn't believe this. This wasn't Grant. This wasn't the man I'd fallen for.

But when we had started talking, he hadn't been in this position. I hadn't been worried about the groupies before, but these girls were professionals.

I opened my mouth to contradict him, but he cut me off. "It's a hard lesson to learn. You seem like a nice girl. If you want my advice, it would be to turn around and get out of here. Find a nice guy who will take care of that pretty face and not break your heart. Grant…he's in a league of his own. He's going places. You're just going to hold him back."

"I don't believe you," I said as strong as I could muster.

"It doesn't matter to me whether you believe me or not," Hollis said with shrug.

I pushed away my fears. I didn't need all of this clouding my mind. I just…I couldn't believe what he was saying. If Grant cared about me, if he loved me, we could make it work.

"Whatever. Grant has been messaging me all break. He wrote that song for me. I just need to talk to him. So, if you don't know where he is, I'll keep looking."

"Feel free to keep looking, but he's already gone. He left with Jaci ten minutes ago."

I shook my head and stumbled away from Hollis. I had to find Grant. He couldn't have left with another woman. He wouldn't do that to me. Sure, we were on a break, but we weren't broken up. I knew that I hadn't responded to his messages. I knew that things were kind of fucked-up. I just couldn't fathom that they were over.

When I finally found the back exit, I pushed it open and gazed out at the small parking lot. I didn't see Grant's truck, but that didn't mean anything. He could have parked somewhere else. I felt like I was grasping at straws, but I just couldn't let any of those things be true.

I heard a commotion behind me, and I slowly turned in hopes that Grant was still inside. But it was just Donovan fending off a group of girls. I rolled my eyes and looked away.

"Ari, good to see you," he called out when he saw me. "Jesus, it's freezing. Let's close that door."

With a sigh, I let him shut it behind me. It wasn't like staring out in the cold was going to bring Grant back. I just couldn't believe that he was with a girl. I'd meant to surprise him by showing up, but maybe I should have just given in and texted him.

"Everything all right?" Donovan asked.

My heart beat in my chest as I looked up at Donovan. I didn't want to ask him what I was about to ask. I couldn't have him confirm it, but I just had to know. Maybe Donovan wouldn't even know.

"Have you seen Grant?"

Donovan looked uncomfortable for a minute. "Uh...yeah, I saw him."

"Do you know where he is?" Hope sparked in me.

"I'm sorry, Ari."

And he did look sorry. *Shit.*

"What are you sorry about?"

"I saw him leave."

"Oh," I whispered. "Are you sure?"

"When I was out with him last night, he told me that you guys broke up."

"We…wait, he *said* that?"

I was not going to get upset about this again. I'd thought that we were just on a break, but he must have assumed it was an official breakup…that we'd talk about getting back together when I came home. I'd never given him any indication otherwise.

"Yeah, he did." Donovan's hand dropped onto my shoulder, and he looked at me sympathetically. "Just so you know…I think he's crazy." His other hand came up and pushed a loose strand of hair behind my ear. "If I had a girl as beautiful as you, I'd never let you out of my sight, seventeenth-century antiquated ideals or not."

I stepped away from his touch, and my back hit the door. "Thanks for your concern. I'm sure you have hundreds of girls much more beautiful than me throwing themselves at you."

"None as beautiful as you who are turning me down."

"I bet you don't have *any* others doing that."

Donovan shrugged. He knew that I was right. "Why don't you forget McDermott tonight? Stay for my show. Haven't you ever wanted to see a Drift show from the side of the stage? We could hang out after. We'd have a good time."

For some reason, I had a feeling that his definition of a good time and my definition of a good time weren't the same thing. And the only person I wanted to be with was Grant. Even if he was off with someone else tonight, I still wanted him.

"Appreciate the offer, but—"

My words were cut off when Donovan bent down and brushed his lips against mine. Fire alarms went off in my mind. This was wrong. This wasn't Grant. Even if Grant was with someone else, I didn't want to kiss someone that he knew. I didn't want to be around people who were associated with Grant. I needed to get out and get out now.

I pushed against the door I was leaning on and opened it into the cold. Donovan stumbled through it with me, breaking our kiss. His green eyes were fierce.

"I appreciate the offer, but no, I'm not interested," I said, my voice hard.

"You're wasting your time on Grant."

"If I'm wasting it on a man who loves me, then I'd obviously be wasting my time with someone who doesn't."

And with that, I shoved past him, back inside, back through the crowd of girls, and out into the arena. I texted Cheyenne to let her know that I was getting a cab back to the airport. She seemed frantic, but there was nothing else she could do at this point. I just wanted to be back in Boston.

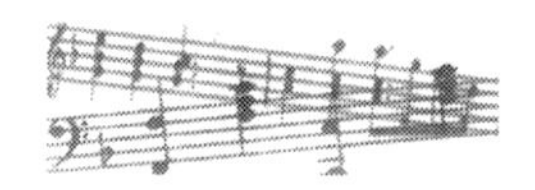

The clock chimed midnight soon after the plane touched down. I waited anxiously for a text message from Grant, like I'd gotten over Christmas, but it never came. I hadn't wanted to believe he was with someone else, but somehow, his silence convinced me more than anything else ever could. When I got home, I crawled into bed, determined to forget Grant McDermott.

45 GRANT

I typed out ten messages to Ari but deleted them all.

She didn't want to hear from me on New Year's. She hadn't wanted to hear from me on Christmas. She hadn't wanted to hear from me every day before that. I should just give up and let her move on with her life, but I couldn't.

I'd been onstage, singing the song I'd written for her, when it just hit me how fucked-up all of this was. I was in love with her. I'd said as much onstage, but the lyrics had just driven it home. I was in love with Aribel Graham, and she wanted nothing to do with me.

After I'd finished the song, I'd stormed offstage, unable to continue. I was over it. I'd just wanted to be alone.

But no, even then, I couldn't get what I'd wanted. Hollis had stopped me at the exit, wondering what the fuck I was doing. We weren't signed with Pacific, and I was ruining my chances of ever getting picked up with them.

That was fine with me. If we got picked up, who knew when I'd get to see Ari anyway? Didn't seem like a fair trade to me.

Hollis obviously hadn't seen it that way. He couldn't understand how I felt about Ari. He never would. He talked about girls the way I had before Ari. I might be a total fucking asshole, but Ari came first. If by some fucking miracle I could salvage this with her, then I was going to do everything I could to make sure that was a possibility.

I'd had it out with Hollis backstage, and then I'd gotten into my truck and driven straight home. The drive had taken fucking forever since everyone and their mother was out in New York City for New Year's, but I hadn't cared. I'd just needed to get out of there. I'd needed to think, and I couldn't do it surrounded by thousands of people.

Being all alone, holed up in my house, didn't seem to help much either. I just wanted Ari here with me. I wanted to get a New Year's kiss I'd remember. But if Ari didn't want me around, I wasn't sure how much more of my antics would change her mind. If it came down to that, I'd have to resign myself to move on.

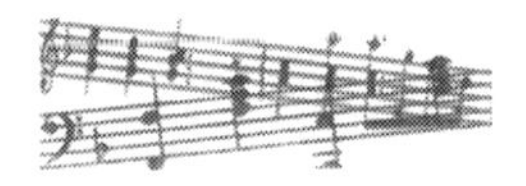

Hollis hadn't been the only one pissed that I'd walked out of the show. The guys had returned from the city early afternoon on New Year's Day, and they had promptly gone about ignoring my existence every time I tried to talk to them. I'd fucking wanted to be alone to think, and now, they were giving me all the space I needed.

I wandered into the garage, and everyone seemed to have calmed down by the time regular band rehearsal was supposed to start. They were seated on the couches. McAvoy had his laptop open. He was the tech-savvy one of the bunch, and we generally just left him alone when he got in the zone. Miller looked up when I walked in, but Vin didn't even spare me a glance. He must really be pissed.

I took a seat next to McAvoy. I decided to take a direct approach. "Sorry about last night."

"What the fuck happened?" Vin asked. He looked like he'd doped up on steroids this morning, and he was even more of a loose cannon. "You just fucking left us out there. We had three more songs to go, and you ditched us! What the fucking fuck kind of band member ditches his band onstage with no motherfucking warning?"

"I know. I should have told you guys."

"You fucking think? You humiliated us out there!"

"I didn't humiliate you," I argued. "We played the majority of our set. No one even knew the difference."

"Hollis knew the difference," Miller cut in. "He was pretty pissed."

"Fuck Hollis," I said with a shake of my head. "I'm so tired of these label people thinking they can mold us into these perfect shapes. They can't define us by dangling a contract in front of our eyes."

Vin cursed under his breath, but Miller was the one who spoke up, "Hollis isn't trying to fit us into a certain mold. He's been pretty lenient as far as I'm concerned, and I like him. Now, after that performance and your argument, we might not get signed."

"Good. I don't want to get signed," I said without thinking.

The silence in the room was deafening. Even McAvoy stopped clicking away at his computer to look up at me. All of the guys stared at me with a range of shocked expressions. I'd never voiced that thought out loud to anyone before. I hadn't even really thought about it much until recently. After the Frank Boseley incident, I'd been feeling more and more constrained by the pressure of fitting into a traditional record mold. Then, with the added fear of losing Ari, it had only amped up that feeling.

"You what?" Miller asked.

"I don't want to get signed."

"Since when?"

"This whole experience is ruining me for wanting to sign with anyone."

"Is this about Ari?" Miller asked, just laying it out there.

"Oh, come on, man. Just forget that girl," Vin complained.

"I'm not forgetting about her!" I yelled back at Vin. "Can we just drop the subject?"

"You just dropped a bomb on us, and you want to just walk away from that?" Miller asked in disbelief.

"Guys," McAvoy said, speaking up, "you might want to shut the fuck up and look at this."

"At what?" I asked. I leaned over his computer and tried to make out what I was looking at. It just looked like a spreadsheet with random words and numbers on it.

"Well, we sold about ten-thousand more copies of our 'Life Raft' demo than we've sold of every other song combined."

"What? Since when?"

"Since…today," McAvoy said.

I looked at him, stunned. "How is that possible?"

"I can only assume it's because of the show last night."

My mind ran away with me. *Ten-thousand more copies.* Of course it had to be that fucking song. It had to be that one. I didn't ever want to sing that song again at this point, but it was the one that over *ten-thousand* people had purchased within twenty-four hours. *Fuck!*

Aaron finally coaxed me out of bed a couple of days later. He insisted I come out with him. The last thing I wanted to do was party.

I'd been sulking around the house exactly like the lovesick puppy I was. My mother had seemed concerned and tried to get me to see a doctor, but I wasn't sick. I'd just shooed her away and closed the door. She'd never seen behavior like this from me before, so she was rightfully worried. There wasn't much she could do at this point though.

Even if I didn't want to go out with Aaron, I was kind of ready to get out of the house. Sitting around in my room all day meant that I thought about Grant all day. I figured it might be good to get him off my mind.

Around ten o'clock, we arrived at Le Petit Parlor, a ritzy French bar that catered to an elite crowd. I'd been here a couple of times before but mostly with high school friends, who I preferred not to see tonight. The room was extremely dark with red velvet booths that were dimly lit and a small dance floor in an adjoining room. Unlike the Princeton crowd I was used to, the people here were drinking scotch rather than beer and Grey Goose or champagne rather than hunch punch. I'd dressed the part in a fitted knee-length dress, matching my eyes, and pumps.

Aaron didn't hesitate when we entered, and he walked us right over to a booth where six of his friends sat around a bottle of scotch. He wrapped an arm around a girl sitting with them. She was clearly not Sarah, the girlfriend he'd brought with him to the Christmas party. I frowned, unsure what to make of that.

The guys were all smoking cigars, and my nose crinkled at the smell. Aaron made no introductions as I'd known everyone, aside from the girl, since grade school.

"I'm going to get a drink," I said after a minute.

They already had scotch, but I wasn't going to drink that. I wouldn't get carded here anyway.

"All right," Aaron said with a nod.

I made my way to the bar. The bartender smiled at me and passed over a flute of champagne without me asking for it. I had wanted something stronger, but this would do. Maybe if I had four or five more, they would numb the pain or something. I handed him my credit card and told him to leave it open.

"Let me get that," someone said, coming up next to me.

"Oh, that's not necessary." I turned toward the person who was trying to buy my drink and froze.

Henry smiled at my stunned look and switched out our cards with the bartender. "Good to see you again, Aribel."

"I thought you were in Paris, not just a French-themed bar."

He chuckled. "I was, but I came back on New Year's Eve."

"Oh, right," I said, snippets of our conversation coming back to me.

"How have you been?"

He gestured for me to walk with him, and I complied.

"Fine." Hardly, but he didn't need to know that. "How was Paris?"

"Enchanting. Have you been?"

"Mmm…yes. Lots of museums."

I noticed he was walking me away from where Aaron was seated, but at this point, it didn't really matter. Henry was handsome and intelligent, and he'd just bought me a drink. I wasn't going to think about anything else right now.

"Ah, you've only seen a tourist's view. I can show you a side of Paris the tourists never see," he said with a charming smile.

We took a seat at a small empty booth in the back of the room. He started chatting some more about his Paris trip just as a waiter came to our table. To my surprise, he dropped off a bottle of champagne. I hadn't even realized that Henry had ordered the bottle.

Our conversation moved from Paris to his time at Harvard to the work that he did for my father. I drank one glass after another, finding myself enjoying the conversation more and more, as the night went on. My head felt as light as the bubbles. The room was suddenly so loud that I had to lean in to listen to him talk.

And God, he had a nice mouth with perfectly straight white teeth and full lips. I bet he was a great kisser. Something was nagging at me, telling me that I shouldn't even be thinking about that, but I pushed that thought away. I'd been so sad for so long, and I just wanted to be…carefree. *Not a word I'd ever use to describe myself, but I could be that tonight, right?*

Henry made some joke that I honestly didn't even follow, but I giggled anyway, and he only smiled wider. I glanced up into his blue eyes and saw something that should have made me back off, but I didn't. I wasn't sure what it was. Maybe…predatory. But that was ridiculous! This was Le Petit Parlor, not some backroom at The League. Plus, I hadn't had *that* much to drink anyway.

A waiter came by and took the bottle of champagne.

I started to protest, but Henry put his hand out to stop me. "Would you like another?"

"We weren't finished with the first one."

He smiled at me, and his hand landed on my knee. "We could get another, or we could have the bottle I have chilling at my place. It's not too far from here."

"I mean…I'd have to let my brother know." I knew I sounded like a kid, but I had driven out here with him.

Henry chuckled. "He already knows. It'll be fine."

"All right," I said softly.

I stood to leave, but he pulled me back down toward him. I was nearly sitting on top of him at this point, and good Lord, did he smell good. He was wearing some really, really fancy cologne. He'd probably picked it up in Paris. It was intoxicating, and I was already drunk.

One hand held my leg tightly in his grasp while the other moved my chin up until I was looking at him. There was that look again, but I had no time to think about it as he dropped his lips down on mine.

He was kissing me.

No, I was kissing him back.

No, I wouldn't do that.

But he tasted so good, and he really *was* as good of a kisser as I'd thought he'd be. My head swam with the energy of it all.

Yet, something wasn't right. It wasn't Henry I wanted to be kissing. It was hot. He was hot. But it just didn't feel right. Kisses were supposed to feel like a burst of electricity mixed with fireworks and crackling infernos coursing through my system. The intensity and passion was supposed to radiate from me until I couldn't breathe or think about anything but that moment.

And I'd been kissed like that—like it was life or death to feel his lips against mine, like there was nothing else that would ever exist in the world, like it was the only source of true happiness.

I broke away from Henry with a gasp. His returning smirk told me that he thought that was a good thing. After all, my face was flush, and my heart was pounding. But I felt wrong, all wrong. I felt like spiders had just crawled under my skin.

"I'm sorry. I…I can't," I whispered breathily through my drunken haze.

"Can't or won't?"

"Does it matter?"

"No," he decided.

"I'm sorry. There's someone else."

Well, that took him by surprise, and he finally released me.

"I didn't realize you were dating someone else. Funny how that didn't come up until just now."

"We're kind of broken up…" *And he's sleeping around with other people.*

He arched an eyebrow. "So, then…you're not dating someone else."

"The technicalities of it don't really matter," I slurred. "I'm not really all with it. So, it's probably best for us to stop… whatever this." I put some more space between us to emphasize my point.

"I was kind of enjoying…this." He scooted closer to me. "So, maybe you should find out what's going on with the technicalities. I'd like to get back to this." His mouth dropped down on mine again. "And I think you'd like to as well."

I pulled back again and stood. I didn't want that. I didn't want whatever he was offering. My parents had set up this entire thing. There was no real attraction between us. As far as I was concerned, this was an arranged-marriage deal that I was being forced into at the hands of my mother.

The heat of his gaze told me that he didn't believe my unspoken thoughts.

With that, I turned around and walked out.

I would catch a cab home. I couldn't be there a second longer. The point of the night out had been for me to stop thinking about Grant. And while I had momentarily forgotten him, it was only because I was drunk, not because I felt anything less for him.

The whole thing left me wondering what I was going to do when I had to return to Princeton next week.

Ari had been back from break for three days, and I hadn't gone over there and busted down the door, demanding to speak to her. I thought that was pretty good.

It helped that I'd gotten a gig at a recording studio in Trenton to pass the time during the day. The money wasn't that great, but I felt better being in the studio, working and learning, than I did sitting around, obsessing about Ari. Not to mention, I didn't have to think about whatever the fuck we were going to do with the band. We hadn't heard from Hollis since New Year's Eve, and I wasn't all that surprised. At least, I still kept in touch with Donovan. The Drift would be in New York this afternoon for some talk-show appearance, and we were set to chill afterward. It meant another way to keep my mind off of Ari.

Though, I knew it was only a matter of time before I made my way over there to try to convince her that she had made a terrible mistake. Until my resolve broke, I was going to try to give her the space she had requested. I didn't know what I'd do if she turned me down. I'd probably keep trying.

I left the studio early and drove home to shower before going into the city. The guys were playing video games in the living room, and it all felt so normal. It was a nice change of pace from how we'd all been acting since New Year's.

Miller nodded at me when I walked in the door. "How was work?"

I shrugged. "I bet we could get some free studio time next week."

"Nice."

"What are you up to tonight? I'm meeting up with Donovan in the city for a few drinks. You interested?"

Miller shifted his gaze and fidgeted in his seat. I looked over at McAvoy, and he also seemed uncomfortable. Even Vin wouldn't meet my eyes.

"Okay…what's going on?"

"We already have plans," Miller said.

"Doing what?"

"We're, uh…going over to Ari's place tonight—"

"What?" I bellowed, completely blowing up. "You're going over there? I haven't even been over there!"

McAvoy sighed and nodded. "I'm sort of seeing her roommate, Gabi, and Vin is seeing Cheyenne. Miller was planning to hang out with Shelby."

I stared at Miller, waiting for him to respond. "What about Sydney?"

"Sydney wants what she wants when she wants it. Right now, she's back in Knoxville, probably fucking half the school. And before you blow up on me, just think about it. You know it's true."

"Whatever. So…you're all just going over to hang out at Ari's house, and I'm just here?"

"Bro, we want you there," McAvoy said.

"But she doesn't," I finished for him.

McAvoy shrugged in apology.

Ari didn't want me there. She hadn't asked for me. *Fuck, things were really over.*

"All right," I said, slowly backing away. "I'll just go visit Donovan in the city. You guys have a good time."

The guys looked at me with varying levels of sympathetic faces. They knew I'd been fucked-up about Ari. They knew I'd been beating myself up about it. But there was nothing to be done.

I'd just go see her later this week. I'd let her tell me to my face that it was over, and then I'd find a bottle and drown myself in it.

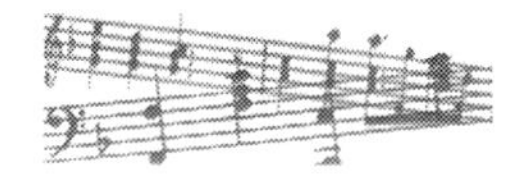

I met Donovan in the penthouse suite he was staying in. He was shirtless with a bottle of whiskey out in front of him and his guitar in his lap. The rest of the band was there as well with nearly naked girls hanging all over them. Donovan had two girls in nothing more than sheer lingerie sitting at his feet, staring up at him with idol worship.

"McDermott!" Donovan said, waving me over. "Just in time!"

"For what?"

"The party."

It appeared that the party was already well underway, but Donovan might be on something a little harder than that whiskey sitting in front of him.

"Didn't realize I'd be walking in on a…pajama party," I said.

"Guess the invite got mixed up. Girls, maybe you can help McDermott out of his shirt?"

The girls got up automatically. There was no hesitation. They were just going to take my clothes off because Donovan had told them to.

"Uh…no. I got it."

I slipped out of my shirt, and the girls looked disappointed, like they really had wanted to do it for me.

I dropped into the seat next to Donovan. "Quite a place you have here."

"Yeah. Hollis wanted the best."

"Nice."

I crossed my arms and looked at all the girls. I knew that there were girls like this at the shows, and damn, it was pretty easy to come by girls who wanted to fuck me. I was sure it was easier to get girls for The Drift, who were legit rock stars, but still, it wasn't even dinner yet, and there were at least thirty hot-as-shit girls in lingerie in his hotel room.

"Where do the girls come from?"

Donovan was playing a new tune on his guitar, and he stopped at my question. "Oh, Hollis finds them. Most are regulars. I mean, you know Jaci," Donovan said with a wink as he pointed at a girl across the room, who was wearing nothing but a black lace thong.

"She looks familiar," I said. I remembered Vin had wanted to get with her, and Hollis had tried to push her on me, but that was it.

"Well, you fucked her on New Year's. I'd hope she looked familiar."

Time froze. I reacted without another thought. "What? I didn't fuck anyone on New Year's!"

Donovan gave me a knowing look. "Oh, come on. Were you that fucked-up? You left with her right after you got offstage. Hollis saw you leave."

Anger started to settle into the pit of my stomach. "I went home after the show. Straight home. I didn't have anyone with me."

I didn't know why I was trying to defend this to Donovan. He probably thought it was good that I'd fucked one of the groupies after the show. That was commonplace after all.

"All right, man. Whatever you want me to believe. I won't fault you for fucking a groupie. I got some good action with that Ari girl you were hanging out with at the lodge."

All semblance of control that I'd had earlier evaporated. "What the fuck are you talking about?" I asked, rising to my feet. "You fucked Ari? I'll fucking kill you."

Donovan raised his eyebrows at my reaction, but he didn't actually look that surprised. He looked smug. "Big reaction for the status of one groupie."

"Ari is *not* a groupie. She's my girlfriend," I growled, fighting for control.

"She didn't *seem* like anyone's girlfriend when she was backstage at the New Year's Eve show," Donovan said, standing up to face me. "If you get what I mean…"

I didn't think. I just acted. I lunged for Donovan, catching him off guard and connecting my fist with his face. It snapped his head backward, and he stumbled into the chair. But I wasn't finished. All the pent-up anger from the weeks without Ari came flooding into me in an overwhelming quantity. I couldn't even control it all. He had touched her, and I would fucking destroy him, just like I'd said the first time he'd tried something.

"What the fuck is wrong with you?" Donovan yelled.

All that did was bring more attention on us, but I was too far into this to care.

I'd lost the element of surprise, and Donovan was already back up on his feet. I reached for him again, but he blocked my punch. I pivoted and got a shot to his kidney that caused him to double over. I sent my fist into his face again. He fell flat on his back in the hotel room.

The rest of the band showed up at that moment and dragged me away from Donovan. I could see his face was bloody, but I hadn't broken anything. My chest was heaving, and all I could think about was the bloodlust. He couldn't touch her. I'd fucking murder him.

"Get him out of here!" Donovan cried as girls flocked to his side to check on him.

"I told you that I'd destroy you if you touched her, you motherfucker."

"You're fucking insane. She's just some girl. If you ever get signed—and that's a big *fucking* if at this point—you're going to see this for what it really is. You're going to leave her, or she's going to get tired of you cheating on her. You'll look back on this moment and know I was fucking right."

"That just shows how different you and I really are, Donovan. Because I love Ari. I respect her. I'd give her the world, the moon, the stars, the whole fucking universe.

When I get signed, and I really do mean *when*," I growled, shaking off the guys who were holding me, "I'm coming for your ass, just to prove you wrong."

I already had organic chemistry homework.

It was a bit of relief to be back on a normal schedule again. The break had seemed like some kind of strange dream, something someone else had gone through and not me. I'd lost my virginity, lost my boyfriend, been kissed by a rock star, and been propositioned by someone whose relationship with me bordered on an arranged marriage.

At least some things always stayed the same—like homework. I had a tough class schedule this semester, and I needed to make sure that I stayed on top of everything. There was an introductory study session later tonight. I couldn't decide if it was better to get involved from the get-go or try to do everything myself…like normal.

A knock at the door kept me from deciding. My heart rate shot through the roof as I wondered if today would be the day that I'd have to face Grant. I'd decided that I would do it this weekend. I'd let him break my heart this weekend.

Cheyenne came out of her room and jumped when she saw me. "I thought you were going to a study session!"

I narrowed my eyes. "I decided not to."

Shelby and Gabi appeared a minute later. They were equally surprised to find me sitting in the dining room. They shot questioning looks at Cheyenne.

"What's going on?"

"We're having some people over to watch a movie," Shelby said.

"Some people…as in?"

Gabi sighed. "I invited McAvoy over. We saw a lot of each other over break, and well, I guess we're kind of together."

I just stared at my friends. McAvoy…and that probably meant Vin and Miller and…

I shot out of my seat. "Are you saying Grant is going to be in our house?"

"No!" Shelby and Cheyenne said at once.

Gabi was shaking her head. "We told them not to bring him, but we thought you'd be gone."

"You can't just hide this stuff from me! I don't want to be blindsided that his friends are going to be here in our house!" I started packing up all of my papers and throwing the stuff into my backpack.

The guys started knocking again, and Shelby rushed over to answer it.

Cheyenne gave me a pleading look. "Please don't freak out about this."

"Freak out? Why would I freak out? It's every day that my roommates invite over my…whatever. This is stupid," I grumbled. "Fuck Grant McDermott."

Cheyenne giggled, and I glared at her.

"Sorry, I shouldn't have made that dirty," she said.

"I swear, you just can't help yourself."

Our conversation cut off as Miller, McAvoy, and Vin walked into our apartment. They looked pretty shocked to see me there as well, so the girls must have said I'd be gone. Well, lucky for them, I was leaving.

"Hey, Ari," Miller said cordially.

I nodded my head at him and then continued to pack up.

The group moved to the living room, and I stomped into my room to find my boots. It was still cold out there. When I returned, they were all cuddled up together. Cheyenne was sitting on Vin's lap on the couch. Gabi had her head on McAvoy's shoulder. Shelby and Miller were sitting side-by-side. I wondered how much Shelby knew about Miller and Sydney, but I didn't care to bring that up right now.

After grabbing my peacoat off the back of the chair, I put it on and threw my backpack over it.

"Hey, Ari?" McAvoy said.

Our eyes met across the room.

"Yeah?"

Miller sat up straight. "McAvoy, no."

"Shut up, Miller. No one else is going to talk about it. We need our brother back, so seriously, just shut up."

I resolutely stood there, wondering what the hell they were talking about.

"So, are you going to talk to Grant?"

"It's not like he wants to talk to me."

"Really?" McAvoy asked incredulously. "That's the line of reasoning you're going to go with?"

"What else am I supposed to think?" I asked, feeling my frustration turning to anger. "If Grant wants to talk to me, he knows where to find me."

"Maybe you should remind him. He's been acting like a fucking idiot since you left, and he might have forgotten." McAvoy sighed and shook his head. "We've been trying to get signed for years, and now that we're this close, Grant is talking about *quitting* because he's so fucked-up about your relationship. Maybe think that over, and stop being so selfish."

My mouth dropped open. "Selfish? He cheated on me!"

"Not the way we've heard the story," Miller piped up. "I think you have a lot of things to talk about."

"Whatever," I ended lamely. I didn't know what else to say. There was too much of what they'd said that didn't make sense, and I needed to process.

Everything that the guys had said was swirling around in my mind. *Grant was thinking about quitting ContraBand? Why the hell would he do that?* He loved the band and his brothers and everything about music. It simply couldn't be about me. That made no sense.

And the guys had said that he hadn't cheated? I'd been there on New Year's. Donovan and Hollis had told me that he'd gone off with someone else, and he'd never messaged me. I'd never messaged him…but still. It seemed likely with Grant's track record. *Did the guys just not know he'd slept with someone on New Year's? And if he hadn't slept with someone…did that mean I'd cheated with Henry?*

No. I hadn't wanted that kiss. Well, a part of me had, a drunk part of me, but I'd stopped it.

God, there are too many things to think about. I didn't want to go rushing over to Grant's house like a dog with my tail between my legs. We had a lot to talk about. The few weeks of us being apart had felt like an eternity, and at this point, there was so much that needed to be said. It felt like we'd built a wall between us, and I wasn't sure how ready I was to climb that. It might be easier to try to tear it down with my bare hands.

Deciding that O-chem took precedence over my floundering love life, I drove to the library in a hurry. I found the study group with ease, but I stopped myself from joining them at the last minute. Not only did I not want to have to deal with teaching the group instead of actually learning anything myself…Kristin was with them.

Her mousy brown hair was in a braid over her shoulder, and she was tugging on it as she flirted with some guy from our class. Disgust washed over me. *Did the girl never stop?*

I hated that I kept seeing her…that I would continue to see her. We had organic chemistry together as well as molecular biology and calc IV. I seriously couldn't escape the conniving bitch.

Backpedaling, I found a secluded spot on the same level and pulled out my assignment. I quickly got lost in the equations before me. I was finishing up the assignment, my head buried in my book, when I heard someone clear her throat next to me.

I glanced up and groaned. "What do *you* want?"

"Hey, Aribel," Kristin said, rocking back and forth on her toes. "I thought you might have been at the study session."

"Well, I wasn't. And you're free to go now."

"Mind if I take a seat?" She gestured to the chair in front of me.

"Yes, I do mind," I snapped.

"Is someone else meeting you?"

"If this is you trying to get to Grant, then you can turn around right now and leave. I don't want to talk to you. I don't want to see you. Just leave me alone."

"This isn't…I mean, that's not why I'm here," she said hastily.

"Then, why are you here? Simply to annoy me?"

"No!" she cried. She quickly glanced around and lowered her voice as she said, "I came to apologize."

"What for? Being a slutbag whore? Or did you do something else to me that I don't know about?"

Kristin pulled out the chair and sat down, ignoring the fact that I hadn't given her permission to do so. "I know I deserve that."

"You think?"

"Yes," she said flatly. "I just…I acted like a crazy person. I don't even know what was wrong with me. I was just so set on hooking up with Grant, and I felt so slighted that he didn't want me…that he wanted you."

"Oh, yes, that's a great way to apologize—dismiss the fact that Grant could want *me*! I'm just the girl who thinks she's better than everyone else, right?"

"I'm sorry," Kristin said earnestly. "And I know that you have no reason to forgive me. I don't expect you to, but I am sorry."

I shrugged. I wanted out of this conversation. I wanted her to leave me alone. "You're right. You have no reason to be forgiven. You accomplished your mission anyway. Grant and I aren't together."

"What? Why?"

"Why do you think?" I asked. I started putting my papers back together. The assignment was basically completed. I just needed to get out of here.

"Because of what I did? But nothing happened. He didn't even touch me."

"Whatever, Kristin. I don't know what made you have a change of heart in the last couple of weeks, but I don't want to hear it. Just leave me alone."

"All right. I just saw what happened at the New Year's Eve show."

My mood darkened. I didn't want to talk about *that* either. "About what?"

"Him saying that he loves you. I thought it was really romantic. It's what made me see how wrong I've been," she whispered.

I sighed and closed my eyes, remembering how I'd felt when Grant had dedicated "Life Raft"— shocked, excited, hopeful. Then, I'd gone backstage to find out Grant had left with someone else. But the guys had said that wasn't the case. They'd said he hadn't cheated on me. And I just didn't know what to believe.

My head hurt, and my heart hurt. My whole world felt like it was crashing down around me. There was only one person who could pick up the pieces, only one person with the answers I needed. I was tired of hiding. I needed to go find Grant.

"Thanks, Kristin," I said, shooting out of my seat.

"Wh-what?" she asked, surprised.

"I have to go talk to Grant. I mean…he loves me. He basically said he loves me, right?"

"I mean, yeah…I assumed that's what he meant when he dedicated the song. He's definitely never said anything like that onstage before."

Yeah, and she would know since she was a groupie. The anger flared up in me again, but I pushed it back down. There was nothing I could do about that right now. I just needed to find Grant.

"I don't forgive you for what you did," I told her bluntly. "But thank you for apologizing and for reminding me."

"Um…you're welcome."

Then, I was dashing out of the building and through the parking lot to my car. I drove recklessly to Grant's apartment. I knew he'd be alone since all the guys were at my place, but that nagging suspicion crept up in me, wondering if maybe he *wouldn't* be alone. I tried to squash that. I could only deal with that when the time came. There was no use in worrying about it now.

The lights were out, and Grant's truck was missing when I arrived, but I decided to try knocking anyway. When he didn't answer, I slumped back against the door in defeat. I didn't know where else he could be. He could be anywhere really. It would probably be best just to call him and find a place for us to meet up. But I wasn't going to do that tonight.

I had a hunch about his whereabouts, and even though it felt totally insane because he really could be *anywhere*, I still started up my car and followed my gut instincts.

"This fucking sucks," I grumbled into the wind.

I rested my hands on my knees as I sat on the blanket, and I stared out at the ocean. My foot absentmindedly kicked at the cold sand. I'd brought extra blankets with me, but I was just suffering through the icy temperatures.

After threatening Donovan and getting thrown from the party, I'd driven straight down the shore. I didn't have anywhere else to go. My friends were hanging out at Ari's apartment, a place where I didn't belong. I didn't want to be in Princeton where I could sit around and be miserable. The only place I ever wanted to think was the beach. And I had a lot to think about.

I hadn't been out here long, but already, I was questioning if it was helping any. A lot of demons were chasing me, and none of this was making it any better. I suddenly wished that I'd brought a bottle out with me or at least a joint. Any of my old vices would have done the trick. Anything to numb the pain, but I didn't have anything with me. I'd more or less given everything up cold turkey when Ari had walked out.

I just had the sand, the water, the moon, and a million tiny stars to mock me. *Congratulations on ruining your entire life, fuck up. You're a good-for-nothing, worthless waste of space. How you managed to get this far in life, we'll never understand.*

I rolled my eyes at my own thoughts, dropped back onto the blanket, and threw my arms over my face. *Maybe I'll just sleep out here. Hypothermia sounds preferable to this shit.*

Footsteps echoed in the sand behind me. Hopefully, it wasn't a cop who was going to tell me to get the fuck off the beach. That would just be my luck.

I thought the person had passed by until a shadow fell over me. There wasn't much light out here, but there was enough to know someone was standing over me.

I dropped my hands and started to sit up to explain to the cop that I was going to leave, but I just stopped everything I was doing and stared.

"Ari," I whispered. My voice was strained.

She was here.

How?

No. This didn't make any sense.

She was a vision, a beautiful ethereal vision.

Before I knew what was happening, I scrambled to my feet and reached my hand out to touch her cheek. Her skin was warm beneath my icy fingers, and she shivered. *Oh God, she's real.* She was so soft, and fuck did I want her. It wasn't just physical need either. I wanted to fuck her, but I wanted *her*. I just wanted to pull her into my arms and know that she wasn't fucking going anywhere.

"Hey, Grant," Aribel finally murmured.

"How did you know I would be here?"

"I didn't." She sighed softly. "Can I sit with you?"

"Sure." I gestured for her to take a seat on the blanket. "So…if you didn't know I'd be here, why did you come?"

"I just had a feeling, and I needed to talk to you."

"So, now, you can talk to me?" I didn't know why those words had left my mouth, but I couldn't help it. I'd pounded down her door. I'd been messaging her for weeks. She hadn't said a word. Now, she was just showing up with no explanation? Fuck that.

"Yes," she snapped. "Now, I can talk to you."

"How did that space work out for you, Princess? You have a good time? Go to any fancy parties?" Yeah, I was pretty much purposely antagonizing her. I had no fucking clue why.

"Would you shut up?"

"Not likely, darlin'. You drove all the way out here to see me. You're going to have to sit here and have a conversation with me."

"This isn't a conversation! This is us yelling at each other again!"

"Well, I'm just trying to figure out why it was so damn hard for you to use your fucking phone in the last three weeks. Is it broken? Did you not get any of my messages?"

"No, my phone is not broken! I just needed some space. I believe I told you that."

"I didn't think space meant you were going to ignore all your problems for three fucking weeks."

"And I didn't think space meant that you were going to go and fuck someone else!"

I snorted. "That's good coming from you."

"What the fuck does that mean?" she shouted.

"You fucked Donovan, Princess! Did you think he wouldn't tell me?"

"Now, you *are* being ridiculous!" Her hurricane blue eyes were so dark, and she looked fucking shocked at my suggestion. "When would I have slept with Donovan? And even if I *had* the opportunity, you think I'd just sleep with *anyone*?"

"How the hell am I supposed to know? You disappear without a word for three weeks, and then I get wind that you slept with Donovan. To be honest, I beat the shit out of him for it."

"He deserved the ass-beating. He kissed me, but I didn't sleep with him!" she cried. "I would never sleep with someone I just met. But you would…and did on New Year's."

It was my turn to look shocked. "Why does everyone keep saying that? I didn't sleep with anyone on New Year's. And how would you even know if I had?"

"I was there."

"At the show?" I asked in disbelief.

She nodded. "I came backstage to find you after…well, after you stormed offstage, but you were already gone. Donovan and some Hollis guy told me that you'd left with someone else."

I grabbed her hands in mine and forced her to look at me. "And you just fucking believed them? You didn't think to call me?"

"I wouldn't want to interrupt your good time," she said darkly.

"I was fucking miserable without you. I wanted to give you the space you'd asked for, but I fucking wanted you with me every goddamn second you were away, Ari. I don't know what else I can say to prove that to you."

The truth was that there wasn't anything else I could say. She either knew, or she didn't. And right then, looking into her eyes on our beach…she knew. She'd come here for me. She fucking wanted me. She had said that she had fallen for me completely. That shit hadn't gone away in three weeks.

My lips dropped onto hers before she had a chance to reply. There was no hesitation on her part. She kissed me right back as hard as she possibly could while grabbing my jacket tightly between her fingers. Her lips were like a double shot of espresso to my exhausted system.

The energy crackled between us, heating the crisp night air. There was too much space and decidedly too much clothing between us. The weeks of pent-up frustration was colliding into this one moment, and neither of us could keep our hands off the other. I just wanted to touch her, feel her, consume her, bury myself in her. I needed her. I fucking needed all of her.

My lips moved to her neck greedily as I pushed her back onto the blanket. Her fingers deftly dragged the zipper down on my jacket. She was already shaking from the cold or from what we were doing, so I threw the remaining blankets over us. My hands found the waistline of her jeans, and after unzipping them, I dragged them down her legs.

"Shit!" she hissed. "It's cold."

"Not for long, Princess."

I trailed my hands down her legs until I found her waiting opening. I circled my fingers around her and then finger-fucked her pussy until she was all warmed up for me. I didn't want to hurt her, but I wasn't exactly patient. She squirmed underneath me until her breathing turned labored, and I felt her walls tightening all around me. *Fuck, that's hot.*

She was so damn close to an orgasm, and I knew that I was going to push her right over the edge any minute. As I circled her clit, she came undone at my insistence.

"Grant…"

"I know, babe," I said before covering her mouth with mine. "I'm going to fuck you now."

Her eyes were wide. She wanted what I was offering, but a spark of fear still crept into her features. Everything about her was fucking hot. Just the way she had her mouth opened slightly like that made me want to shove my dick down her throat. But it was too cold, and I wanted her around me—hot and wet and tight.

I slipped on a condom, and without warning, I thrust forward inside her. She yelped as she expanded to fit me. *Fucking hell, she feels so fucking amazing.* Everything else paled in comparison. There was only Ari and me.

My fingers locked in her hair, and as I slowly slid out of her, I brushed my lips against her. "Princess, open your eyes."

She complied, and those big blue eyes stared up at me.

I started up a steady rhythm. "Tell me if I hurt you."

"Okay," she whispered throatily.

"Because I'm not going to be gentle."

Her eyes widened as I took what was mine, and I slammed back into her, hard. She made a small cry, but she didn't tell me to stop. And I had no plans to. Our bodies met over and over as I picked up the pace. I could tell that I was close to coming, but I needed to hold out long enough for her. I could hold out for her second orgasm…even if it felt like I might explode any second.

"Fuck, Ari."

"Grant," she breathed.

"Louder," I encouraged, and I thrust into her harder.

"Oh God," she cried a little louder.

"My name. Scream my name."

She bit on her lip, so I slammed into her again and again until her eyes rolled back into her head, and she really was calling out my name. She probably didn't even know how loud she was.

Fuck, I couldn't hold out any longer. I came as soon as I felt her walls contracting around me.

"Fuck, fuck, fuck," I said, leaning over Ari. I shuddered, and then I was spent.

Her breathing was ragged, and to my surprise, so was mine.

I pushed her hair out of her face, kissed her lips lightly, and sighed. "I love you."

She smiled up at me in a dreamy haze. "I love you, too."

After our escapade, we retreated back to Duffie's for warmth. Grant still had keys to the restaurant. He started a fire in the fireplace, dropped the blankets down on the ground, and snuggled us up in front of it. There was so much that needed to be said, yet…it felt right. Things felt right again.

It wasn't just the sex. *But holy shit, the sex…*

My body flushed from just thinking about what had happened outside. As cold as I was, my whole body was also super heated with energy. I'd come here to talk to Grant, and somehow, he'd just unraveled all my plans. Now, we had to decide where to go from here.

Grant's mouth found mine again, and just when I thought we might have a repeat performance, he pulled back and just stared into my eyes. There was longing, pain, desperation, and desire all rolled into one.

"Ari, about what happened at the lodge…"

"No, you don't have to say anything," I said quickly. "Kristin told me nothing happened."

"I don't mean about that. I mean, about what I said. I was so angry, and you just laid out every reason I'd been telling myself why I didn't deserve you. I shouldn't have said those things. I shouldn't begrudge you the good life you had growing up. You deserve everything that you have. I love your fucking mouth, and I love how smart you are. I'd never change that because those are the things that made me fall in love with you in the first place."

I smiled slowly and then glanced down. "I shouldn't have said you were worthless. That's not fair to you. You are ambitious. It's just not what I'd been raised to believe ambition was." Henry's face appeared before my eyes, and I shuddered.

"I've actually been thinking a lot about what you said, and on some level, I think you're right. I've been coasting most of my life because of what happened. It consumed me, and I never let myself get past it. And…I might not be the CEO of a company, but I got a job."

"You did?" My mouth dropped open. I wasn't sure why I was so surprised, but I'd just never thought about Grant working. "Doing what?"

"Working at a recording studio. It's not a big deal right now, but I like the work. Plus, I wanted to do better, be more for you."

"Grant," I said with a smile, "you're already everything I want."

"That's not true, Princess, and we both know it. You deserve a CEO."

"But I want you."

"And I'll be thankful every day for that, but I still have to try."

He was so earnest that I really believed him. I didn't think he needed to better himself for me, but I had told him that he wasn't good enough and that he hadn't done anything to prove he had changed. Well, here was proof.

"I appreciate that," I said finally. "But you know you can't quit the band, Grant."

"What? Why would I quit?" he asked, shocked.

"McAvoy said you were thinking about it."

He ran his hand back through his hair and cursed. "No, that's not what I meant. I'm not quitting the band. I'd never quit the band."

"Good, that's really good." I breathed a sigh of relief.

I couldn't be the reason he gave up music. He'd eventually regret the decision and blame it all on me. It was a part of him just as I was.

Still, I had one nagging question. "And you…really weren't with any other women?" I asked, feeling vulnerable.

His hands found the sides of my face, and I stared up into his dark brown eyes. "You are the only person in this world that I want to be with. Other women don't even exist since I've been with you, Ari."

My heart skipped a beat at his admission. "You took me for granted," I whispered before I could stop myself.

He nodded solemnly. "And it probably won't be the last time. But I'm trying to make it better every day."

I believed him. Things wouldn't always be perfect. We were too stubborn, too strong-willed, but we could work through them if we tried, if we really wanted to. And oh, I wanted to. I'd never felt like this with anyone else. I'd never let myself open up enough to be hurt, but I'd also never opened myself up to be loved. And I loved Grant McDermott with everything that I was.

"I can live with that."

He laughed and kissed my forehead. "I sure hope so because I'm not letting you go again. Next time you want space, can you not jet off to Boston for a few weeks?"

I laughed, taking it lightly. "Yeah, but I don't think I'm going to need space again."

"Oh, you underestimate me."

I smacked him on the arm and rolled my eyes. "Why do I like you again?"

"Something to do with my charm."

Charm. Right.

"What made you decide to come out here anyway?" I asked. "I mean…it's freezing. I stopped by your place first, but obviously, you weren't there."

"I, uh…" He sighed. "I got into a fight with Donovan. He said that…well, that we wouldn't work out, and I'd never get signed. I, more or less, told him to go to hell and that I'd prove him wrong."

"With your fist?"

"He deserved it."

"I'm sure he did." I remembered the kiss Donovan had taken from me, and I pushed it out of my mind. I hadn't wanted that one either. "You know you don't have to prove anything to anyone."

I reached out and laced our fingers together. He looked like he had more to say, but he couldn't decide whether to tell me or not. I didn't like the haunted look in his eyes, but I gave him the time he needed.

"There's more…"

I squeezed his hand when he paused. "You can tell me," I said, bracing myself for the worst.

"My dad is getting out of jail."

"What?" I gasped. "When? How did this happen?"

"I just heard from my uncle today. I don't know all the details."

"Are you going to go see him?"

Grant's eyes hardened. "No."

"Do you think…he's going to try to see you?"

After a moment, he answered, "Yes."

I swallowed the fear that settled over me.

His father was a murderer, and he blamed Grant for what had happened.

"Do you think he'll try to hurt you?"

"Yes," he said flatly.

THE END

Acknowledgments

This book would have never come to be if it hadn't been for Bridget Peoples. So thank you for listening to my ranting, raving ridiculousness and letting me vent in the form of a book.

To Jessica Carnes, Trish Brinkley, and Taryn Cellucci, who suffered through reading this book chapter by agonizingly short chapter, thank you! Thank you for giving my asshole manwhore a shot, for loving Ari as a spitfire and not a doormat, and for believing that I could write first person even when I wasn't sure.

Katie Miller and Amy McAvoy—thank you for letting me use your names and make awesome rockers out of them. #blackandgoldforever

Thank you to the people who read this book in an early version and giving me feedback—Jessica Sotelo, Lori Francis, Ashley Truelove, Heather Maven. As well as the support from my fellow authors Gail McHugh and Jenn Sterling. Also Jaci and Jennifer for allowing me to make them groupie whores. Be careful what you wish for ladies!

I can't thank Najla Qamber enough for the masterpiece she made for my cover, and Jovana Shirley for making the inside match.

As always, I couldn't have done with this without my love, Joel, and our two puppies who keep me company while I write—Riker and Lucy.

About the Author

K.A Linde grew up a military brat traveling the United States and Australia. While studying political science and philosophy at the University of Georgia, she founded the Georgia Dance Team--which she still coaches. After graduation, she served as campus campaign director for the 2012 presidential campaign at UNC Chapel Hill. She is the bestselling author of the Avoiding Series, the Record Series, and Following Me.

An avid traveler, reader, and bargain hunter, K.A. lives in Athens, Georgia, with her boyfriend and two puppies.

OTHER TITLES BY K.A. LINDE

Avoiding Series
Avoiding Commitment (#1)
Avoiding Responsibility (#2)
Avoiding Intimacy (#2.5)
Avoiding Decisions (#1.5)
Avoiding Temptation

Record Series
Off the Record
On the Record

Following Me

You can contact K.A. Linde here:

kalinde45@gmail.com
www.kalinde.com
www.facebook.com/authorkalinde
@authorkalinde

CPSIA information can be obtained at www.ICGtesting.com
Printed in the USA
LVOW10s1733160115

423151LV00019B/982/P